Advanced praise for The God of New York

The God of New York is a novel written with a persuasive cadence in which the characters mobilized by Fontanella's authorial verve take on a role of their own and enter with narrative functionality into the heart of the story.

Dante Della Terza, Harvard University

As the figure of Pascal emerges from the pages of this book, the vivid portrait of this character touches the very heights of poetic creation, engaging the reader's attention for the literary passion of this young man, as well as the painful struggle experienced by an entire generation of Italian immigrants in the United States during the early 20th century.

Pietro Frassica, Princeton University

Luigi Fontanella's vivid novel *The God of New York* tells the heroic story of Pascal D'Angelo, an Abruzzese immigrant who against all odds achieved recognition as a poet and memoirist in the harsh xenophobic arena of 1920s New York. Fontanella's book brings alive a myth of literary transcendence and assimilation that is rich in pathos and tragic irony.

Jonathan Galassi

Fontanella's novel [...] delves deep into the story and, above all, into the soul of Pascal and the guys who worked with him. It is a text in which one feels the cold, the hunger, the filth of the houses, but also Pascal's joy in discovering literature, his frenzy in consulting his little shredded dictionary, New York Library's warmth. [...] A very hard novel, full of pain and emotion, yet not gloomy, because it is a novel about one's attachment to life.

Emanuele Pettener
from "Breve passeggiata nel giardino
della letteratura italoamericana"

The God of New York gives Pascal D'Angelo the literary glory he longed for in his short and difficult immigrant existence. Fontanella treats him as a colleague and a friend, using the present tense, resurrecting him in the places of his life and kindling his feelings as only a fellow poet can do. Pascal dreamed to be remembered in literature. Fontanella gives him eternal life in a novel.

Ilaria Serra, Florida Atlantic University

Fact and fiction, biography and creative writing, manual labor and literary vocation converge in this new novel, in which Luigi Fontanella chisels every word with the crafty attention his protagonist used in his daily toiling. A true story of migration, *The God of New York* is also a novel about the pilgrimage of life, where Pascal D'Angelo's discovery of his own identity becomes a metaphor for the hard reality Italian immigrants faced when reaching the shores of America. This book is a must-read for those who care about the intersection of life and literature.

Alessandro Vettori, Rutgers University

CROSSINGS 33

The God of New York

The God of New York

A Novel

Luigi Fontanella

Translation into English by Siân E. Gibby

BORDIGHERA PRESS

Library of Congress Control Number: 2021953534

Cover Photo: Bernard Titowsky Collection
John D. Calandra Italian American Institute, Queens College
The City University of New York

Printed in the United States.

Published by
BORDIGHERA PRESS
John D. Calandra Italian American Institute
25 West 43rd Street, 17th Floor
New York, NY 10036

CROSSINGS 33
ISBN 978-1-59954-177-8

TABLE OF CONTENTS

New York, 1910. Pasquale D'Angelo, a sixteen-year-old native of Abruzzo, arrives at Ellis Island together with his father and a group of their companions in search of a better life. The shock of the New World is brutal, one of the worst experienced by our emigrants; but at the same time, for Pasquale (who becomes "Pascal") it's powerfully attractive, electrifying. Unlike his buddies, whose sole aim is to improve their condition and to send some money back home to their families in Italy, Pascal develops a desire to become a writer, an American poet. In order to do so, he studies English assiduously, night and day, utilizing every free moment he gets during his merciless schedule at work as a stone cutter, a manual laborer, a pick and shovel man. With titanic amounts of perseverance and an indestructible faith in poetry, Pascal will carry on until he reaches the limit of his sufferings. Over time, he will become convinced of having a mission that he has been destined for since birth, with a responsibility to obey his internal voice in the face of the enormously difficult life circumstances and countless sacrifices he must bear, of a new language learned with a crumbling Webster's Dictionary and with the help of sublime teachers like Keats and Shelley—teachers who light the way along his path and give him the strength to keep going. It's a promethean struggle, made more difficult by crippling poverty, a struggle that will lead the young stone cutter to leave his friends after a long and exhausting stint of manual labor and to retreat in the end to a miserable hovel in Brooklyn in order to take on the challenge of New York City and the "god" that rules it.

Luigi Fontanella, among the most notable essayists and poets of his generation, has brought together papers and other documentation about this life lived in America a century ago by our countryman, creating from it a compelling, epic, and moving novel, following the entire arc of D'Angelo's life from his wretched origins to his tragic yet also glorious ending. The facts of the narrative come, in part, from D'Angelo's autobiography, *Son of Italy*, published in New York in 1924.

Born in Introdacqua (L'Aquila) in 1894, Pascal emigrated to the US at sixteen and died in Brooklyn, in desperate poverty, in 1932. Many of the events in *Il dio di New York* are authentic, as are some of the characters with whom D'Angelo shared his emigrant's tale. Various other episodes described in the novel are invented, based upon research undertaken by Fontanella and on the cultural and historical record of New York in the 1920s. The novel has been originally published by Passigli Editore in Firenze in 2017 and has received numerous excellent reviews in all major Italian journals and newspapers. The translation into English is by Siân E. Gibby, John D. Calandra Italian American Institute, Queens College.

The God of New York

PROLOGUE

A man makes his way toward Times Square, having spent the whole day in the Reading Room of the New York Public Library.

Reaching the subway ticket booth, he sticks his hand mechanically into the pocket of his threadbare overcoat but doesn't find the few cents he needs for the fare. Suddenly he realizes that someone robbed him in the library, taking advantage of his momentary absence from the reading room.

There's an embarrassing moment as the young man (he is 28, but his appearance shows signs of a life filled with struggle and privations) confronts the impassive ticket-seller who, in the face of his confusion, informs him that the BRT (Brooklyn Rapid Transit) isn't a charitable organization. The man smiles slightly; without further comment he goes back up the steps and reemerges onto the street. It's 8pm. He glances at the starless sky as if to inquire about the weather. Anyway, he thinks, why rush to get home to that freezing little hovel where he lives all by himself?

He wraps his overcoat more tightly around himself and turns toward Fifth Avenue, suddenly battered by a furious blast of wind. It's a frigid evening: December 31, 1921.

He walks without stopping for more than an hour till he reaches the Union Square area. Another couple of side streets and here he is on Broadway. But here all hell breaks loose: a mixture of snow, hail, and freezing rain engulfs him, leaving him nowhere to escape to.

Uncertain what to do, the man huddles under the eaves of a building, but only for a few moments. He resumes his trek and makes it to Canal Street. He knows that from Canal he can reach Forsyth Street quickly and from there get to the Manhattan Bridge, which will take him to Brooklyn, where he lives.

Arriving at the bridge, he is violently lashed in the face by snow; within moments his coat is covered with a diffuse glittering, but the man doesn't stop, partly because now he has only the bridge in front of him, and there's nowhere to take refuge from the fury of the elements.

Robotically he crosses the two miles of the Manhattan Bridge, while snow and freezing rain drench his clothes to the bone. He glances incuriously down at the wildly foaming waters of the East River.

Reaching Flatbush Station, the man pauses inside the waiting room to catch his breath after more than two hours of walking. Through the large window he watches, paralyzed with cold, exhausted, and hungry, as the snow blandly continues to come down. His eyes half close and he thinks about the piece of stale bread he's left under his bed. At that moment his miserable little room, which had previously been used as a storage closet for firewood, seems to him infinitely better than this lobby that doesn't have so much as a living soul in it. He plucks up his courage and, skirting the walls of isolated structures, crumbling apartment buildings, shacks, and modest stores, makes his interminably long way up Flatbush Avenue, which at this time is the outskirts of New York.

He finally reaches Fourth Avenue, at one time the outer edge of the Brooklyn suburb. Little more than a shadow by now, he still has ahead of him a little over a mile in the dark of the night. Fifteenth Street, 16th Street, Prospect Avenue, 17th 18th, 19th ... the man at last reaches 20th and No. 210, where his home is.

It's almost midnight.

To get into his little room he has to go through an outhouse used by other tenants of the apartment building. Frequently from this latrine come discharges of dirty water and other filth that flow under the doorway of his room. On this night, with the rain and the snow, as well as the usual leaks, semi-frozen pools have formed. The man opens the door to his room and, in the dark, sinks his feet into a puddle. The window is wide open; the snow's blown in in gusts, and a ferocious whirl of it continues to enter. One part of the bed is sopping wet, as is the floor, which is covered with the shambles of his papers, his few books, and his meager furnishings. Everything is wet or muddy. Also soggy are a pair of pants and some other spare clothes that he usually keeps under the cot. The bread, soaked with water and filth, emits a stench that makes it inedible.

Freezing cold, shivering, and deathly tired after his great efforts, the man closes the window, curls himself up on the one part of the bed that is still dry, and wraps his coat (which also serves as his blanket) around him. He closes his eyes and lets his thoughts take him back to his childhood, when he lived with his family in an isolated little hamlet in Abruzzo.

This man is named Pascal D'Angelo. My grandfather Giorgio Vanno was like a brother to him his whole life, and now I want to share his history in the same moving way he told it to me and as I've been able to reconstruct it through my research.

PART ONE

Introdacqua, Abruzzo, 1910

1

A little more than a hundred years ago Introdacqua was, and to a large degree is still today, a little area in the Abruzzese Appenines sheltered between two mountain ranges in the southern part of what's known as the Conca Peligna. Situated just a few miles from Sulmona, the town has an unusual name that alludes to the fact that it was built between two bodies of water (*inter aquarum cursus*). The banner of the commune, originating in a 1751 ink drawing by Giuseppe Lafolla, shows three crenellated towers and, beneath them, the flowing streams.

The idea of constructing the village so high, between two deep valleys on the slopes of Colle Rotondo, was surely a result of the need for security in past centuries, in case of wartime attacks.

The mountain that dominates the whole area is the Genzana, nearly seven thousand feet high, so named because of its abundance of gentians, a flower with beautiful blue funnel-shaped blossoms. According to Pliny the Elder, the first to discover the curative properties of this plant was Genzio, King of Illiria (180–168 BC). From the summit of this mountain, about four hours' hike from Introdacqua, one can enjoy a panorama of exquisite beauty: You can clearly see in the distance the Gran Sasso, the Maiella, the Morrone, the Colle Mitra, and the Fucino riverbed, and looking further down, the entire Conca Peligna. Almost all of these mountains are blanketed with a lush expanse of ground cover and forest, consisting mostly of beech trees, oak, pine, and spruce. In the clearings of these ranges there used to come—and they still do come, though in smaller numbers—shepherds from various interior valleys around Introdacqua to graze their flocks during the spring and summer. The clearings were sought out for the quality and abundance of their grasses and streams. The region is rich with rising springs; just as numerous are the natural caves and grottoes in the mountainsides, which were formed by continual water seepage.

There was a time when, in order to reach Introdacqua from Sulmona, you had to go a few miles down a path that cut its way through woods and along mule tracks. This path became a driveable road in 1874, exactly twenty years before the birth of Pascal D'Angelo.

October 10, 2010. I'm in a car, having left Sulmona, and heading down the 479 on the way to Introdacqua. It's the second time I find myself in this place. The first time occurred almost by accident ten years earlier, even though I had wanted to come for a long time, ever since my grandfather had talked to me about Pascal, whom he had known in the 1920s in New York.

Besides my grandfather's memories, my curiosity about Pascal had certainly grown some years ago as a result of reading his autobiography, which was published in 1924 by an important American press. Yet that first visit had been very short and casual. I went to Pescara to meet a friend, and from there I was supposed to go via the A25 to Termoli, where I would have sailed for the Tremiti Islands for a short vacation. Through a series of unforeseen circumstances, I wasn't able to see my friend. That's how I unexpectedly found myself with an entire day at my disposal. Why not, I said to myself, take a detour and add a brief visit to my grandfather's hometown?

Very different is the spirit in which I am going to Introdacqua this time. I want to try to find Pascal's childhood home, to visit calmly and attentively the places of his childhood and youth and gather some data and possibly even some documents. In particular, I'd like to meet with Rino Panza, an elderly, affable man whom I had occasion to meet and become friendly with on my first trip. He talked enthusiastically about Pascal; he seemed amazed that someone would come from New York just to find out about him.

Rino took me to see the place where Pascal was born: a tiny spot, outside of town, called Cauza, consisting basically of a widening of the road lined with a few small houses. In one of these had lived the D'Angelo family. He also told me, in an intelligent and passionate manner, something of the history of emigration from this area, on the subject of which he had written some articles and accrued valuable documentation. Today I want to consult his files in hopes of finding useful information. On my way I am thinking about our first encounter, which took place in the main piazza of the town.

Rino, a fanciful and genial person, a multifaceted spirit, a poet, philosopher, and musician, had been working at that time on a revised study of Pascal D'Angelo's troubled life story. But he spoke to me vigorously about matters beyond Pascal, and especially about another illustrious man from the same town, Francesco Ventresca, who left for the United States in 1891, aged 19, and immediately spent all the money he had with him on a book of English grammar. Two years later, he made a new start in Western Springs, Illinois, beginning a long academic career from elementary to university education, all the while working at a series of humble jobs: laborer, stonecutter, bricklayer, railroad worker—all of them jobs Pascal and his father would undertake a few years later—and dedicating his nights to the study and acquisition of the English language and culture. In the end, having graduated with a specialization in interpretation and translation, he became a professional in the US Department of the Navy and War.

I come to a crossroads: To the left there's the sign saying "Introdacqua, 1 kilometer"; to the right a country road: Via Torre San Pietro. I turn left, and before me opens up a long, sloping, tree-lined road.

Just before getting to town I ask someone loading bags into a van if he knows where Rino Panza lives. He tells me to turn around and go back to the intersection and take Via Torre, which leads to a little neighborhood named, if I understand him right, "Doctors' Homes." There I'll find some cottages, and my friend lives in one of them.

2

An elderly woman comes up to me at the closed gate. She peers at me through the bars, more perplexed than curious. I apologize for having come without calling first; I tell her, somewhat hesitantly, that I come from New York, that I am here to visit Introdacqua, where my grandfather, Giorgio Vanno, was born, and that I would very much like to see Rino Panza (mentally assuming he is her husband) to ask for information about Pascal D'Angelo. A slight grimace passes over the woman's face, as of pain mixed with suspicion and hesitation: But it's only a moment, and it's possible I am misinterpreting her reticence. I add, as thoughtfully as possible: "I beg your pardon for bothering you ... it's just that I really must see Rino again" (I emphasize that "again" with my tone and use his first name to indicate to her a certain familiarity that would link me to him in time). "You know, we met ten years ago right here in Introdacqua. Your husband ... Rino is your husband, isn't he? He told me about a book that he was writing on Pascal D'Angelo and the subject of emigration. Right now I am doing some research on D'Angelo's time here in Introdacqua before he emigrated to America with his father. My grandfather emigrated with the two of them."

"My husband is ill, very ill ... he can't speak, he has trouble speaking clearly." The woman stops abruptly, but she does so with grace and what seems like an old-fashioned patience. She adds nothing more. Maybe she is waiting for me to leave or to show some sign that I've understood her. Then, as though lost in thought, almost as if speaking to herself, she murmurs, "He's bedridden ... he had a stroke."

She says the last words looking me in the eyes, making a small gesture as if she wanted to pull something out of her hair, which was coiled into a neat white bun at the nape of her neck.

"I'm so very sorry ... I didn't know; I am really very sorry to hear this," I don't know what else to say.

She gives me a look that is at once humble and kindly.

"All right, come in, come in," she says in a low voice and, almost as though breathing a sigh of relief, she opens the gate for me.

We cross a small garden, and I feel a vague sense of shame for intruding like this. For a second it occurs to me to stop, excuse myself, and go back to the car. All around us is an unearthly silence, interrupted only by the sound of our footsteps on the stones of the path leading from the gate to the house. We enter a tiny vestibule that opens into a corridor. I am immediately struck by the heavy shadow that envelops the space. To my right is a large sitting room, to the left the kitchen. Then the hallway goes on and I spy other rooms and at the end a large window that looks out onto a garden with a nice pergola in the middle.

I follow the woman into the sitting room. In the center, a long table like the ones found in monasteries, with benches, and off to the side a parlor with a sofa, a low table, and two armchairs facing a stone fireplace. One corner of the room is dominated by a display cabinet whose base is a writing table made of heavy wood. Some old paintings, mostly landscapes, complete the furnishings.

The entire space is shrouded in heavy darkness; the two side windows are shut with the blinds almost completely drawn. A few slivers of afternoon light filter through the slats.

"Make yourself at home," she says. "I'll go tell him. What's your name?"

Embarrassed, I reply, "Excuse me, I didn't introduce myself. I'm Giorgio Vanno. I have the same name as my grandfather from Introdacqua. Maybe your husband knew some of my family. There's no one left here now—they've all gone to America years ago."

The woman disappears down the corridor. I look around me. There's a distinct smell of the fireplace mixed with some scents coming from the kitchen, which I can see clearly from this room. Smells of burned wood blending with others: first mushrooms and dried tomatoes, chestnuts, olive oil, and oregano. I hear little pieces of sentences, fragments of the woman's dialect, which are countered by short guttural sounds from the man. There's a transistor radio on low in the kitchen.

"Come in. Rino wants to see you." The quiet voice of the woman surprises me, coming from behind my back while I am glancing at the display case, which contains the usual things, put there somewhat hastily, it seems: books, cards, clippings, notebooks, pads of paper, and newspapers of various kinds.

We go into a small, simply furnished room: a bed, a nightstand, and a little dresser. Pungent odors of camphor, alcohol, urine, medicine, and mildew fill the air. Stretched out, immobile, on the bed is a man with a dazed expression on his face, a bit of white hair plastered on his mostly bald head, his mouth slightly agape with a grimace at once fixed and also trembling slightly.

Pointlessly I take his hand and introduce myself, reminding him of our previous meeting. The old man's eyes flash. Maybe he is trying to say something indecipherable to me, as I am succinctly explaining the reason for my visit. It's a surreal situation, accentuated by his complete immobility. A bright rectangle of light, coming from the room's single, small window, bisects the bed he's lying on.

At a certain point, some kind of dialogue is exchanged between him and his wife, consisting of visual signals and bits of words in dialect. The woman seems to get what her husband is trying to communicate; she motions me to follow her into the sitting room. Here she opens the shutter on one of the display case windows. She removes two books and hands them to me in silence. I don't know if she wants me to look through them or is simply giving them to me as a gift. I quickly read on the cover of one of them the author's name (Rino Panza) and the title: *The World of Pascal D'Angelo*. Presumably it's the book he told me about when we met before.

"Thank you," I say a bit awkwardly, "May I ... could I examine these?"

"Please take them," the woman replies immediately, but with immense kindness. "Rino told me to give them to you; I'm sorry it's all he can do. He's half paralyzed ... as you could see ... he has tremendous difficulty talking but I think he recognized you."

All I can do is say goodbye to this woman, to this house, to this man: the only person in Introdacqua with whom I could have spoken about what's in my heart—the only person, maybe, who could have told me what the flesh-and-blood Pascal was really like.

Having reached the front door, I thank the woman and convey to her, as much as is possible, my sympathies. I get back in the car and, behind me, hear the gate close.

3

No one knows who built the Castle (really it's more of a watch-tower) or when they did it; it reaches some 2,425 feet high and 358 feet from the bottom of the valley (Piazza di Contra), at the highest point of Introdacqua, between two large valleys that at one time marked the northern and southern limits of the town. It's hard to imagine a more ideal strategic place for spotting potential enemies from afar and taking in the whole territory of the domain, from Rupe di San Nicolo to the slopes of Tassito Piccolo.

The most likely story has it that it was the counts Di Sangro who built the tower; allies of the Normans, they managed to found a feudal dynasty that was among the most powerful and enduring in Abruzzo. Simone di Sangro distinguished himself in 1173 by extending his dominion not only over Introdacqua but also over the so-called Conca Peligna. Most likely he was the one who constructed the tower, not as a home for himself and his family but rather merely as a last refuge and defense point for his soldiers in case of danger. Later on, it was used as a prison, and it's in this capacity that it is described in the Catasto Onciario at the Università della Terra in Introdacqua "castle at the land's highest point for use as a prison."

It was the custom of lesser feudal lords (minor vassals and their own vassals in turn) not to organize jousts or other tournaments but simply to steal money, giving themselves over to armed robbery—actual acts of brigandage—in nearby areas, stripping of their wares shopkeepers, priests, women, and any person of any wealth whatsoever who found themselves within the territory—people who, having been captured and locked up in the Castle's tunnels, were constrained to come up with bounties or ransom taxes if they wanted to be released. Exceptions: beggars, who were poor; and musicians, who were constrained to roam the lands, performing.

I get these bits of information from one of the two books I was given by Rino Panza: a weighty volume some 600 pages long and with 43 color plates (*Introdacqua in History and Tradition*), published by

Gaetano Susi in 1994 as a reissue of a 1970 edition. This enormous book sits on the table in my hotel room, just steps away from the tower, together with other books, letters, documents, and notes that I brought with me from New York.

The hotel is located in the heart of the old section of town, a zone the locals call simply "the Castle." More than a hotel, it's really an inn with some bedrooms for rent on the top floor. Mine is the last in a small group of them that offer glimpses of panoramas of wild and exquisite beauty.

4

It's six in the evening, and I'm in my little hotel room reorganizing and putting in chronological order the cards and books in my possession: first of all, the photocopies of the first edition of the autobiography Pascal published in 1924 (*Son of Italy*), which I was able to find at the New York Public Library; a pad on which I wrote down some notes I made in that glorious library; a booklet from 1989 published (after a manner of speaking) by the Università degli Studi di Sassari and edited by Francesco Mulas (*Le Poesie di Pascal D'Angelo*); photocopies of some reviews that came out the same year the autobiography was published; and some bibliographical materials, among which, very precious to me, are copies of the letters Pascal wrote to Carl Van Doren, preserved by the Firestone Library at Princeton University.

To these materials must be added the two books Rino Panza gave me: his work, *Il Mondo di Pascal D'Angelo*, and the ponderous Gaetano Susi volume. Besides this, I have a complete set of printouts from Google as well as three brochures, in reality not very significant, that they gave me at the Pro Loco in Introdacqua. The first, from 1997, has poetry in dialect and related music composed by Rino Panza (*Lu file de la vite*); the second one, generically titled Introdacqua 2000, which seems to have come out around then, since it includes the calendar for that year. That one offers brief writings about and photographs of Introdacqua by Antonio Giammarco. A group of these texts have to do with Saint Feliciano, the patron saint of Introdacqua. There's a charming legend tied to this martyred saint that is related in this publication by Bernardino Ferri. Here's the tale, which is worth noting for its lively spirit.

The people of Introdacqua desired to have the relics of a saint to venerate in their town. When the bishop of Sulmona in 1755 finally authorized the parish of Introdacqua to send a delegation to Rome to obtain there the body of a martyred saint of the Church, the emotion among the general population was very great. The word spread from house to house, finally reaching as far as the last houses of the

Castle and, as quick as the sound of a bell, spread to every house in the area. In every Mass celebrated on Sundays there was official confirmation of the news.

They immediately put together a committee to solemnly greet the arrival of the relics and to prepare festivities for this long-awaited event.

Six men, all of them young and strong, formed a group that would go to Rome in order to collect the saint. They also gathered funds for the expenses of the trip and for the acquisition of an urn.

The body of the martyr was buried in the catacombs; he had been a Roman soldier who had refused to burn incense in front of the stature of the emperor because for a Christian such an act of devotion was reserved for God alone.

This young Roman had been a pagan his entire life until he reached the age of twenty, but then he learned of the new religion and became a Christian. With this refusal he understood what he was risking, but he wished to give testimony to his faith and so he became a martyr. His name was Feliciano, and this name became instantly lucky for Introdacqua's citizens; with his arrival there would be much peace and serenity and happiness in the land.

From that time many newborn babies were baptized Feliciano, Felice, Felicetta, Felicia, Anna Felicia, as a sign of devotion and homage to the region's new protector.

The group of young Introdacquesi left for Rome under the safe conduct of the bishop, having been given the precise address of where to find the body. When they crossed the border into the Papal State they did so without difficulty, and the trip continued to seem auspicious.

Many of the men were familiar with the road, having a number of times had occasion to take it in order to do labor in the Roman countryside. This time, however, they weren't on foot; they were equipped with three mules, and, possibly for that reason, the way seemed shorter.

Rome was still a small city at that time, no more than 200,000 people, all gathered together within the old walls.

These pilgrims readily found the church in which the body of the martyr was lying and, in the short span of just a few hours, managed to secure the holy relic, taken from the catacombs of S. Callisto.

Such emotion for the young highlanders! They now were in possession of the body of a saint, the body of a man who had given testimony to his belief and had paid for the act with his life.

The holy relics were washed, carefully dried, and placed in a great chest covered by a silken cloth.

5

Pasquale D'Angelo is born in Introdacqua on January 20, 1894, to parents living in extreme poverty. His father, Angelo D'Angelo, born November 18, 1859, is a peasant; he has six sheep, four goats, and a tiny piece of land. He'll die on November 24, 1935. He came to be known by the locals as Ze' 'Ngelelelle (Uncle Angelino), according to a local custom whereby older people are addressed with a certain respect. In the birth register of the district where Pasquale's birth is listed, one finds his signature. This doesn't indicate that he knew how to read and write, in the sense in which we understand it today. In the last decades of the nineteenth century, illiteracy in Italy hovered around 60 percent, on average. In some regions, such as Abruzzo and Puglia, it approached 80 percent; the majority of the inhabitants never progressed beyond being able to sign their own names.

Pascal's mother, Anna Felicia, is born on March 1, 1864, and dies on December 6, 1932. Pascal has a younger brother, who is mentioned every so often in the first sections of the autobiography. The four of them lived wretchedly as laborers, "the most miserable class existing in Italy at the end of the nineteenth century," says Vincenzo Padula in one of his books. He goes on, "Up to the age of eight, a boy walks behind the donkey, the sheep, and the sow; at nine his father hands him a shovel and a hoe, he brings him along with him to work and sets him up to earn 42 cents a day. At age fifteen his earnings increase and he gets 67; at twenty he's no longer hoeing with a small tool but with a large one, and breaking his back morning to night he gets 85 cents and a meal, or $1.25 with no meal. At that point he feels like a real laborer, and, to lessen or increase his misery, he takes a wife."

The alternative to this miserable existence is to emigrate somewhere. And that's what father and son will do in 1910, together with some of their neighbors, and that's what my grandfather Giorgio does as well. But after six years of excruciating manual labor, an ordeal lived out in inhuman working conditions in numerous places in the northeastern United States—New York, New Jersey, Maryland, Connecticut, Massachusetts, Vermont, and Virginia—the group splits up: Two are crushed to death on the job site; Pascal's father (in America *Pasquale* quickly became *Pascal*), exhausted and discouraged, decides to go back to his homeland. His son, however, stays in New York. He is already fiercely determined to leave his work as a pick and shovel man and undertake the career of writing, despite the difficulty he will have in achieving his goals. An experience that, for a poor young Italian farm boy emigrating to America a hundred years ago, has about it something of both the heroic and the sublime.

6

It's already 8pm. I put those cards, books, and other papers concerning Pascal back in a box in the closet.

I go back over my first Abruzzese day in my mind, starting with my arrival, in the late morning, in Sulmona. Here I stayed just for a couple of hours searching for some of the splendors of Ovid. But nothing is left of the great poet, apart from some archeological ruins, an infinite number of commercial signs bearing his name, and an improbable bronze statue in the Piazza XX Settembre, just a little way off from the beautiful Church of Saint Annunziata. I think also about the last, sorrowful days of his life, spent confined in Tomis (now Costanza) on the shores of the Black Sea.

Up until just a few hours ago I was filled with enthusiasm and anticipation, but after the visit to Rino Panza they've been gradually replaced in my soul by a certain sadness mixed with apathy. And now I am beginning to ask myself what I am doing in this little town stuck out in the middle of the Abruzzi mountains, since I will certainly not find here any documents or written statements about Pascal.

This afternoon, after my visit to Rino Panza, I went to the Pro Loco. The woman in charge of this office gave me a look both quizzical and doubtful, but also kind. At the beginning of our conversation she thought I was looking for a bed and breakfast (in Introdacqua there are about a dozen of them). Then, when she realized exactly what had brought me here, she was even more friendly and gave me, in addition to those documents I already mentioned, a folder with a light blue cover, a big one, like a photograph album. Inside this folder was a pamphlet containing historical and geographical information about the area, notes about its greatest monuments, and finally a list of ten "famous people" set down in chronological order: Giuseppe Pronio, called "le grand diable, who led the Introdacquians of the three Abruzzis after the French occupation of 1799"; Ernesto Giammarco, "linguist and scholar of matters relating to Abbruzzo," with a citation by Ettor Paratore: "The Abruzzo region could not boast a more significant, more complete, and more deeply influential example of its ethnic and cultural values" (these were the bombastic words of the illustrious Latin scholar, who was one of my most feared professors at La Sapienza University); Francesco Ventresca, the writer much beloved by Rino Panza, remembered as a "student of Romance languages, professor at American universities, and author of *Personal Reminiscences*." And there, after him, our Pascal D'Angelo, of whom it says, and blessings on whoever wrote this, that "in the 1920s his poetry amazed the American literary world. He was the author of the autobiography *Son of Italy*, the first significant testimony of Italian immigration to America."

There follow Ilio Di Paolo, "emigrant to North America, wrestling champion in the 1950s and '60s"; Robert J. Di Pietro, "scholar of linguistics and university professor in the United States"; Ivo Garrani, "noted actor and voice-over artist"; Pat Tiberi, "US congressman who lives in the state of Ohio"; Tony Monaco, "jazz organist who lives in the United States, where he gives concerts and spreads the study of the Hammon-Suzuki B3"; and finally Beverly D'Angelo, "actress, singer, and voice-over actor living in Hollywood, famous for having been in the movie *Hair*."

Of these ten "famous people," fully seven are immigrants or children of immigrants to America. The last four, with the exception of Ivo Garrani, who stayed in Italy, are alive and well and working in the US, each in his or her own field. The woman at the Pro Loco made sure, with a trace of inexplicable self-satisfaction, that I noticed this fact. Then she added that she herself has been to New York twice and proceeded to launch into an account of her travels.

I interrupted her with the utmost politeness, asking if she didn't by any chance have anything else to show me that had to do with Pascal D'Angelo. She looked at me, slightly taken aback, and then, as though a bulb had gone on in her head, she went over to a cupboard and took from it, almost furtively, a DVD and some cards. She gave all this to me, calling them "very special documents."

Astonished, I asked her, "What is it? Is it a documentary about D'Angelo? Does it by any chance have any personal photos of his? Who made this video? When did it come out?"

I pressed her with my questions even as an immense desire to see the video rose up in me, though I showed nothing on my face of what I was feeling.

She was smiling, very pleased: "You'll see and judge for yourself."

Then she handed me the cards, which were already stamped, and which showed images from the town. On the back of each one was written *Introdacqua. Tourist site.* Two of them are particularly interesting: one that shows the River Road, a long tree-lined street that goes straight up to the center of town; and another that shows the entire town tucked under the hill with the tower looming over it.

At this point, all I can think of is discovering on this video something about Pascal that I didn't know before, since the only direct information I could have gotten about him would have come from a man who couldn't speak, at this point possibly lying on his deathbed.

Even the so-called Regional Museum of the Immigrant, close to Palazzo Trasmondi, named in honor of Pascal D'Angelo and fairly interesting on the subject of the history and themes of Abruzzese emigration in the early years of the twentieth century, doesn't have documents pertaining to Pascal. And also, now that I think about it, Pascal lived in this area only the first sixteen years of his life. And maybe he didn't even come into town that often, given that his little shack was out in the country outside Introdacqua, more than a half hour by foot from the center of town, as he himself tells us in his autobiography ("When I was about six, my mother had to go to the town, which was a little more than half an hour's walk away").

And finally one needs to remember that the daily work that his family did—though scarce—of leading the flocks out to pasture typically brought him up into the mountains, outside the town.

Who knows if he might have even come to this little hotel, which, as the proprietor told me, was already in existence at the beginning of the century, although at the time it was just a simple stop along the way for travelers.

I turn to the window and a wave of icy air hits my face. The cobalt blue sky, almost black, is covered by clouds and you can't see even a single star.

7

I'm sitting in a corner of the hotel's restaurant enjoying some *frescherielle*: a local dish characteristic of these parts, basically made of a mixture of cornmeal and water, boiled in a copper pot; it's similar to polenta, but it isn't polenta, because of the finer grain size. It's flavored with the local sausage.

Nearby there's a nicely lit fireplace. It's only the tenth of October, but here it already feels like the middle of winter.

There are just two customers: me and a man seated at the bar drinking something brought to him by a waitress. Hanging from the walls are various objects of wrought iron, some baskets, and other trinkets not easily identifiable. Above all of it hangs some type of embroidered white drapery or tablecloth and, next to that, a piece of fabric of a reddish color and made with an elegant simplicity: two objects that stand out immediately from the others for their gracefulness and plain beauty. I ask the hotelier, who is also the host, waiter, and jack of all trades of the place, what it is.

"It's the *mantricchia*," he explains to me affably. "It used to be used just as women's clothes, mainly as a sheet to cover the face, all handmade ... You know, it needs to be folded in a very particular way. Usually it was made of linen or hemp with a long fringe on the edges ... it would frame the face and fall down behind the shoulders all the way to the hips. This one you're looking at here, though, next to it is the *fasciaturo*: a woolen cloth, also made by hand, that goes over the *mantricchia* during the wintertime to protect against the cold. They're things that aren't used anymore, except on special occasions or at folklore shows. If you should happen to end up here again in Introdacqua, say on the last Sunday in August, which is the feast day of our patron saint San Feliciano and Saint Anthony, or January 17 for the Fires of St. Anthony, you can see it. These are very important holidays for our town. It's also when we have the Flying Madonna ..."

"Flying Madonna ... in what sense, flying?"

"On Easter Sunday the Flying Madonna is when the statue of Mary, carried aloft by four hardy young townsmen, moves toward the risen Christ … a really moving ceremony that you can only see here. Some years ago I was one of those hardy young men …"

Encouraged by the good-natured cordiality of the innkeeper, who clearly possessed knowledge of the local lore and whose commentary sometimes sounded like it came from a book, I asked him, "And what are those rounded rocks there by the chimney?"

"Ah, those are the bocce, balls of stone … Every once in a while they'll find another one of them up on the heights of the hills. Archeological evidence of the Neozoic era. Maybe they're linked to some cultic magic or maybe they're elements of some kind of defense, who knows?"

In fact, as the host is learnedly explaining the origins of these spheres, I am remembering that in the afternoon, as I was wandering about the town, I saw a number of these orbs stuck into the external walls of houses; but is it really possible that they could have been placed there to protect against evil energies, or what even today in certain areas in the South of our country is generally called "the evil eye"? Or instead were they just simple, crude cannonballs, antiques used in the Middle Ages to attack towers and fortresses, possibly even the one that looms over the town right nearby? In any case, these "bocce" rocks are certainly interesting and possess an enigmatic magic of their own.

Taking advantage of the friendly familiarity that I've quickly achieved with this man, I ask him, beckoning him to come over, if there is any way I could watch the DVD about Pascal D'Angelo in the hotel. I explain, briefly, without drawing it out too much, my reasons for coming to Introdacqua. I try not to go too much into detail to avoid useless chatter and the usual walk down memory lane of this or that person in the village.

He replies that he and his wife, Anna, will be honored to let me use their television, which is equipped with a DVD player. Their apartment is attached to the restaurant, and he gestures toward the bar where at that moment his wife, who had been serving the other customer, is now casually flipping through a magazine. I turn to look at her and in fact I see, beyond the bar, a door that most likely leads to their apartment.

We continue our conversation from one dish to the next. The man, about 50 years of age, sturdy and portly, tells me his name is Alfredo, shakes my hand with his own strong and plump one, and invites me to call him by his given name. He tells me it's been twenty years already since he took over this restaurant, which he retrofitted to be a hotel also.

I thank him warmly for the DVD player and meanwhile compliment him on his restaurant and the food, which is truly delicious.

After the *frescherielle* I decide against a second course and now am enjoying some ricotta made from goat cheese, which Alfredo serves me accompanied by a little bowl of a sauce made from chestnut honey: a honey reddish in color, almost like amber, dark and with a slightly bitter flavor that goes very well with the ricotta.

"A delicacy," Alfredo explains to me, "prepared by my brother Raffaele; he has a large farm a few kilometers from here."

Alfredo is a charming storyteller. He tells me, among other things, about an ancestor of theirs during the first years of the nineteenth century who planted some special chestnut trees that he had brought with him from the Catanese countryside. A passionate botanist enamored of that volcanic region, he had once upon a time spent some months there learning various cultivation techniques from the peasants of the area.

"It's the Cento Cavalli [100 horses] chestnut, considered the grandfather of all the trees in Europe."

"Cento Cavalli in what sense?"

"In the sense that there's an old legend connected to this magnificent tree, a legend of a mysterious queen who had at her service a hundred knights. One day this queen and her 100 knights on their 100 steeds found shelter beneath this tree in a storm. It's a kind of chestnut of enormous size, bigger than any other tree in Europe or possibly the world."

I end my dinner with a *malterrate*, which, the worthy Alfredo continues in his explanations, literally means "knocked-down almonds"; it's a typical local dessert made by mixing thick chocolate with sweet roasted almonds and moistening it with maraschino.

By this time it's 10:00 and there's been just the three of us left for quite a while: Alfredo, Anna, and me.

We are moving over to their apartment, but not before Alfredo has a quick word with the cook, giving him some final instructions for the day. After which he places a grate in front of the mouth of the fireplace and turns out the lights, and we go into their lodgings.

Anna makes me comfortable on the couch, across from which sits the TV. The room, which serves as living room, sitting room, and dining room all at once, is modestly decorated. Four large black-and-white portraits dominate one wall; they are probably grandparents and great-grandparents of Alfredo and Anna. A small lamp, lit and sitting on a leaved dresser in front of a picture (I can't tell if it's a saint or some relative), contributes to making the atmosphere seem even more timeless.

Anna asks me if I would like a coffee or maybe some tea, but Alfredo quickly stops her, exclaiming, "What do you mean, coffee or tea, Anna?" And here, looking at me with his large friendly face he adds, "My dear Giorgio, what would you say to a small glass of the best nocino? I make it myself with my own hands every year, gathering the nuts when they're still green ... June 24 ... the feast of San Giovanni. Meantime, give me your DVD and I'll take care of it ..."

"Thank you, but I don't want you to go to any trouble ..." I respond, almost distractedly. I am consumed with curiosity to see the video.

The titles scroll by and then the first images. The video was made in 2003 by Mediacom of Pescara. It's directed by Stefano Falco. The voice-over for the documentary is by Claudio Capone.

At the beginning it seems like a meticulous and pleasant-looking study of Abruzzo's ethnological and anthropological culture, shot in the middle of Piazza Vittorio Emanuele and introducing the figure of Pascal D'Angelo in the context of emigration from Introdacquas. It explains the societal conditions of the region in the first decades of the twentieth century that mark the most intense period of emigration from Abruzzo. Areas that in that period were almost completely emptied out. It is a fact that between the end of the nineteenth century and the first years of the twentieth, one third of the entire population of Abruzzo emigrated to America. It's enough to know that on a single day, April 17, 1907 (barely three years before Pascal arrived in New York), there were 12,000 immigrants registered at Ellis Island!

But my curiosity quickly begins to slacken and become disappointment instead. The documentary presents a serviceable reconstruction, even if it is a bit formulaic, of the Abruzzese expatriation to America, with interesting historical images and even some moving moments, especially when they show interior shots of the enormous building at Ellis Island where our compatriots were forced to go through a 40-day period of total quarantine.

The disappointment basically comes down to the fact that the film (which is only 20 minutes long) doesn't have a single image of Pascal. For one moment, I thought I might be able to see my man in the flesh (even though being played by an actor) or at least that the film might show some photograph of him with or without his family, when he lived in this town as a child.

The video wasn't badly made, however. It's just a bit short and doesn't have enough in it about the times Pascal spent in so many places in America, places he was forced to stay in, working, during this exhausting experience as a manual laborer and a humble rock-splitter.

Still, there was a nice surprise: an interview with Rino Panza. It proves to be not a little captivating to me, especially if I compare this man, restrained in attitude and in speech, to the one I had encountered just a few hours earlier in his sickroom. Before my eyes I see a lucid man speaking, elderly but not as decrepit as I saw him this afternoon; a man who, sitting calmly behind his desk, amiably tells his interviewer the history of Pascal and of the emigration from Introdacqua.

And thus it is that I come to think bitterly that it is only seven years that separate today, October 10, 2010, from the day on which Rino did the interview for this documentary. Glancing at his desk, I instantly recognize by its dust jacket design a copy of his book *The World of Pascal D'Angelo*, which his wife handed to me as a gift. The cover shows one of the extremely rare photos of Pascal in America, holding a pickaxe in one hand and working with three other laborers on the railroad tracks in who knows what North American location. One of the three workers is my grandfather Giorgio Vanno.

Alfredo must have intuited my dissatisfaction, mixed with a certain amount of bitterness, and when handing me back the disc he says, "Look, my dear Giorgio, in this town there's nothing that can help your research; all there is here are things to look at and clean air to breathe. Emigration was both a blessing and a curse at the same time. Emigration is basically the history of all of us."

8

I had a strange dream, distressing and fragmented. I'm trying to describe it while it's still fresh in my mind, while this morning (it's about 8:00) the rain's pouring down outside: torrential, whirling rain. A fascinating sight and yet terrifying at the same time. For a moment I open the window and see an apocalyptic scene: overwhelming water pounding down, hurling itself with shocking violence on the town and all the surrounding countryside; all the little lanes are transformed suddenly into streams; the mountaintops are veiled in a cloudy luminosity that seems unreal—something terrible, catastrophic, and yet also of a brutal, indefinable beauty.

So, this is the dream, or what I can remember of it.

I find myself in an unknown Mediterranean city: a cosmopolitan city, attractive, exotic, that seems Spanish-Arab. Maybe Tangiers? Cadiz? Now that I think about it, last night after leaving Alfredo and Anna I read some pages of *The Sheltering Sky*, by Paul Bowles, a moving novel, one I'd call almost menacing. Many years ago I read it in Italian (*Il tè nel deserto*), and I saw Bertolucci's film of the same name, but recently I decided I wanted to read it in the original.

Back to the dream. I find myself at a police station, which is situated inside a white building facing the sea. Here, on the beach, right at the water's edge, someone has made a likeness of me out of sand. A kind of bas-relief or sculpture that reproduces my face exactly, with some doodles in the sand to embellish it, making it more extravagant. So, all in all a real portrait of my face made out of sand.

At this police station a photographer needs to make me an ID, which I will use as a passport. In effect, I find myself in this police precinct for the purpose of finishing up what needs to be done in order to get this passport; it's a document I must have in order to travel somewhere, I don't know where. But suddenly the photographer decides to take a picture of the sand portrait (as I have said, the station was right on the beach). The photographer tells me that, with regard to any photo I might need, this one will be more "artistic."

Some time passes, with people coming and going and police entering and leaving the room. The commissioner is sitting behind a desk, facing me. On his left there's a large window overlooking the beach. On his right there's a hallway with various doors that lead to other offices. Still a lot of people roaming around and hubbub. Finally, the passport is ready and gets delivered to the commissioner so he can give it some stamp and sign it. He looks intently at the photo and then at me. Then he turns his head to look out the window at the "sculpture" in the sand of my face. In the meantime, the surf, although mild, has blunted and smoothed the lines of my face, so much so that the official says severely to me, "But this photograph isn't you!" brusquely shouting in my face, "It's not valid! This passport is not valid! Get out of here!"

I flee the room and run through the streets of this city. I get to a hospital, or some kind of clinic. A gloomy, gray atmosphere. I'm in the waiting room. I hear rumbling, as though someone were banging on the walls of a nearby room. In this crumbling clinic, my friend F.D., one of my dearest childhood friends, is a patient. With me are also A. and M. I understand that A. has come every day to visit F.D.

At some point I leave A. and M. and, after going through various hallways, get to the room where F.D. is. I have a vivid, clear memory of this room: There's just one small window with the shutters half-closed; meager furnishings composed of a cot on which F.D. is lying among bandages, rags, and sheets; a scrawny bedside table and some kind of chest of drawers, which I can scarcely make out in the gloom, to my right. Next to the bed there is a huge man, tall and stocky, with a decisive manner but not rude. He's F.D.'s doctor. F.D. is huddled up, as though curled into the fetal position. He's complaining weakly; he breathes heavily, monotonously, painfully. Every so often he emits a guttural sound, as if he wanted to tell me something.

Suddenly the doctor (a madman) jumps on the bed and straddles it, facing F.D. He seems to be rummaging among the sheets or else somehow trying to straighten out the tangle of rags, gauze, sheets, and blankets. He shows clear signs of rage and impatience because, he says, F.D. has wet the bed. He shakes his head, and from his clipped speech, sprinkled with curses, I realize that F.D. is in terrible shape, possibly even dying. Again I hear the beating sounds, like dry thuds, or deep and sudden blasts, coming from a room close by.

I return, dejected, to the waiting room where M. and A. remain; inside me there is a terrible feeling of helplessness of not being able to relieve the suffering of my dear friend. I ask M. (this is an inexplicable paradox) to lend me his cell phone so I can call him. I need to tell him that F.D. is dying, to hurry up, to come quickly to this hospital, and I give him the directions, while he is right in front of me!

In the meantime, A. is looking at me and around us with a smile that's inexplicably cynical and disillusioned. And yet I know that he's been coming every day to see our mutual and beloved friend.

M. isn't surprised at my request, he mildly hands me his phone, which has on the end of it a small wire with a cap on it; the other wire ends in a plug. I grasp the plug and stick it into the wall socket, but oddly, the plug detaches from the wire and stays stuck in the socket! I feel my anxiety taking over my whole being, and I shake spasmodically.

M. says to me, "But you don't need that plug; I already charged my phone!" In an atmosphere that is getting more and more ambiguous and hallucinatory, I dial M.'s number—M., I repeat, is right there next to me—and I tell him to come immediately because F.D. is dying and there's no time to lose.

Finally all of us head toward F.D.'s room. Behind us another couple of people appear; I feel as though I recognize them in the shadow, that one of them is P., another good friend of F.D. (but who told him to come and how did he know about F.D.'s illness?).

We go into F.D.'s room. The first thing I see is his face all stained with black spots, with here and there a splotch of blood. It almost doesn't look like him. It is a very upsetting, terrible, horrific scene. The same doctor is there, big and beefy, at the sickbed, absolutely still, with his arms crossed, observing the sick man impassively. The entire room now is in a state of incredible disarray. In a corner, on the floor, I glimpse bloodied gauze and shreds of rags.

At a certain point, abruptly, the doctor jumps on the bed again and, straddling the agonized body of F.D., turns his powerful shoulders to face him. Then again the deafening and continuous bangs and thuds from the wall. I burst into tears and wake up with a start.

9

It's 8 am. I go down to the hotel hall that also serves as a dining room and head toward the bar, where I find Anna polishing the counter. I order a cappuccino and a brioche. I ask after Alfredo.

"He went to Sulmona. On Mondays there's the general market. He should be back around noon. Is there anything you need?"

"I don't suppose you have today's paper?"

"Right here," and she points to the end of the bar, where the paper is lying next to some brochures for the hotel. Beside them there's a kind of a perch with toys, charms, and other souvenirs hanging from it.

"Is it all right if I read it in my room? I'll bring it back later." Just at that moment a clap of incredibly loud thunder seems to shatter the entire space. "What the hell?" escapes my lips, and I quickly soften it by adding an ironic "Nice weather today, eh?"

"What can you do? It's the season. We're used to it. It'll be like this the whole blessed day and maybe tomorrow too. As far as the paper goes, no problem, please take it. You're our only guest ..."

I finish my cappuccino. I take the paper and head back to my room, accompanied by the clamorous pounding and a lightning strike that suddenly illuminates the whole dining room.

I sit down in the only chair in my room and open the paper. I'm uneasy, nervous, preoccupied, maybe on account of the dream, which left me with a strange and persistent apprehension. From time to time I get up to inspect the scene outside the window, the torrential rain that never for a moment ceases cascading down on the entire town, with lightning and thunder that resounds gloomily, like relentless thuds. And I begin to think about some pages in Pascal's autobiography.

It's an autumn day like this one. His mother needs to go into town to take care of some errands. His father is working in the fields. Pascal, a child of about five (it's 1899), kicks up a fuss because he wants to go with his mother, who tries in vain to dissuade him: It's too long a trip by foot and she's afraid he's not up to it. But Pascal is stubborn and doesn't let up with the sweet talking and promises to his mother. He insists the distance to town isn't any too long for him if they can hear the bells from there every evening. So, he makes such a to-do that finally his mother has to give in, even as she keeps a worried eye on a "ruddy cloud that was growing in the softened blue" of the sky: The word *ruddy* carries with it both the connotation of the heavy redness as well as of the concepts of being accursed or damned.

It's at that moment that the boy would absorb and keep always with him the unforgettable comforting beauty of the anxious, expressive look on his mother's face.

The two of them set off. We can see them leaving the country lane hand in hand and going up the path, which is today called Viale Fiume, and which more than a hundred years ago certainly had no paving and not even the double rows of trees that line it today.

But after they have gone just a few hundred meters that cloud has become black and pressing. Now the cloud takes up the whole sky and throws everything into shadow. Mother and son pick up their pace. They have neither umbrella nor any other means of protection in case of rain. Here come the first lightning strikes: luminous bursts that tear at the sky and the mountains that form a circle around the town. Then, suddenly, the rain: impetuous, inexorable, whirling. His mother takes Pascal in her arms and starts looking around for shelter.

If you go across Viale Fiume today you can see on both sides all the way down the street gracious cottages with flowered yards and even some modestly beautiful porticoes. A century ago none of that was here, and therefore this draining trek Pascal's mother is on at this moment can be seen in all its desperate and lonely desolation, in all its blind tragedy.

Finally, on this crazed path between thunder and lightning, the mother spies a tiny stone hut. It could be a good place to take cover, but just as she is nearing the shack, two horrendous hounds jump out, snarling, ready to pounce on her. Pascal bursts into tears, and his mother lets out an inhuman shriek to get the attention of whoever might be living in the hut. An old man appears at the doorway and looks disdainfully at the two fugitives begging for help. In the town it was said that he was a bad-tempered old wretch, a sort of witch doctor who lived alone and apart from the rest of the world.

Snickering cruelly, the cynical old villain calls his dogs. But it's at this precise moment that the tops of two skeletal trees on either side of the house explode into flame, like the spray of a shooting star at the doorway, directly over the head of the old man. Immediately after, an immense eruption of thunder. The man falls to the ground; "the old man had been struck by the fires of heaven."

Pascal's mother, still with the boy in her arms, begins shouting at the top of her voice and hurls herself down the slope. Having crossed the street, she discovers a tangle of water and mud. She finally reaches the first houses; someone dashes out and hustles the two inside.

10

Magic, sorcery, superstitions, enchantments, and occult rituals were very common in the Abruzzese backcountry when our Pascal was a young boy. He would have seen witchcraft and divining arts that coexisted—and still do so in some remote little villages not only in Abruzzo—with the South's purely religious traditions.

Many of these magical, which to Pascal's young eyes exerted a certain fascination mixed with terror, involved plants, herbs, and local flora and fauna, or were linked to certain distinct individuals considered soothsayers, magicians, witch doctors, or even vampires. Even today, for example, one can find rituals, like the one of water and olive oil, that date back many centuries, used against the evil eye: perhaps the greatest of the malignant influences that, according to popular belief and superstition, result from the simple gaze of certain people (principally magicians and witches) in order to impose (from the regional verb *iettare*, from which the word *jinx* derives) misfortune onto someone. It should be noted that the word *mago/magician* (masculine) has positive connotations (at one time *magician* meant wise man or scientist), whereas *strega/witch* (feminine) comes from the term *strinx, strigis*, which is a predatory nocturnal bird and therefore carries a negative connotation in which women (generally old ones) come to be identified with relationships to sinister, diabolical power and are accused of evil actions harmful to society.

"Tales of happenings and scenes," Gaetano Susi writes, "which the inhabitants of Introdacqua swear they witnessed or took part in were the order of the day. The one who told about having been followed at night by two men who suddenly and mysteriously vanished, as though they dissolved into thin air; the one who declared himself to have been followed one night in the country on his way home by a strange animal which, even though he hit it many times with a pitchfork, nonetheless crossed from one side of the road to the other unharmed; the one who swore to have heard, while harvesting his crops on a piece of his land in the mountains, a voice repeating from a small nearby wood, 'Come back to God for your time is near!'; someone who insisted that, having once fallen asleep in a confessional in the church, he was able to witness a midnight Mass celebrated by a priest who had been dead many years, responding to the 'Dominus vobiscum' and hearing the priest say, 'Blessed may you be! It's been years and years since I said Mass at this altar and no one has responded to free me from the sin I committed, when alive, of making a mistake in the liturgy'; more than one woman asserted that, while going to collect wood in the mountains, she saw a hen with her chicks, or else a Mother Superior with her nuns; the man who, positive he was telling the truth, stated that more than once he saw a prominent person throw himself into the pool of the courtyard at night and splash around; a smith who attested that he was present when the priest tried to prepare to give extreme unction to the impenitent Andrea Scompiglio and who witnessed the sight of a black chicken that came down from somewhere near the tower and pecked insistently on the exposed chest of the dying man; a sick man, not delirious, told of having seen his dead mother go around his bed several times in the nighttime and then stop to look at the brightly burning candle in front of a religious relic; another who repeatedly swore that he asked for a pinch of tobacco from a monk who was walking down a country road and then declined it once he saw the monk had the hooves of a cow; another, finally, who related having seen, close to the Witches' Stream, a group of disheveled-looking women dancing in a great circle around an enormous fire."

"It was later ascertained that the soul of a murdered man wandered near the place where his life was taken; it was generally believed that on the night of Saint Simon (November 17) processions of the dead moved through the streets of the town; in order to be able to see them, however, you had to light a candle made of earwax; it was demonstrated from experience that spending the night in the cemetery one could have the surprise of being terrorized by the unquiet spirit of someone who had died, or else by a witch who suddenly appeared. It's for this reason that women would sing when they walked on their way up the mountain to collect firewood: a surefire way to appease the spirits of the dead and avoid being frightened by them."

11

In his autobiography Pascal dwells on this witch-laden atmosphere, these obscure popular superstitions and events with magical aspects, recounting one of them, in particular, having to do with the curious figure of an old crone who would appear from time to time in the town. Pascal was six years old the first time he saw her and has an intense memory of her.

The daughter of a powerful conjurer who lived on the Montagna Madre (which is what the Abruzzesi still call the Maiella), she had a look that was as sharp as it was authoritative, terrifying, as Pascal remembered it.

As soon as she appeared in town, everyone showed a profound fear of her and hastened to give her something: potatoes, pieces of bread or portions of lard, corn, and other foodstuffs; the old lady amassed a giant sack of them, which, once she'd gathered it, she placed on top of her head and took back to her hovel at the outskirts of town, while glancing furtively all around her.

Once her provisions were exhausted, you could see her again haunting the town in order to scrape together more food, which would be quickly proffered by the townspeople in order to avoid any curse falling upon their house or on some member of their own family.

It was rumored, besides, that this old hag was also a vampire; if anyone managed to put salt on her head or else to stab her with a needle, her power would be annihilated.

Some years later this state of affairs caused Pascal and his closest friends to come up with the idea of ambushing her, but every time they tried to do it, they were quickly thwarted, probably also because of the terror they felt when they went to approach her. Every time, the witch managed to figure out that they were creeping toward her, and she'd stoop down and grab a stone and fling it at them, all the while yelling curses.

Some more years go by and one day in September they find the witch. She is in a field, squatting in the shadow of a fig tree, mumbling broken phrases, incomprehensible, almost grumbling to herself. The boys cautiously approach and before long a small crowd of villagers forms around her trying to understand her, as though they are drawn hypnotically by her and what she's saying. No one can grasp her gibberish; finally, breaking off her soliloquy suddenly, the old lady gets up, her eyes half closed, and sets off for the town to do her usual begging. A little cortege of people follows her, confused.

One evening (Pascal by this time is about thirteen), at an inn, possibly even the same one where I am staying now, a group of men is happily boozing it up and joking around. The occasion is the feast day of the patron saints of the town.

It is late; celebration, jokes, smoke, confusion, and drinks haven't let up. At a certain point the wife of one of them shows up to beg him to come home. The drunkest of the group yells at her not to fear: There are no women in the bar who could rob her of her husband. Next to him, leaning up against the wall, another man is snoozing. The drunkard turns to him, starts snickering, and, turning back to the group, yells: "What's up with him? Look at him! Maybe last night he was walking around like a vampire and didn't get any sleep?"

From that moment on, the group's rowdy conversation turns to vampires and witches. Everyone has some story, more or less horrific, to tell, and little by little the atmosphere in the place gets increasingly animated, heated, uneasy.

More wives arrive, some bringing their kids with them. Pascal, who is there with his father, Angelo, remembers the night vividly and powerfully, and he presents it to us, in his own particular English that has a lively narrative tension. In just a few pages he creates an atmosphere that feels morbidly disconcerting and that—of course with the obvious differences—would not be out of place, as far as suspense goes, in certain of Edgar Allan Poe's horror stories.

The animated conversation reaches its peak when one of the women, certainly the bravest and most eloquent, exclaims: "Hey, it's the vampire hour now!" Another one quickly replies, "Yeah, but you're not the witch of the Maiella!"

At that point one of the men, a young buck with flashing eyes and curly black hair, rises on unstable legs and in a voice thick with drink, brusquely orders his wife from that moment on not to give anything further to that old hag, not even a crumb of bread, or else she will have to deal with him! And, growling insults and curses against the witch, he pounds a fist on the table, as though to seal the order. His wife, a little blue-eyed woman, is accustomed to obeying him without a peep. The two of them, who have been married only for a couple of years, have a beautiful baby boy.

The conversation comes to a close, everyone speaking against the witch or hurling abuse of one kind or another upon her.

Finally, bit by bit the group leaves the tavern. As is the way in the best scary stories, an insistent moon stands out in the sky, calm and sinister, with all the mountains around it, and casts a greenish glow over the little street in front of the bar. In this spectral light, someone spies for a moment the outline of the old witch. A murmur ensues among them, and the woman who spied the hag whispers, "She was here! And she heard everything we said against her!" Everyone imagines the most dire consequences, and the next day the witch receives lavish gifts. Everyone, that is, apart from the wife of the hot-blooded young buck, whose drastic commands are still ringing in his young wife's ears.

Undaunted and stubborn, the old lady comes back the next day to visit their house, but the bold youth is there to greet her with a pitchfork in hand, and he chases her away with ferocious insults. The hag flees, but not without cursing the house in some fragmented words, accompanied by mysterious hand gestures.

Some time passes, and the couple's baby, barely six months old, falls ill; all treatments and cures heaped upon him by the doctor and the local healer are useless.

In town and all throughout the area there's talk of the "strange" illness of the baby. Prisoners to their own beliefs and superstitions, everyone is convinced that the child is a victim of the old lady's witchcraft: Word goes around in fact that one night, thanks to her black magic, the witch managed to shrink herself and get into the house through the keyhole and, with an incantation, not only cast a deep slumber upon the parents but also to kidnap the infant. Then, in a flash, flying, she carried him away to beneath the branches of the celebrated Benevento walnut tree, from whose roots shoot out the flames of hell. All around the tree are other witches taking part in their usual Sabbath; every one of them has a baby with her. Blood is taken from these little ones, and their little naked bodies are passed over the flames—a ritual that doesn't leave them unharmed because, as is handed down in the old country beliefs, it leads to certain death and there is no medicine that can save them.

In Pascal's adolescent soul the scheme to throw salt on the head of this hag and stab her with a needle is strengthened. They just need to solve the problem of how to set up the ambush. Together with Antonio, his best friend, he studies the plan and goes through drills: He obtains a large needle (the ones used to mend mattresses) and quickly becomes a tenacious "salt thrower," though fearing that the witch is well aware of the popular use of this piece of magic.

The boys decide that it's a good idea to take a test run, and they identify a sacrificial "victim," a fat old lady from town who wheezes loudly when she walks. Upon reflection, the two of them convince themselves that she may even be a vampire: Just as well, then, that she should be the one on whom to test their dexterity.

The day of the ambush arrives: One evening, just after dark, the two friends approach her furtively from behind and, coming up beside her, jab the needle in her leg, through various layers of her tunic. The reaction of the old woman is as terrible as it is sudden: Screaming at the top of her lungs, she punches and kicks the two boys, who take off running. A bit of a fiasco, which nevertheless does not deter them from their original plan: stabbing the witch at the opportune moment.

And the moment arrives one moonless night. The two boys, who punctually patrol the town and its surroundings every night, see her in the darkness, walking with a slow and dragging pace close by a low wall.

They approach, slowly and stealthily, barefooted and armed with the salt and the needle. They come up, undetected, just behind her; they hear her panting and hastily saying some words: a sullen, incomprehensible complaint. They are just a few inches away: The two tug at each other; each one wants the other one to strike. Pascal, holding the needle to launch the attack, is just about to jump on her when, suddenly, the old hag wheels around, lets forth an inhuman cry, and, raising her dried arms, pounces on the boy in all her monstrousness, her long nails contorted into hooks, her eyes half-closed, her sharp teeth flashing.

The following month the baby dies. In the town the gossip goes around that the day before he died a black cat was hanging around the foot of the crib. Everyone is convinced it was the witch, who turned herself into the black cat.

The father, devastated by pain and rage, wanders around the town, asking himself out loud why this terrible thing has happened, why an innocent creature had to pay for the folly of his own parents. Finally, at the height of his fury, with a small group of his friends and townsmen, he heads to the house of the old lady. Reaching it, they insult and attack her violently; they beat her and chase her out of town. After that they set fire to her little hovel. A swarm of people, our Pascal among them, rushes to see what is left of the mass of rocks and burnt refuse.

From that day on no one hears anything from the witch, although the fear of some unpredictable reprisal dwells in the hearts of the locals.

Much later—more than a year has gone by—Pascal, who by this time is fifteen, will see her again. This will also be the last time. He is grazing his sheep in the mountains that loom over the town's tower. With his modest flock he clambers higher and higher. From up there the view of the entire valley opens beneath his eyes; he glimpses, somewhat cloaked by fog, Sulmona with its walls and the tiny suburbs that cluster around it.

At a certain point, at the end of a path he catches sight of a dark shape. He comes closer, keeping his staff ready in his hand, and suddenly two skeletal arms burst forth, covered by black rags. It's she, the old witch, who stands trembling in front of him. Pascal's first impulse is to run away and abandon his flock. But just then a new emotion takes hold in his heart, a mixture of terror, curiosity, revulsion, and compassion.

The crone doesn't show any sign of hatred or anger, just a hunted animal's simple fear. Pascal looks at her bony arms. One of her feet, cut from the rocks, is wrapped roughly in a strip of wool. Their gazes meet for a moment, and from the mouth of that pile of rags comes the choking cry: "I'm hungry!" The youth feels himself fill with an infinite suffering, and from a sack he brings out his own small meal, which she immediately snatches and attacks; she finishes it in four mouthfuls. She would like more, but Pascal has nothing left to give her. The two look at each other anew and, for the first time in his entire life, Pascal sees her smile a vague smile. Sobbing then, the old hag moves to hug him in gratitude, but Pascal, horrified, recoils. Her arms rest in midair, her fingers scraped and peeling. Her smile suddenly vanishes. Maybe in that precise moment she realizes how repellent she is and how much disgust her wretched figure must have caused over the course of her entire unhappy existence. Like a mother who has lost her child, the old lady collapses onto the ground, sobbing, feeling acutely her own remorse and the horror of herself. Upset, Pascal takes off with his animals, downstream and home.

Not much later the witch is found bruised and beaten close by a stream. When the marshal tries to question her, she responds only with scattered words, looking off into the distance at nothing.

The following night, a night in which the clarity of the moon rains down in splendor on the snowy mountain peaks, the witch dies. Pascal will never again see her, but her figure remains indelible in his memory, and certainly she has helped him take a step further into maturity. That encounter, which caused pity and compassion to spring up in him, would have not only a cathartic effect on him, it would also constitute a deliberate distancing of himself from superstition, from folk beliefs, from certain popular rituals and habits, and, in a word, from a state of ignorance that dominated his village culture. In his adolescent soul of just fifteen years, Pascal intuits, even if in a slightly confused way, that there are still other horizons of knowledge that he needs to, and wants to, reach for.

12

It's four in the afternoon, and I haven't even moved from my room, apart from a brief break when I went down and had a sandwich, provided by Anna.

The rain is now noticeably reduced in its intensity, and the atmosphere outside has become calm. I open the window of my room and breathe in the crisp air, rich with the feelings and smells of the surrounding countryside. I decide to go out for a walk in town. I go down into the room below, which serves as the restaurant. A strange silence has enveloped the space in shadow. There's no trace of Alfredo or Anna. The tables are all neatly laid out with their tablecloths and everything else.

I examine one by one the various objects affectionately hung on the walls, passed down by who knows how many hands before reaching Alfredo's, who decided twenty years or so ago to use them as decorations in his restaurant. Now, here in their places as though frozen in time, having survived more than one generation, they clearly present me with tangible signs of a culture already on its way to extinction. Their nakedness has something sacred and untouchable about it. And who knows if some of them, even having been, for the most part, handed down directly to Alfredo from his parents or grandparents (I am reminded of those four enormous portraits in black and white in the sitting room of their apartment), may have been acquired by him from country houses that were emptying on account of the great emigration in the years just before and just after World War I. Who knows, I say to myself, if among these objects there might be something belonging to my grandfather Giorgio, or to his family, who left in 1919 for the United States, of whom nothing remains apart from me, who am searching now for traces and documents relating to a man who was his friend and travel companion in American lands: I who am roaming like a shadow, looking for some fragment that might have to do with my ancestors here, in this little town about which until just a few years ago I knew nothing but its name.

I walk along randomly through the streets of the town, and I try to imagine what it was like a century ago when Introdacqua, like so many other places in the Abruzzo and Molise backcountry, began to empty itself via a continuous exodus—when entire regions, like Veneto, Calabria, and Abruzzo saw more than 30 percent of their own populations take off for the Americas between 1900 and 1920: a true hemorrhage of Italians dispersed among far-off lands that signifies a tremendous historical violence.

13

On account of the rainstorm that, from last night up until just a short while ago, has raged across the town, the lane I am walking down is filled with mud, stones, and puddles. The roadway, although it had been covered in asphalt at one time, is filled with holes and sudden bumps and, just now, an incredible mass of wet leaves, crumpled and stuck together, rotten fruit, plastic bags, branches and shoots that the fury of water ripped up and dashed from the trees.

At a certain point the little road ends and becomes a simple country path, all hollows, dips, and marshy spikes that it would be almost impossible to drive over.

From the documentation and reconstruction I have, I know that there is a place after about a quarter of a mile where the path becomes even smaller, and there's a turn, practically a hairpin curve, to the left and just a little further on you reach some shacks. This is a handful of buildings that even now is outside the inhabited part of the town that had been built, casually and illegally, in the middle of the countryside. I also know that on the right there should be a small cornfield, some fruit trees, a little section of vegetable garden, and a tiny tool shed.

I reach the crossroads. I turn to the left and there it is, just about fifty feet away, at a small rest stop, with some crumbling shanties on one side surrounded by trees, hedges, and a general tangle of greenery.

The building I am headed toward is the third and last one. A deep and otherworldly silence pervades the whole space. The houses, or what is left of them, are utterly uninhabited.

I reach a main doorway, eaten away by time; I push it open and go into a hallway or a kind of dining room with a ruined stairway on the left. The notice on the decrepit main door warned me not to go any further. The walls are barely standing upright and are marked by gashes and noticeable fissures; some of these are actual holes where birds have made nests. The floor, which is made up of dirt and cement pieces, is completely covered with trash, flakes of plaster, and garbage of every kind. To the right side of the stairs there is a rough fireplace on which one can still plainly see the stains of fire and smoke. The space is completely empty: no trace of furniture or decorations, just more stones, slivers of wood, pieces of broken glass, dusty empty bottles, rusty cans, grimy rags, scraps and remains of every sort. Here and there, some timid little plant shoots, growing out of nothing.

The stairway, after a few broken steps, turns to the right and leads into a fairly large room, presumably the bedroom of the people who lived here. Here too are garbage and plaster on the floor. In a corner is a tarp filled with holes and, next to it, a gaunt-looking plant. But the most noticeable thing is the wall on the left; it's made of … air, completely destroyed, as though it had evaporated. Outside this invisible wall looms a panorama of incredible beauty, like a landscape painting, framed in a rectangle by the other remaining walls and depicting an immense, infinite green, as far as the eye can see. Far away there are birds flying around the peaks of the snowy mountains.

My grandparents lived in this house. It was my grandfather Giorgio himself who built it, brick by brick, in 1895, with the assistance of the capable hands of his old father. He was twenty years old and was about to marry Giulia, a young woman of eighteen with whom he had been madly in love since childhood. In this little house, just rocks and broken walls now, Giulia would wait seven long years, starting in February 1910, for the return of her Giorgio from America.

14

It's my third day in Introdacqua. I throw open the window of my room and let in the light and invigorating fresh air.

It's a day filled with sunshine and the sky is extremely blue; there's a soft, soothing glow that stretches from the town all the way up to the mountains. I think of some lines of Pascal's: "The mountains like mighty giants lift themselves/ with a regal haughtiness out of the ruling gloom." Proud, magnificent, imposing mountains, like the Montagna Madre, la Maiella, which thrust up their millions of calyxes.

And yet I am not happy, not satisfied with what I see and hear. A feeling of deep uneasiness, mixed with detachment, is consuming me. In the end, am I not just an intruder who doesn't have anything in common with this place? Truly, I say to myself, I don't know what I was looking for in Introdacqua. I never lived here; nothing is familiar to me except for memories of my grandfather Giorgio, and clearly I am not going to uncover any documents or evidence useful to me in reconstructing the childhood and youth of Pascal. Everything's been destroyed or scattered, by wars, floods, earthquakes. Nor would I ever be able to track down some 100-year-old who might remember him. And even if I did find one, what could that old man tell me that I don't already know from Pascal's autobiography and from stories I heard myself from my grandfather? What could he tell me about a boy, barely seventeen, who left for America with his father and never came back?

And yet I had to come here, I couldn't not *see* these places where Pascal lived from 1894 to 1910. I couldn't not visit the house where my grandfather and grandmother lived—my grandfather until 1910, and she who waited alone for his return until 1917, when Giorgio came back to Introdacqua to get her and bring her back with him to America to stay.

I couldn't not breathe the air they breathed here, I couldn't—using a lot of imagination, of course—not look with my own eyes at the landscapes that, a hundred years ago, nourished their own gazes.

But I can't leave it without visiting the house, or what remains of the house, where Pascal's family lived. This is what I propose to do, calmly, today, on this boisterously sunny day.

I decide to leave the car in the hotel parking lot. I want to walk the whole length of the road to Cauze, the district where Pascal was born and lived. I want to take the same path that he took who knows how many times, alone or with his buddies.

I go down Via Fiume, today a delightful street filled with flowers, trees, and cottages. In Pascal's time, as I've already said, it was just a simple country lane. Today it takes you from Introdacqua to state road 479, the one I took three days ago coming from Sulmona.

I have my notebook in hand and some sheets I printed out from Google Maps. The page that deals just with Cauze informs me curtly that: a) the district of Cauze is 2.77 kilometers from the commune of Introdacqua, of which it is a part; b) the Comune of Introdacqua has no other districts apart from Cauze (however, also on the Internet, I saw someone say that Introdacqua leads to districts and small towns including Cantone, Mastroiacovo, Pannate, and Santa Maria Frascati; c) the district of Cauze reaches 506 meters above sea level; d) the district has seventeen inhabitants. This is all there is, officially, to say about Cauze.

After about a half hour I reach the little intersection, which a passerby kindly told me was coming up, and which would bring me to Cauze. I cross a dirt road and I can't help but think of the fact that Pascal walked down this very road many times, a century ago.

On my left before getting to the opening in the road where the few houses of Cauze sit (by the way, it may not be out of the question that the name given to this spot derives from the word *case/houses*, pronounced in the local dialect), there is a fresh spring that almost certainly in days gone by would have served as a watering and drinking trough for the district. After quenching my thirst I listen to the silvery sound of the fountain. The water is amazingly fresh, and even now, writing these lines, I remember its taste in my mouth.

And here it is, at long last: the place where my Pascal was born, in this silent and deserted clearing overlooked by this scattering of humble shacks. There is not a single person around. I get the sudden eerie impression that the district itself has been abandoned by its few inhabitants (as I said, according to the Internet, there should be seventeen!).

I approach the entrance to the house I immediately recognize. With me I have the book Rino Panza gave me, which on page 32 has an accurate drawing of Pascal's birthplace; the caption reads, "This picture, drawn in the '80s by V. Annino, does a better job than any photograph of illustrating the exterior of the poor dwelling."

And here, to the left, the famous three steps where mother and son were sitting the night they said goodbye just before he, together with his father, Angelo, departed for Naples and then sailed to America.

Three humble stone steps, worn down by time, speak just to themselves. Above them stands a small doorway, all corroded. I stand on the steps and peer through some cracks into the squalid interior. On the right, on the main floor, there's a room where some piles of wood are gathered, here and there, in unlikely ways, and lots and lots of trash of every variety, miserable objects, ratty remains of what was already an extremely humble dwelling. Everything chaotically and pathetically heaped up, helter-skelter.

In this smaller room, which functioned as sitting room, kitchen, and dining room, humans and animals lived side by side. After dinner, in fact, the space served as shelter at night for the few goats and sheep the D'Angelo family kept.

I observe through the slits in the gaunt planks of the door the ladder that leads to the loft, which served as a bedroom for the whole family. This extremely modest windowless space was and is divided into unequal parts: In the forward one, in the center, was the bed on which all four members of the family slept. At the top were the parents, in the middle was the smallest son, and at the bottom, sideways, Pascal, who sometimes would be kicked off the bed during the night by his parents' feet, which resulted in his finding himself in the mornings with lumps on his head. He was "lucky" in that his parents typically got up at dawn; once they had left the loft, he could curl up in the warm space they left next to his brother and they could sleep as long as they liked, unless, of course, a storm arose and the raindrops coming through the roof woke the two brothers up. Further inside the loft, whose ceiling fell just about to the floor, were piles of wood, the only source of energy in the house and also typically the home of mice.

I realize simply describing this place the way it was in Pascal's day and the way I saw it spying through the spaces in the decrepit door, that it could be easily the kind of thing one might find in the pages of *Oliver Twist*, except that those sordid scenes so magisterially rendered by Dickens took place a hundred years before the ones in which the D'Angelo family lived.

I stare as though in a dream at this tattered ladder that leads to the loft in Pascal's house. A child of four is slowly climbing it ... the child is followed by his grandma, who lovingly urges him from half-way up the ladder as he goes to get an onion from under the bed. "Go on, Pasquale, get the onion from under the bed so we can roast it in the fire pit and eat it."

The little boy has reached the top of the ladder, while the grandma, behind him, says the last encouraging words, partly to alleviate his terror of finding himself face to face with the mice that are scampering around among the loose roof tiles.

15

"Who are you? Whaddaya want?" The ill-mannered voice of a woman behind me shakes me out of my daydream.

I come down the steps and turn toward her. I try to explain very succinctly my reason for being here. Our brief conversation, which was difficult for both of us to follow, is continually interrupted by the scratching about of some chickens and a dog's insistent barking.

I walk around the clearing, lingering a while longer in this place that has changed so little from a century ago until now. It's here, in the small world that brought it to life, that games, dreams, and adventures took place, all in the mind of the young Pascal.

His closest pal is Giulio, a slender, undernourished boy. One day Giulio stumbles on a stone and takes a bad fall. Blood springs from his face and Giulio bursts into tears. Enraged, his mother comes out of her shack and immediately lays into Pascal, thinking he's the one who caused the accident. She grabs him by the ear and starts to shake him as if he were a rabbit. Terrorized, he somehow manages to explain that he didn't make her son fall and invites her to confirm as much directly with Giulio, meanwhile thinking, "Just wait till I am bigger, and if something happens, I'll show you I can escape!"

Another bloody head, this time that of another boy, would also involve our innocent Pascal some years later, at age eleven. Here, in this little clearing, possibly even right where I am walking now. This time there are three boys. Besides Pascal there's a rough bigger boy three years older than him and another, littler child. Some squabble begins among them and the bigger boy at a certain point starts mistreating the little one, who defends himself as best he can. The big one throws him on the ground and sticks a rock in Pascal's hand, inciting him to strike him, for no reason. Pascal, who by nature is against any kind of violence, refuses, but here's where suddenly everything happens very fast: Pascal no longer is holding the rock, the bigger boy is snickering ferociously, and the little one's on the ground with a bloody head. It's almost noon.

A moment later the child gets up and launches himself toward home, covered in tears and with an uncertain step, his forehead streaked with blood. Pascal is consumed with terror. He feels responsible for having taken part in the incident, although as if in some kind of trance. In his heart he knows that if the little boy's father comes over to beat him, he can add Pascal's parents' blows to his, since they had always told him to avoid certain of his friends, and especially that coarse ruffian, the older boy.

Pascal therefore resolves not to go home and instead to flee to the open countryside, looking for some safe place to hide. He goes along quite a while, his shoes halfway destroyed, sinking alternately into muddy and marshy ground.

At last he reaches an area where various streets intersect; he notices a bridge under which is a dry gully and he curls himself up in a corner of it, still keeping an eye out in case anyone should appear. Pascal is afraid not only of some reprisal but of being seen by some passerby here, under the viaduct, and their going to report him to his parents, who certainly would never forgive this flight of his.

This childish and agitated wait of Pascal's is suddenly interrupted by the appearance of a girl, with her flock of about a dozen sheep and lambs. Pascal curls up into the smallest ball possible in his little hiding place, but the young girl sees him.

"What're you doing here?"

Terrified, Pascal comes slowly out into the open; he doesn't know what to say, he hears only the long-distance sound of the jingle of the sheep and the soft baa of a lamb: sounds that at that moment make him hope that no one is out hunting. Not far from him is the shepherdess, a bit older than him, whom he recognizes as the sister of the injured boy. Knowing nothing of what has happened, she asks him again what he's doing hiding in his little den.

Pascal says nothing, overcome by myriad conflicting feelings, and he doesn't want his behavior to betray anything. Instead he moves away from her, without saying a word. The puzzled girl follows him with her eyes; she doesn't know what to make of this reticence tinged with fear. Having reached a certain distance, Pascal proceeds to yell to her what happened and why he fled. The shepherdess doesn't want to believe him despite the fact that Pascal, in all his disarming candor (the kind an eleven-year-old boy could have a hundred years ago in a remote village in Abruzzo), insists on confessing to her his noninvolvement in what happened and his innocence.

The young girl, at first a bit hesitant, bursts into laughter, genuine but still puzzled, and then moves away, shaking her head.

Everything around Pascal sinks back into silence interrupted only by the distant and muffled baaing of a sheep.

He goes back to his hiding place, by this time prey to complete dismay, and, whimpering softly, he gives himself up to a drowsy torpor that eventually makes him forget lunch. In his childish and dreamy soul, as he falls asleep, the idea begins to take root that maybe as the hours go by everything in his little community will return to normal, and there won't be anyone who is looking for him anymore to confront him and do him harm.

In his sleep Pascal is running frantically amid some uproar that from time to time seems like it wants to run him over or else drag him to the edge of a cliff. In the midst of the din he can clearly make out the fervent braying of a donkey, a braying that reaches him no matter where he is on this frenetic, breathtakingly fast run. At a certain point he arrives at the slopes of a majestic mountain, more majestic than the mother mountain Maiella. An irresistible impulse pulls him forward to climb this imposing mountain, to do whatever it takes to reach the top. He feels like something is slowing him down, however, as though he can't make his legs go on, but he's already close to the peak, and in the end he reaches the highest point.

From up there, looking around at the vast panorama, he has the impression that he has grasped the heart of the mystery of the universe. At the top of the mountain is a gigantic, leafy tree, filled with birds of many colors, the likes of which he has never seen before. Their chatter seems to invite him to climb the tree. Pascal climbs, but at a certain point he feels the mountain splitting beneath him; the boy desperately grabs hold of a limb, but it falls apart and he begins to fall further and further down, down, still further down … and suddenly he wakes with a start.

It's raining hard and Pascal realizes that night is falling. The rain grows more intense and so does his fear, fear of being out in the middle of the countryside alone in the imminent darkness of evening. He's also feeling hunger, but even stronger than this is the desire to be at home.

Once again he begins running crazily. A little ways ahead he has to cross a stream that seems to be getting bigger right before his eyes. He wades in up to his knees, but at this point nothing matters to him anymore. His sole objective is to get home as soon as possible. He thinks that by this time the sister of the wounded boy has already gotten back and almost certainly will have reported her strange encounter with him to her parents.

Finally he is back at the tiny village; Pascal sees in the distance a grouping of houses that looks familiar. A plume of smoke hovers over one of them; through the windows you can even glimpse the pale lights inside.

The boy gets closer to his home. In front of the door there's someone yelling his name; someone else echoes the cry. He feels better; in his heart he knows he hasn't done anyone harm; he'll head straight for the house, ignoring these people who certainly won't have the guts to bar him from the door. With his heart in his throat he moves through a group of people and in a flash reaches the three steps of his house, just at the moment when he feels a hand grabbing hold of him, but then he hears the unmistakable voice of his mother commanding: "Leave him alone! You know perfectly well he's done nothing."

The hand, which belongs to the older brother of the hurt boy, immediately lets go.

"Don't worry, Aunt Naflice; I'm just joking." And then turning to Pascal, "I know you didn't do anything. Otherwise I would have tracked you down no matter where you were hiding."

16

It's almost three p.m. and I've come back to my room: a bit too early and too late to do much of anything. It's the hour that in the meridionale in Italy they call *controra*, especially in the summer when in the first part of the afternoon the heat is still intense, and people stay in their houses to laze around or doze. The air itself, in these long, suspended, lethargic hours, seems to stop for a metaphysical waiting period before the freshness of the evening brings life back into the townspeople.

I put my odds and ends in order, folding my clothes and everything else in my suitcase. At this point there's nothing keeping me here in Introdacqua. I'll continue my research in the northeastern United States, in New York and Brooklyn, in New Jersey, Connecticut, Vermont, and the Cumberland Valley of Virginia, where the most tragic and dreadful periods of Pascal's American experience unfolded.

I carefully put all the material I have on Pascal D'Angelo in a separate bag and take some final notes on my visit to Cauze and on its ghostly and phantasmagorical atmosphere that has occupied my thoughts ever since.

An hour later I go downstairs, where I find Alfredo organizing the wood pile next to the fireplace. He's got a nice pile there, and he's now tidying it up in the wood-stacker.

I stop to chat with him a bit; I laugh at the fact that he's already starting up the heating engine for warming up the room. Alfredo says that here in Introdacqua the chill comes early, and by November, and sometimes even in October, you have to put on the heat. He adds that even today here in the local houses the fireplace serves as a fundamental source of heating in the wintertime. In a lot of the homes, especially the ones further out, they place a pot in the middle of the fireplace that gets used for mixing stews and other kinds of foodstuffs. It's the custom to leave this pot out continually and every day to put something into it: greens, potatoes, herbs, salt, peppers, oil, and water; meanwhile the embers serve for roasting various types of meat, onions, potatoes, and delicious *scarmorze* cheeses. Every day something new goes in, and so the pot becomes a constant resource, a means of perennial refueling for anyone who wants access to something edible during the course of the day.

We chat about the weather, and I express my amazement at yesterday's catastrophic thunderstorm.

"It's a blessing!" he says. "Here rain is always a blessing, my dear Giorgio."

He explains that, in effect, the worst wound the entire area has suffered is its dryness. The streams stay dry, the fields become deserted, and many harvests are dried out and ruined.

"I see the farmers, and I am one of them, who, during a season that's completely suffocated by the sun, turn their eyes up to the skies that are always blue and serene, as they are now, and just like my grandfather did in his day, beg for rain!" He makes a grimace almost of annoyance, wrinkling his brow, and adds, "Here's what it is, my dear Giorgio: This is one of the main things that pushed our peasants to emigrate ... which is also linked to another important reason— when the harvest was little or nothing on account of the drought there wasn't enough money to pay the land rent to the landlords, and these guys don't want excuses. A tragedy. Around here not everyone owned his own land. Many of them in order to keep going rented parcels and had to pay a certain amount every year. My grandfather was in that same situation. He started it ... then my father managed to purchase a plot. When the crop would turn out really bad, someone, pushed to the limit, would chuck it all up and move abroad, leaving behind lands, house, and sometimes even wife and kids."

"Of course ... I know," I don't what else to say.

And so, out of a spirit of solidarity and also to launch myself into the topic of emigration, I tell him about my excursion to Cauze, using the D'Angelo family itself as an example, and I mention, fleetingly, my research on Pascal, alluding also to the video we watched together in his apartment.

Alfredo listens attentively and with an air of interest. Then he says, "Here in town there's Rino Panza who might have been helpful. Unfortunately he just died this morning."

I am completely knocked out by this blunt piece of news. I tell him I saw Rino just two days earlier and that it was from him, and also his wife, that I obtained certain materials that could prove useful. But then I stop, overcome. My distress is so strong that I can't say anything further.

"I'm sorry," Alfredo says. "Rino took a bad turn and ..." He stops piling the wood and invites me to sit with him. He goes to get a bottle of wine and pours me a glass of it. This is his way, simple and direct, of cushioning for me my sudden and evident sorrow.

17

It's the morning of October 13. I'm leaving the hotel. I drink a cappuccino at the bar. I've already loaded my few bags into the car. Anna keeps me company. Alfredo went to Sulmona and won't be back before lunchtime. I say goodbye to this friendly and hard-working woman; I thank her again for her hospitality, pay my bill, and ask her to give my affectionate goodbyes to Alfredo.

In the car I think again about Pascal and his father's separation from the family. Pascal had just turned sixteen. It's February of 1910. I go through, moment by moment as in a film in my head, his last evening in Introdacqua, the emotional farewell between him and his mother. The two are sitting on those chipped steps to the front door of the house; I can almost hear the promises the boy makes in vain to his mother about his future return, while she knows only too well that her son, like a bird whose wings are strong and who's learned to fly, won't be coming back to the nest.

I go down highway 479, skirting for a few seconds the Via Torre San Pietro, where up until yesterday lived Rino Panza, keeper of the only documents about Pascal that remain in this town.

Eventually I get to Sulmona, and I decide to take a look at the train station in the Piazza Vittime Civili di Guerra, built in 1888. It was from this place that, twenty-two years later, Pascal, his father, and a small group of men from their town took the train for Naples, the city they sailed from to reach New York.

Today to get to Naples from Sulmona takes something like five hours, provided you take the "red arrow" and change at Teramo and at Rome. But if one takes the normal train, switching at Avezzano, Cassino, and Caserta, it takes more than twelve hours, four hours longer than flying from New York to Rome.

In February of 1910 there weren't any "red arrows" or "silver" or "Eurostar" or "intercity" or any other type of "high velocity" trains. I can reasonably assume, then, that the train Pascal took at Sulmona, with all the multiple changes and a slower speed, would have taken at least fifteen to twenty hours to arrive at Campania's capital.

In the piazza outside the station there's a steam locomotive, like a monument, a train from the 835 group, third series, which was put into commercial use between 1907 and 1911. The first series, of twenty trains, was ordered in 1905; in 1906 another order was placed.

The train Pascal and his Introdacquesi group took was most likely equipped with an 835 locomotive, possibly even the same one on display at the station (to be exact it's the 835, 092 locomotive) that I am looking at here, in the semi-deserted Piazza Vittime.

In this piazza, on the morning of April 2, 1910, a group of men from Introdacqua arrived. Having left their town before dawn, following the last emotional farewells from their families, in the midst of a heartrendingly sorrowful atmosphere, which one of the relatives tried, in vain, to lighten by making some funny quip, this meager handful reached Sulmona just about dawn, having walked around five kilometers along the country lane, the lane that, decades later, would become the 479.

It's Pascal's first time on a train.

At the station the band of men from Introdacqua mixes with many other people (also on their way to Naples to take the same ship) in the middle of a general clamor—a confusion of men, women, and children, a chaos made up of weeping, shouting, amazement, and uncertainty.

18

What exactly were the reasons that caused hundreds of thousands of Italians, many of them peasants from Veneto, Abruzzo and Molise, Calabria and Sicily, to emigrate to America during the first twenty years of the last century? Aside from the usual causes that everyone can imagine (the poverty of so many Italian areas, unemployment, the difficulty of earning a decent living from farming, the dreams of the goodly and lauded "promised land"), I am more and more convinced that, in the last analysis, there are two factors that Italian emigration in that period is founded on, and they boil down to the landowners and the loan sharks. The first were the wealthy landlords who a century ago rented out big or small parcels of land to farmers. They in turn cultivated them as best they could, but they were obligated to pay very high rents, earning just half (and sometimes even just a quarter) of what they harvested. Not only that. They also had to trust that the unpredictable weather conditions would continue to keep the land fertile.

The second were the greedy loan sharks who intervened to lend money to the farmers who needed it. At the ready, like leeches, they knew they could count on the urgent necessity of these predicaments.

In this scheme of things the most unfortunate were the so-called day-laborers. The most abased and denigrated of those who worked in the fields were paid a miserable wage by farmers, given that they themselves weren't able to earn substantial amounts of money.

This doesn't happen anymore, but only up to a certain point, if we consider the exploitation of so many immigrants in our country (for the most part undocumented), used variously in the regular harvest of fruits and vegetables. But this phenomenon, particularly in our southern regions, is also on the way out because it's too costly for the farmers to hire these day-laborers, even if they own their own land. What results is increasing neglect and abandonment of the fields, where every year tons of various fruits rot; or else their sale to new growers coming from Morocco, from Tunisia, or elsewhere in North Africa.

In other cases, the sale is not final; it sometimes happens that, after some years, certain fields—having been improved under the cultivation of foreigners who have managed to produce, at great personal cost, a more efficient system of growing and harvest—are reclaimed by their former owners, who can then retake possession of their lands and immediately sell them again, for a higher price, to different growers. A vicious cycle that actually conceals a very bitter truth, which is the utter inability of our farmers in the South (I am thinking specifically of those in Calabria and even more of those in Sicily) to band together: the inability to create an effective collective that can work together and bring about a system that will benefit everyone.

Between 1908 and 1909, although just a boy, Pascal understands the difficulties his father is facing in trying to improve his family's quality of life. Pascal has already worked with him for three years now. He had had to quit school at age eleven in order to help the family out. In the spring of 1908 his father decides to rent two sizable portions of arable land. He kills himself every day from dawn until dusk. He doesn't have enough money to pay his first installment and is forced to borrow at a high interest rate. At the end of the season, after having sold the entire crop, once he has paid his workers, paid the rent, and paid off the loan, he finds himself with almost empty pockets.

Here we return to the harmful effects of the landowners and the loansharks, the vampires who infested the countryside in Abruzzo a hundred years ago. Forget about the evil eye spells against jinxes, the faith healers, the fixers, the miserable witches like the old "vampire" of Introdacqua!

And finally, one must not forget, in the general atmosphere that preceded emigration to another country—an atmosphere made up of misery, anger, sadness, and uprooting from one's own land—a new and important element: the positive one of curiosity.

What I mean is that in this anger or indignation that is widely felt by emigrants, whether it be toward the land that can't provide the most basic things they need to survive or toward the unknown country they're moving to (*America* in this sense taken in its widest geographic meaning), which separates fathers from their families, an unfamiliar and increasingly positive emotion takes hold: adventure, the awareness that this voyage will lead to learning about other places, other ways of life, other cultures.

It's precisely this combination of sentiments—in which emotions, fears, rage, sadness, and dreams of the future mix together—that these half-asleep people on the train are feeling, having left Sulmona, having left their little village, perhaps forever.

The noisy confusion of the station has disappeared, and now the passengers, almost emigrants, are silent, wrapped up in their own thoughts as the train carries them to Naples. It's a strange silence brought about by their uncertain feelings, which no one wants to confess to his seatmate. Maybe some of them are thinking again about the images they've seen in some photographs, not very remarkable ones, of relatives who have emigrated. In one of these there's a fellow who's pushing a handcart loaded with gigantic onions; each one of them surely weighs a kilo at least! In another, a boy points at a countertop covered with pumpkins of colossal size. On the reverse of the photo someone has written, "Look at this pumpkin; it weighs more than 100 kilos!"

Photographs like these must have fed the imaginations of our farmers on their journey to America.

19

In Naples our Pascal—having lived up to that moment as a shepherd in the mountains of the Peligna Valley—will see the ocean for the first time in his life. It will be an imposing sight, magical, seductive, and repellent at the same time, something that remains in the imagination of the emigrant forever: the immense, infinite sea.

Edmondo De Amicis, in a memorable if sometimes sketchy and didactic book (*Sull'oceano*), tells of the experience he had on a similar voyage, though bound for Buenos Aires: the atmosphere of setting out from Genoa, the sea, the Atlantic crossing, the ship conceived of as a microcosm of "exoticism" and "eroticism" (fascinatingly and significantly representative of a diverse social, national, anthropological, and linguistic world), life on board and the diversified typology of the passengers, depending on whether they were in first class (wealthy tourists, haute-bourgeois, and cosmopolitan aristocrats), second class (petit-bourgeois, modest businessmen who were possibly on the edge of bankruptcy and tempted by new prospects of well-being for their families, thieves, the disinherited, "hotheads," and fugitives from justice), or third class (the most dejected, mostly poor emigrants and tramps, manual laborers, and other people of no significance—in sum, the lumpenproletariat, half-illiterate peasants, the man who will content himself with the most humble and degrading work, who will contribute to the construction of pre-industrial America with roads, bridges, water mains, tunnels, buildings).

Sull'oceano was one of the most successful of De Amicis's works, a true best-seller (ten editions in two weeks), whose book launch was capably handled by the Treves publishing house in 1889; the book's publication came twenty years before Pascal came over himself. I don't think the feverish atmosphere among the great masses of emigrants, as well as the procedural dynamics at the port of Genoa, related by De Amicis in an animated and picturesque—but also sometimes rough and emotionally engaging—way, were so very different from those that our Introdacquesi heroes confronted at Naples. In his succinct autobiography, Pascal deals in just a few lines with the things that happened before they set sail on the ship. He was evidently more interested in narrating his experiences in the United States, the encounter with the new world, the hard work he had before him, the agonizing sacrifices, the oppressions, the hardship, the abuse he suffered, but also the dreams, the resolutions, and the ambitions—which were for him undeniable—that would mark the years in America for someone like him who would never return home. Certainly he, his father, and some of their townsmen were capable of spending those three days before embarkation (devoted to paperwork of various kinds) doing something besdies "curling up like dogs" (De Amicis) outside in the Neapolitan streets, like derelicts in the area around the Spanish Quarter.

An employee of the maritime company, whom the Intradacquesi men had been assigned to, met them at the station and took them to a *pensione*, where they stayed for the days before their departure.

All the paperwork having been dispensed with, on the morning of the fourth day they got in line in the third and final group to go aboard the great steamship *Cedric*, one of the jewels of the British mercantile marine, managed by the White Star Line, to join many emigrants like them in the belly of the ship.

Into that belly would go almost a thousand people, most of them coming from regions like Veneto, Abruzzo and Molise, Campania, Calabria, and Sicily.

It's only too easy to imagine the climate of general chaos at the moment of boarding the ship (which was coming from Alexandria, Egypt; the usual route for these transatlantic ships was Alexandria to Naples to New York): shouts, rebukes, dins of various kinds, arguments, people calling out to one another, entire families with children and luggage clustered together, attached one to the other, as though in fear of being suddenly separated amid that human bedlam.

20

My grandpa Giorgio, in the stories he told me when I was little, never spoke about the transatlantic voyage.

I don't know if that was because of an instinctive reticence or if he'd removed the experience from his memories, excited as he was at telling me about what life in America was like, how he himself had seen it and lived it in the first decades of the twentieth century.

Pascal too in his diary barely touches on the Atlantic crossing. In just a few pages he tells us merely what is essential, and some things are more or less negligible. As regards the great steamship that carried him from Naples to New York, he tells us only its name: *Cedric*.

There are photographs (faded ones, which may even contribute to their appeal) of this colossal ship, which, like its twin the *Celtic*, was a true pearl of the British Merchant Navy. At the beginning of the twentieth century these were the most powerful transport ships in the world, second only to the *Titanic*, which was built ten years later; the launch, proclaimed in all the newspapers and rotogravures of the period, took place on May 31, 1911.

The first decade of the twentieth century witnessed a feverish race to construct transatlantic steamships, above all by Germany and England, which had two companies that operated powerfully and in reciprocal competition: the White Star Line and the Cunard Line.

The first could boast a quartet of ships that would quickly become legendary: the *Celtic*, as we've said, from 1901; immediately followed by the *Cedric*; and then the *Baltic* and the *Adriatic*.

The Cunard could counterstrike with the *Lusitania* and the *Mauritania*, two superbly outfitted, enormous transatlantic ships, even a bit bigger than those of the White Star Line. This glorious company was founded in 1850 by Henry Threlfail Wilson and John Pilkington and originally named the Oceanic Steam Navigation Company. Its two primary presidents were Thomas Henry Ismay and his son Joseph Bruce Ismay. Over the course of their lives both Thomas and Joseph would strive mightily to make their naval company the most famous and utilized in the world.

In 1933, after a turn of events culminating in the two disasters of the *Titanic* (on April 14, 1912, more than 1,500 people died) and the *Britannic* (which sank in 1916 after colliding with a mine—about a thousand people were killed there as well), the company was taken over by the rival Cunard Line, a move that was aided by the British government, which was taking care of the interests of the latter.

The *Cedric*, the vessel carrying our heroes on their way to New York, was described by the British press at the time as "the biggest and most splendid transatlantic ship on earth, or rather, on the sea."

Launched on August 21, 1902, near the Belfast coast, the *Cedric* was constructed, as the *Celtic* had been, according to the most modern systems of naval architecture. Both transatlantic steamers were 698 feet meters long, 75 feet wide, and with a depth of more than 49 feet. They were supplied with equipment of a size never before seen. The two gigantic smokestacks measured, from the keel, 135 feet high, and the weight of each ship was close to 21,000 tons.

If you look closely at the photographs of these two ocean liners, what strikes you are their perfectly harmonious and elegant forms, which will instantly remind you of our *Rex*, immortalized in Fellini's *Amarcord* (although the *Rex* was built thirty years after the two English ships).

Notwithstanding their great size, the *Cedric* and the *Celtic* possessed a maximum of strength and security and were divided up into numerous water-tight compartments in case of accident. They had an astounding capacity of almost 3,000 people (2,875, to be precise). First class, with plush, luxurious interiors, could hold around 365 passengers; second class, from 160 to 200; third class, huddled together in the belly of the ship, more than 1,000. The rest of the passengers (about 800) were the varied and cosmopolitan crew.

Looking at photographs of the interiors and exteriors of these ships, it's impossible not to admire the refined manner in which they were outfitted and the detailed internal arrangements that the vessels had in common. Instantly striking, among the many chambers, is the sumptuous, elegant dining room, featuring huge chandeliers; but also the numerous sitting rooms and powder rooms, the dignified smoking room, the library, the enormous and completely stocked bar, the elevators, the various staterooms and cabins (for families or individuals, according to the numbers of people and whether they traveled together or alone), and the numerous other areas delicately decorated and kept fresh by electrical ventilation.

The first-class rooms, in addition to the wide variety of comforts, were furnished with equipment for wireless telegraphs, which allowed travelers to stay in communication with land for the entirety of the crossing. These passengers, certainly privileged, walked on floors covered by carpets and rubber that muted every sound.

I'm describing rooms and spaces that the passengers in third class, stuffed all together for almost the entire ten days of the ocean crossing, would never have a chance to see, very likely not even being aware of the splendor and the luxurious elegance.

The "space" reserved for these travelers in third class consisted basically of a bunk made of iron to sleep on, or else to lie on for hours fantasizing about their present and future and using these fantasies to keep at bay thoughts, worries, stress, anxiety, and anguish, particularly every time the ship pitched and noises of various kinds became as deafening as they were mysterious.

There wasn't a dining room for this army of ragamuffins, just a long and tortuous route into the very belly of the ocean liner. After making this trek one got to a place where it was necessary to stand in a very long line until reaching a sort of counter, behind which was someone who brusquely gave you some unappetizing soup. But hunger wasn't the worst enemy for these passengers. The worst enemy, the greatest discomfort, came as a result of their isolation, of being constrained to stay almost the entire time in the bowels of the ship and to see through the portholes the constant violent splashes of water hitting it.

I can picture these dispossessed figures: some eating a hunk of bread kept in their pocket; some playing *scopa*, *brisola*, or *tressette*, using a worn-out bundle of cards; some writing letters; some sleeping in the midst of all the coming and going; some who are making the time pass just by talking. Someone sings one of the songs of his village.

If a terrible rainstorm hit—as in fact did happen during Pascal's crossing—the bowels they were stuffed into in third class became an inferno. In those moments it might happen that some passenger, in the grip of terror, would become hysterical, irrational, and the slightest thing could start a ferocious brawl. Somehow a knife would appear in Tizio's or Caio's hand ... above the general chaos one could hear the massive, unending din of the waves continuing to batter against the portholes.

It sometimes happened in these conditions that a woman gave birth, or that someone died of a heart attack or for some other reason. In those cases regulations insisted that the body be wrapped in a suitable covering and dropped into the sea.

These moments alternated with some others of relative calm, such as Pascal experienced when the ship passed the Azores—islands that, to his eyes, looked like floating toys; or the really happy, and rare, occasion when our group of men was allowed to go up to the deck to stretch their legs.

From up there, even for a few moments, one could breathe in the fresh sea air, feast one's eyes on the blue of the sky, and sometimes be entertained by the innocent pastime of looking at the amazing variety of fish in the sea.

One of our Abruzzesi suddenly yells, "Look, look how many fish!"

"Where, where?"

And here our heroes all lean over the deck railing to see the playful acrobatics of some joyous dolphins who are swimming alongside the ship and who keep up with it for miles and miles.

Ten days of traveling are both long and short, depending on the state of mind of the passengers, in this case depending on which class they're traveling in.

It is a fairly misty day when our emigrants finally spy New York Harbor through the porthole. It's April 18, 1910. First, little white dots appear, barely visible to the naked eye. They're sailboats, the first signs of life in this infinite expanse of water, where up to this moment, for days and days, the only thing visible has been ocean, ocean,

ocean. Then, little by little (by this time the sun is going down) a strip of earth becomes clearer and then slowly disappears, engulfed by the evening darkness and a blanket of heavy fog.

Land finally. It's America.

Seeing it erases the many days of fear and anxiety for our travelers, now impatient to exit this enormous belly, impatient to set foot on the soil that has fed their imagination for so long.

21

While our emigrants are disembarking from the steamship I'd like to say a little bit about that vessel's remaining years, which were not many.

On April 15, 1912, when the tragedy of the *Titanic* was made known to the world, the *Cedric* was anchored in the port of New York, remaining there for four days after having finished the same journey as two years before with Pascal and his friends: Alexandria-Naples-New York.

Many of the survivors of the *Titanic*'s disaster wanted to return to Europe immediately, and they did so on the *Cedric*.

In 1914, after the First World War had broken out, both the *Cedric* and the *Celtic* were converted into battle cruisers. Two years later both ships were used to carry troops to Egypt. In 1918, just before the war's end, the *Cedric* rammed the Canadian ship *Montreal*, sustaining severe damages. In that same year its twin the *Celtic* suffered a violent blow to the bow from a torpedo; six people were killed.

At the end of the war the two ships, completely restored, resumed their regular service, setting sail from Europe to America and back again, transporting thousands and thousands of passengers. They continued on this way until 1923, when, in the midst of an impenetrable fog, the *Cedric* collided with the transatlantic ship *Scythia* of the Cunard Company, just off the coast of Ireland. There were no casualties, but the damage was significant.

Repaired and restored again, our steamship returned once more to her usual transatlantic route until 1928, when she was converted into a cabin-class liner, or a second-class ship. The same year, on December 12, her twin broke up on the rocky coast of Northern Ireland; devastating damages were reported, but no deaths.

By this time we're on the cusp of the Great Depression. It took at least a year for it to fully take hold. One after the other, all the glorious steamships wind up in the scrapyards. The *Cedric* and *Celtic* are no exceptions.

On September 5, 1931, the *Cedric* makes its final crossing to New York, and on its return to Liverpool, it passes the baton to the *Britannic*, not a steamship, but equipped with an extremely powerful turbine engine and four smokestacks, some 187 feet longer and 27,000 tons heavier than our emigrants' steamer.

The history of the *Cedric* ends at the beginning of January 1932, when she is sold for 22,000 pounds sterling to the Thomas W. Ward Company. On January 11, she completes her final, brief voyage from Liverpool to Inverkeithing, across the bay from Edinburgh. Here she is taken apart piece by piece.

The same destiny befalls the *Celtic*. After the incident on the Irish coast in December 1928, she is reduced to mere wreckage, a twisted, shapeless carcass.

PART TWO

New York and East Coast, 1910–1916

1

Our little gang of Introdacquesi is thrown in and mixed into the confused mass of people that pours off the ship at Ellis Island. Among them is a sixteen-year-old boy. It's our Pascal in that torrent of folks that fills the enormous entrance hall, soon to have his identity verified and be given his certificate of good health (in Italy at one time this was the famous certification of a "healthy and robust constitution") so that he may then be added to the list of those who have arrived in the United States. And here, by the way, the official who signed the certificate made two mistakes: The first was when he named, under "ship of travel," the *Celtic*. Our young immigrant states in his autobiography that it was the *Cedric*. I can't believe that Pascal would get the name wrong after having had so much time to observe it on the ship's great hull, in the Port of Naples, and during the long journey of ten days, together with thousands of other people coming from Alexandria, Egypt, and from the Italian ports. But in any case, whether it was the *Celtic* or the *Cedric* really doesn't matter, considering that the two steamships, as I've said, were built at the same time and were absolutely identical: utter and complete twins.

The second mistake on the certificate is Pascal's age: fourteen instead of sixteen. I see these notations on the passenger manifest conserved in the Ellis Island archives. On the same sheet they list the ethnicity of the young man: The zealous official wasn't content to write merely "Italy"; on the same line he writes "Italian South." It's not a case of idle punctiliousness. In the first decades of emigration to America not a few Italians from the South, maybe on account of the darker color of their skin, were employed like Blacks, particularly in Louisiana, for the hardest and most onerous work because they were considered more resistant to fatigue. There's an excellent documentary, *Bitter Bread* (Gianfranco Norelli, 2009), that illustrates this phenomenon.

I try to imagine also, looking at photos and documents from this era, what this endless hall was like, the atmosphere of confusion and the babble of so many languages from the thousands of emigrants arriving in a continuous stream. In a single day more than ten thousand people might arrive. It's been ascertained that between the years 1880 and 1920 five million people, from all over Europe, arrived in America. The peak came in 1906, when in a single year 358,000 arrived.

For the most part, Italian immigrants settled in New York (particularly in lower Manhattan, where they founded the first Little Italy, or further uptown in Harlem and in Riverdale and the rest of the Bronx), Connecticut (Hartford and Bridgeport), Maryland (with the greatest concentration in Baltimore), Pennsylvania, Illinois (mostly Chicago), and Massachusetts (largely in Boston, which had another important Little Italy).

When the Abruzzesi group arrived at Ellis Island in 1910, almost a hundred thousand Italians were already living in New York alone. On the East Coast the Italian community, along with the Irish, was the largest.

It's not difficult to imagine the dazed state of our boys from Introdacqua, in the midst of the bedlam of different kinds of sounds, once they set foot in America; they're feverishly excited but also deathly tired and also afraid of not being approved, or else of being sent home after all the incredible financial sacrifices it took them just to raise the money for the voyage.

Likewise, it was not at all unusual for diligent customs officers and "inspectors" at Ellis Island to observe infectious diseases among the new arrivals who, apart from anything else, if interrogated couldn't respond properly either because of their not knowing English, or because the questions were posed curtly, or simply because they were stunned by the entire situation.

The medical inspection began from the moment the immigrants started in single file to move toward the stairway that would bring them to the large Registry Room. There they were shaken up together, weighed down with their bags and boxes, suitcases, and pieces of furniture of all different kinds often crushed into a rough bundle of cloth slung over their shoulders.

A band of public health service doctors was stationed at the top of the staircase, giving a brief preliminary inspection to those who met them with shortened breath or limping or with vision problems or scratching their heads, or with any other symptoms of illness or disability.

These distinguished doctors had only a few minutes to summarily examine each passenger, and they were extremely faithful to the rules of the Immigration Act, which stated, "The Congress acts to exclude immigrants with mental and physical defects, and prohibits any lunatic, idiot, or any person unable to take care of himself or herself without becoming a public charge."

These provisions were fairly elastic and intentionally vague so that officials of the PHSD could act at their own discretion. If they spotted some symptom of any illness, they noted it with a chalk mark on the back of the jacket or directly on the shoulders of the immigrant: an "L" for lameness; an "E" for eyes; "SC" for anyone suspected of having lice or other problems with their scalp; an "H" for heart; etc., etc.

Those who were marked with these letters were immediately taken from the line and moved to another hall called the Special Examination Room. Here they were examined more thoroughly, but still hastily, given the enormous and unending daily influx of immigrants. Many of those who were marked were sent directly to the Ellis Island Hospital (Marine Hospital Service; in 1912 renamed US Public Health Service).

In this hospital, the immigrants were subjected to more specialized tests and eventually received treatment. Once they were cured, they received their permit to enter the United States. Other immigrants, victims of more serious sicknesses—sometimes people who were members of the same family—were declared excludable and thus held for forty days. After this quarantine, if their health had not returned or had not returned sufficiently, these unfortunate immigrants were called "mandatorily excludable" and then sent without further delay back to their countries of origin, a situation of agony and desperation for the family members with them.

Anyone who passed the medical examination was given an "inspection card" on which was stamped the word "passed."

Naturally, there were frequent cases of corruption, and with sufficient bribes some immigrants managed to elude the medical exam.

It was this regrettable situation of deception, fraud, corruption, and schemes that William Williams, appointed federal commissioner of Ellis Island in 1902, tried to remedy.

Williams served twice in this capacity, first from 1902 to 1905, and then from 1909 to 1914, when our group of Abruzzesi reached Ellis Island. It was this commissioner who, in his official report for 1904, declared that the United Stated was accepting too many immigrants in poor physical condition.

Anyone who visits the Ellis Island buildings and the annexed Museum of Immigration can find beside the entrance a plaque, posted in 1912, containing this statement by William Williams: "Ellis Island is one of the greatest human nature offices in the world; no week passes without its comedies as well as tragedies."

2

Our Pascal's eyes shine while looking at the extraordinary and disjointed spectacle of automobiles, taxicabs, buses, and rivers of people rushing through the streets of Lower Manhattan.

Its late morning on an April day. Our Introdacquesi have made it to the Big Apple. More than almost anything else, their eyes are drawn to the elevated train tracks on which the cars of the New York City metro run unceasingly over their heads with loud clanking noises.

This is the largest public transit system in the world, whose first routes, in the City of New York and its environs, commenced in 1869.

Pascal is overwhelmed by the languages he hears among the crowd, as cars and other vehicles hurtle all around him.

Obviously English is the most common, which the young man heard at Ellis Island from the diligent customs officials and that now is mixed miraculously with the Abruzzese dialect of his companions and also of Mario Lancia, the squad captain who arrived right on time at Battery Park to meet them.

But there's not much time to savor or even to completely absorb all the marvels. The guide marches them along rapidly and knows how to navigate through Manhattan traffic. Nervously checking his watch, Lancia exchanges one or two words with them as he brings them directly to Penn Station and from there, amid all the general confusion, by train to Hillsdale, New Jersey.

This is America, the first America Pascal meets, on April 20, 1910.

Our little group, just arrived in Manhattan, find themselves suddenly in a desolate location, right in the middle of a forest, thick with vegetation and majestic trees as tall as massive statues, trees such as they've never seen in their country. All the hustle and hubbub of Manhattan have vanished, the skyscrapers gone as though by magic: gone the taxis, the public transport, the deafening noise, the nonstop flow of hurrying people.

A truck is waiting at the tiny train station in Hillsdale to pick up our group and now is driving through a long forest until it reaches a clearing. In the center of the clearing is a hut. This will be the first home for our Abruzzesi.

Night is falling, and the new immigrants get their pitiful belongings squared away in this small, smoke-stained wooden shack. Someone is strumming a mandolin, someone else sits on the edge of his cot, lost in his own thoughts; another is paused at the threshold, looking dazed: silent and pensive, he's staring out at the majestic trees all around them. Every once in a while he'll look up at the sky, which is already a dark cobalt color, and try to comprehend this new situation.

Shortly after that, they all sit down around a large table by the light of a kerosene lamp and enjoy a meal of soup.

Let's look a bit more closely at these men, who already seem like brothers united by a single purpose: to work so they may improve their own futures along with those of their families left at home.

There is the easygoing Matteo Rossi, who, during the brief sojourn at Ellis Island, has been nicknamed "ace of hearts." A strong worker, generous, tireless, Matteo is the kind of person who has the highest capacity for hard labor: All he cares about is working hard every day, almost mechanically, in order to earn enough money to send it regularly back to his family. It's his fixation, the constant and only reason for his being here in this alien land.

There's Giovanni Ferraro, a happy bachelor who hopes to find a nice little wife and who in the meantime enjoys hearing tales of married life from his friends.

There's Giacomo Gallina, the most irascible and among the most muscular of the group, exceeded only by Andrea Lenta, a six-foot colossus who's also received a decent education, which he sometimes employs with his comrades, relating to them some history and general cultural knowledge. For our heroes Andrea is the archetypal "gentle giant," who can be counted on in case of any quarrel or scuffle. He's also the only one, apart from the squad leader Mario Lancia, who knows any English.

And here is Antonio Lancia, Mario's father-in-law, who likes to sing famous arias every so often. Certain evenings, when you'd least expect it, in the silence as the men are getting ready to go to sleep, his gentle and serene voice is heard, sweet and yet majestic. As if by magic, the shabby, smoky wooden walls disappear, as well as everything inside. For just a moment, before sleep overtakes them all, it feels as though they are in Italy, at home, surrounded by their dear ones.

And here is Giorgio Vanno, fifteen years younger than Angelo, Pascal's mustachioed father, with whom he likes to talk about work and the future.

Finally, there are Matteo's nephew Filippo Rossi, and Pascal. These last two, sixteen years old, are far and away the youngest of the bunch; they're the mascots of the whole squad of nine men, all of them coming from the same little town.

3

It's a cool morning, April 21, 1910. Our men are up at the first light of dawn. A frugal breakfast of coffee and bagels awaits them. It's the first time they've ever seen this doughnut-shaped roll, Polish in origin and immensely popular in North America, particularly among Jews.

The air is filled with a mixture of strange happiness and a show of indifference: They're joking among themselves to conceal their curiosity and anxiety about the coming day, their first day of work in America.

In one corner there's Matteo Rossi, intently writing to his family. He was up a bit before the others, as has been his habit since they were on the *Cedric*, where he'd curl up on his bed and, all hunched over, write his letters. Some of his buddies teased him about his zeal, but others left him alone, respecting his routine. Maybe more than any of the other Abruzzesi, Matteo is living this American experience as if it didn't affect him. His mind is still stuck in his home town, where he's left his wife, Caterina, and their son, five-year-old Antonio.

Pascal is with his buddy Filippo, a couple of strapping lads who are already men and don't feel any less respected by their elders. Between them the jokes are flying, they're gesticulating, winking, facetiously horsing around to hide their nerves about the workday ahead.

Mario Lancia arrives, and the whole group falls silent. He's respected for his brisk, decisive manner, but the men have also quickly come to like him. He's one of them, and they think of him as a natural guide, their indispensable reference point in this unknown land. Besides, Antonio Lancia, who likes to burst into song, is his close relation.

Lancia talks to them briefly, giving them precise instructions about their tasks for the day and going forward. He tells them there's a truck waiting outside to take them to the job site, not far away. Near the shack there's a cabin containing their tools. Pascal, like all the others, gets assigned a pick and a shovel: These will be the tools he will master and that will go with him faithfully throughout the coming years. Meanwhile, they can hear the rumble of the waiting truck.

One by one they get on. Just two weeks ago they were farmers, handymen, peasants, picking up work in vineyards, or else they were simply unemployed layabouts. Today they're reinvented as manual laborers.

A few miles from Hillsdale, a small rural district surrounded by hills and little lakes that, at the time of their arrival, had a couple hundred inhabitants (this area is close to the border of upstate New York), they're building a long interstate highway, which will meander toward the northwest United States between mountains, lakes, and huge steep-sloped valleys. This is the modern Garden State Parkway, which runs almost parallel to the spectacular New York Thruway, also called Interstate 87, which from New Jersey goes north through state of New York to Canada, where it becomes US Route 15. Today from New York City you can take it all the way to Montreal, a journey of about nine hours.

This morning—a splendid day, April 20, 2014—in a giant time leap, I am driving my car up the Long Island Expressway (Highway 495). I decided to retrace the path (avoiding Manhattan) my grandpa took with his pals from Abruzzo 104 years before, once they arrived in New York City, exhausted and confused, and were summarily hustled out to Hillsdale.

Obviously, the highway system now is infinitely better laid out and complex than it was a hundred years ago. If you wanted to follow the same route as Pascal and the others, it would be a totally different urban and rural journey, although some areas are pretty much the same. Once you leave Manhattan and its northern suburbs behind you, you come up to Cliffside Park, Ridgefield, and Fort Lee. A century ago these were tiny villages with just a few inhabitants, consisting of small rural homes scattered fairly far from one another. Today they are large towns with high population densities and every type of modern building and commodity. Some of the small rural homes have turned into mansions, very stately in the midst of rolling green lawns, with private parks and vast gardens filled with trees and flowers, pools or little artificial ponds, tennis courts and suchlike amenities. Behind these, and not very distant from one another, as though suspended between heaven and earth, are the massive Throgs Neck Bridge, Whitestone Bridge, and George Washington Bridge— spectacular structures that connect New York and New Jersey, built long after the great immigration years of the century's first decade.

Planned by Robert Moses, the Throgs Neck Bridge was opened in 1961, with six lanes, plus an emergency lane in either direction, and spans the East River. Robert Moses—admired by Americans, who have dedicated numerous streets and monuments to him—was "the master builder of New York City." After the Throgs Neck, he planned the picturesque Verrazzano Narrows Bridge (misspelled and mispronounced still in the US as Verrazano), the largest suspension bridge in America, second in length only to the Golden Gate Bridge over San Francisco Bay.

If you want to see Hillsdale, where our Abruzzesi went for their first work assignment, you must go through the delightful Fort Lee and Leonia and from there drive past the Flatrock Nature Center (founded in 1973 as a "Preserve and Education Center," according to its sign). This area was just a forest in Pascal's time, dense with tall, thick-trunked trees and lavish flowers. Not far from here is Ridgefield Park, and then Hackensack, the largest city in Bergen County. Before the Dutch arrived in the middle of the 1600s, a flourishing and prosperous Indian settlement was located here along the banks of the eponymous river. And it's for this tribe, variously called Achkineshcki and Hackensack, that the town is named (in the native language the word means "mouth of a river").

The Hackensack were a rather large tribe that clustered in distinct villages. Each one was self-governed but at the same time enacted a true democracy, particularly when all the members of the various villages came together to make communal decisions affecting all the inhabitants of the area.

When the Dutch came, Oratam, the chief of the Hackensack, negotiated their settlement in a constructive and intelligent way, and the two populations lived together in a peaceful and harmonious manner for many decades. At least until the English came, and then the Americans after them, and destroyed their civilization.

Just a few miles north of Hackensack is Hillsdale, a thoroughly modern small city, neat and orderly and practical, home to more than 11,000 people, which in Pascal's time would have been a very small and isolated village of maybe 100 souls. A completely different scene from what one would find here from the 1940s onward, of pleasant and logical urban development. However, there were some buildings and historic edifices, such as Hillsdale College (today an elegant and expensive private institution) or Hillsdale Manor, standing here when our immigrants came. It's probable that the men didn't set foot in them or even know they existed, as busy as they were with their manual labor outside town.

4

Pasquale (who was quickly redubbed Pascal, a result of the dialect pronunciation Pasca', part of the typical change of names in the new country, the way Giuseppe becomes Joseph or Joe, Luigi becomes Louis if not Lou, Nicola is Nick, and so on) is on the truck that's taking him and his crew to work. He savors for the first time voices and sounds of the rugged and varied American natural landscape, dominated by an intense chirping and the noise of wind in the tall trees bringing about a coolness at once sweet and calming.

Pascal seems to hear nothing but these sounds on the trip, in the midst of the excited chatter of his friends and the noise of the truck engine impinging with sounds of its own. These voices of nature, which he knows well from the mountains of home, feed his imagination, nurturing his poet's soul and his innate tendency to fantasy.

The work our Introdacquesi are assigned to consists of digging out a long and wide passage through a hill, a passage that eventually will become the road. The only tools they have are the pick and shovel, briskly handled by our workers. Many others labor alongside them, almost all of them immigrants, but not only Italians. There are some from Germany, from Ireland, some from Russia. It's a ceaseless mechanical labor, interrupted only by occasional drinks of fresh water: pick, smash, gather up, shovel the soil/stones/trash, and little by little empty it into the trucks, which constantly are coming and going to and from the site.

A motion that seems endless and never-changing. A motion that repeats to infinity, hour after hour, regulated by the short, dry orders of the various squad captains, but also accompanied by singing, whistling, curses, and assorted other incomprehensible shouts from the workers, expressing themselves in their particular dialects, which bear only a slight resemblance to the American tongue. A spoken English springs up among them, vivid, fantastical, a multilingual kaleidoscope of fascinating inventiveness.

And this is the new language that Pascal begins to have a first familiarity with, a language frequently characterized by sudden and fierce insults, affronts, putdowns that often wind up with one worker battling it out with another, forcing the squad captains to intervene to break up the two or three who are beating the crap out of each other.

At midday there is a short pause for lunch and, extremely briefly, to lie down in the shade and recover a bit of their strength. The workday hours are brutal: starting at 7 in the morning and finishing at 6 in the evening. Eleven long hours of work, with a break of a half-hour to devour a hero—a kind of gigantic long roll filled with ham and cheese or roast beef or salami or mortadella (which Pascal will learn quickly, in America is called *bologna* or *baloney*).

And it's during one of these breaks that Pascal learns about a fruit that he's never seen before. He can see that it has the shape of a yellow pod, almost like a broad bean, but much bigger and smoother. One of the other workers is peeling one and offers a piece to our young friend; he loves the taste. This fellow tells him these fruits are called *bananas*, a word Pascal can easily pronounce and remember, and surely one of the first words he learns in this foreign land.

The break is short, and the men return to work.

5

One of the fundamental aspects of immigration from a hundred years ago (I refer not only to Italian immigration) was the strongly communitarian spirit that unified members of a group who came from a single place and that pushed them to remain together once they had landed in America.

The reasons are obviously, first and foremost, both anthropological and linguistic in character: the desire to maintain a psychological link with the land of origin and at the same time a way of mutually protecting oneself in a new and unknown world.

This is how the ethnic communities were born that we still have today; although they are much more diluted by numerous instances of remarriage, they have spread all over North America. From here we have the proliferation of Little Italies, which began in the Bronx and in downtown Manhattan, then spread shortly thereafter to Brooklyn, Astoria, and Long Island (the one in Manhattan has little by little been absorbed by the Chinese community, so that the mythical Little Italy of yesterday is reduced now to a single street, Mulberry Street); those in Boston, Framingham, Hartford, Chicago, Providence, Toronto, and, moving west, those of St. Louis, New Orleans, San Francisco. Just as we have Germantown, Spanish Harlem, Italian Harlem, Chinatown, and other compact communities such as the Greek, Irish, Jewish, Russian, Polish, Puerto Rican, Dominican, Portuguese, and so on.

Today these communities are almost completely integrated into the melting·pot of American society even if, proudly and sometimes even a bit pathetically, laying claim to, in a number of representative ways, the distant belonging to the motherland while the majority of them have lost the expressive lifeblood of their core: the language. Even today one can encounter, especially in Brooklyn, Hartford, and Long Island, "Italians" who have retained from the motherland only their surnames—surnames often mangled over time or by overzealous customs officials, when their grandfathers or great-grandfathers came to Ellis Island, or else mispronounced by the immigrants themselves.

But if you have occasion to ask them, they are all proud to declare "I am Italian!" even if they have never been to Italy and from the language have retained only "bongiorno," "bonassera," "fancul," "muzzrell," and "pastafasul."

Now, I don't want anyone to misunderstand me. I don't mean anything derisive in what I am saying about "italoamericans" of today, for whom I have a great respect for all they've achieved and become in this country, a country that they themselves have helped build (in every sense). I only say that as things stand it would be more correct to call them *American-Italians* or rather *Americans of remote Italian heritage*.

However it may be, the problem of language, as the main mode of human expression, remains fundamental, a principal motivation if a person decides to be a writer.

A parenthesis: When Pascal D'Angelo arrives in New York in 1910, and Emanuel Carnevali in 1914, to cite but two emblematic writers whose names have shamefully been almost forgotten by both Italian and American literatures, and decide to become American writers, they've had to deal with this reality. The former, who brought few linguistic and cultural resources with him, faced a long and agonizing odyssey before reaching his objectives; the latter, much more sophisticated, achieved his as a result of solid personal resolution. It is this idealistic but firm resolution that will lead Emanuel, a mere four years after reaching New York, to announce in a letter, "I want to become an American poet!" The letter in question is from June 11, 1918, and is written to Harriet Monroe, a much-respected American poet and intellectual, and at the time the editor of the historic journal *Poetry*. In this candid declaration, the young Emanuel (just over twenty years old) not only makes an explicit admission about his physical emigration but also as a young writer proclaims a literary ideology, wanting to make it clear that what he is writing and will write not only is and will be written in English but also pertains and will pertain to literature in that language.

To this elemental aspiration add other considerations that may be considered secondary to it: the opportunity to express oneself in a hegemonic language widely in use (this was the dream of the young Mario Soldati), a language that in the meantime has become well assimilated; the advantages and the fertile influences of plural lingualism; the sense of working with more freedom and in greater geoliterary spaces, maybe with the secret desire to contribute to them a "unique" voice.

A conviction, this last, that may seem ingenuous, even fanciful, but that is rooted in the soul of every real poet, particularly when one is conscious (as in the case of a Pascal D'Angelo or an Emanuel Carnevali) of being dominated by a feeling of not belonging, like those who—having lost or having never had their own ethnographical-literary center of gravity—want to gain one that is completely new and on a grander scale, all the while, obviously, managing to overcome the diffidence of the literary establishment of the adopted country, which has always mistrusted and continues to mistrust, with picky disdain, this or that immigrant writer, frequently ethnicizing (actually ghettoizing) him as an "ethnic writer."

This was the bitter destiny of more than a few talented Italian writers who emigrated to the United States, twice ghettoized: both by their native land that didn't recognize them or else cruelly forgot them, and by their adopted country that has always kept them at arm's length.

This is how a language (English) that would have to, and has to, break down ethnic barriers, creating a useful fusion of peoples and cultures that are themselves diverse, may paradoxically (and in a racist way) destroy ideals and let go of history and destinies.

Many pages have been written about mishaps or blunders as a result of ignorance or lack of understanding of the language by our immigrants, and there are also many scientific studies on the theme of the particular and extremely colorful expressive koine that they created, a real and proper mixed idiolect, consisting of the Italianization of English words they used. Some examples: *parcare* (for *parcheggiare*, to park); *la yarda* (from the English *yard*); *la giobba* (for work); *lo storo* (store); *il bisinisso* (business); *il carro* (automobile); *il marchetto* (*mercato*); *la cianza* (a word coming from the English chance); *la stimma* (*heat*, from the English *steam*); *il basamento* (cellar of a house, from English *basement*); *a checa* (*torta*, from the English *cake*), and the list goes on.

Pascal himself, not long after having arrived, is amazed at the incredible religiousness of the Americans, noting that on so many street signs appeared the word *Ave, Ave, Ave*, but with the difference that, whereas in Italy the Ave precedes the saint's name, as in Ave Maria, in America it's bizarrely after the name. "How topsy-turvy," he sardonically would exclaim many years later, recalling this first impression of the Big Apple.

And our Pascal himself has some entertaining mishaps during his first months in the US. Late one afternoon, after the usual work day, he takes upon himself the charge of going into town (the small village of Hillsdale, about a mile away) to buy a dozen eggs. The squad captain repeats for him many times the word *eggs*, and our boy repeats it to himself continually as he goes, so as not to forget it. But the word begins to mutate: eggs, egs, ecs, eks, ekses, axes.

Reaching the drugstore, Pascal, using his fingers to count, makes his request of the clerk, a big older Pole, whose English is most probably only slightly better than that of Pascal. The tough clerk goes to the back of the shop and comes back with twelve axes. Between gestures and mispronounced words Pascal tries to make him understand that they are not what he wants, while the stubborn Pole keeps showing off the great features of the axes, running his thumb over the blade and nodding his big head. Finally, out of the shadows of the store appears his wife, Magda, a large woman who figures out the misunderstanding, partly thanks to the boy, having become exasperated, mimicking a chicken and, that not sufficing, making guttural sounds of *coccodé coccodé* and drawing an oval in the air. At last he gets the dozen eggs and returns triumphant to the bunkhouse.

Another similar mix-up happens a little while after, when the group is transferred to Poughkeepsie, a much bigger city northwest of Hillsdale. It's a freezing day in January 1911 and our workers are laboring in the midst of snow, hail, and gusts of arctic wind. On account of a stupid quarrel, Pascal, who actually hates any kind of violence, is scuffling with his buddy Filippo. The two are laying into each other, rolling around on the frozen ground. Giovanni and Angelo intervene and break it up. Pascal realizes he has a swollen eye and is ashamed to be walking around with a puffy black eye. So, he decides to tell everyone that he was hurt as a result of a fall. He asks the squad captain about the linguistics of it, and he tells him that in English you say "fall down," which he naturally pronounces in his own way. Pascal, as usual, starts repeating the phrase mentally *fall down, fall down*, and it very quickly becomes *fold an, foul dan*, and finally *fou dan, fou dan, fou dan*. As it happens, that same evening (a freezing cold Sunday) Pascal, on his way into town, runs into two Americans arguing. He slows down and then stops to listen to them. One of them rancorously shaking his fist at the other, says, "You're damned! You're damned!" The young man is very impressed by the scene and, by some mysterious alchemy, begins repeating "You damn, you damn!" as the expression that in his mind—wholly ignorant of the radical change in meaning—takes the place of "fall down."

He gets to the city and here encounters an American from his work site, walking around all dressed up. Pascal wants very much to be his friend and when the young guy asks him what happened to his eye, he nonchalantly responds, "You damn!"

"What?" the American exclaims, shocked. And Pascal, trying to stay cool but also with a measure of energy, now repeats, "You damn! You damn!"

The young American laughs doubtfully and, shaking his head, hits him, a move that completely astonishes our boy, who can't make out why his friend went so cold on him all of a sudden.

The same scene repeats itself not long after with a young lady employed by the construction company office, and then once more, a couple of days later, with some other American coworkers.

Finally another man explains to him why the first one hit him. Pascal is in a bad way about the whole thing and before long, running into Filippo in a bad mood, gets into another fight with him.

6

Three years go by quickly when one day follows another monotonously, exactly the same, never changing. The only thing that is
ever altered for our Introdacquesi are the worksites. After Hillside
and Poughkeepsie, the group goes to work in Westwood, then to
Ramsey, Williamsport, Utica, Oneonta: all of them tiny towns, now
flourishing cities, situated in East Coast States: New York, New Jersey, Connecticut, and Maryland.

It's a monotony that also brings with it, as long as the work lasts,
moments of happiness and laughter, generated as a result of whatever
earnings, however modest, our laborers and stonecutters, who are
employed making the great communicating arteries or new reinforced
roads, manage to set aside.

There are days that are hard to get through—apart from the
pleasant sounds of nature that one can absorb during breaks—under
an implacable sun, or beneath the rain, or gusts of frigid wind and
snow; entire days of just the dry, persistent, obsessive pounding of
the pick and the shovel. And after a while you don't even notice the
incessant, mechanical racket. You work almost in a hypnotic state;
thought becomes as liquid as the sweat that pours steadily from your
forehead. Only the squad captains are always alert, ready to intervene
with shouts and threats against anyone—as though they were felons
condemned to forced labor—should they happen, exhausted, to
slacken the work's rhythm every once in a while.

Among the few existing documents relating to Pascal in America
are two photographs. In one, presumably from 1914, there are three
laborers working close to some train tracks. The one on the left holds
a shovel in both hands and in front of him. I can't get his face in focus, but it looks like my grandfather's, though the photo is very worn.
Next to him, right in the center, clear and in focus, there's Pascal in
shirtsleeves. The picture was taken just at the moment when he was
raising the pick, although he's looking toward the person taking the
picture. I look closely at his face, using the magnifying lens. Pascal

looks somewhat proud, and there's also a vague satisfaction visible (pleasure in looking at whoever is "immortalizing" him? satisfaction with regard to the situation he's in? personal pride in being a laborer? or something else?). He holds his chest vigorously straight, the pick in his hand looks almost like a twig.

What is Pascal thinking at this exact moment? Near his feet you can see the train tracks; behind his shoulders, and barely visible (the photo is really in bad shape), are the workers' lodgings; on the left a long and low building, probably the railroad station of whatever town they were working for in those years. Next to Pascal, on the right side of the photo, appear two men. One of them is struggling with some contraption that, even with the magnifier, I can't identify; the other one, who's standing, is wearing a typical canvas overall and isn't holding any tools, his arms dangling, his gaze fixed in front of him.

The other photograph, probably taken at the same time and place, shows Pascal leaning forward dealing with a heavy wooden railroad tie (the kind they use horizontally between the rails). Even when bending, the youth's head is held high and he is looking at whoever is taking the photo. On his left are two men: One, small and skinny, wears coveralls and a beat-up beret (it's definitely Pascal's father, recognizable by his thin face and his big moustache); the other is a large man, tall and broad—it could be Andrea Lenta, the 6-foot-plus colossus of the Introdacquesi group—and he's shoveling topsoil in between the rails. Behind this trio stands a bare freight car.

The simple nakedness of these photos illustrates very effectively—better than could ever be expressed on a written page—one of the many humble workplaces for our laborers and the atmosphere that must have pervaded them.

These first three years are intense and troubled, but they are also the years in which our Pascal begins to learn the spoken language of America. Every month that goes by, the various cities, districts, things, and people seem less and less strange to his growing desire for knowledge. At the same time, every day his desire is growing to return to New York City, the American metropolis that enchanted him right away and that he saw just the once, in passing, when setting foot on Ellis Island, exhausted and bewildered. In his heart he can't wait for the opportunity to present itself for him to go and live there and work. He is tired of hearing in remote rural areas only the repeated clang of the pickaxe, the metallic clink of the shovel, and the insults of the squad captains. The monstrous hero sandwich consumed hurriedly during the half-hour lunch, the return to the workers' housing, the usual chatter of his comrades, and not even a woman to go out with on Sundays, when often he works anyway, whether because his friends are also working or just to scrape together a few more dollars.

His main consolation is when evening comes and the workday—monotonous, crippling—ends. Pascal knows that on those cold roads and on the steel rails on which he has silently spent his best youthful strength no one will ever see a trace of his fantasies, his efforts, his hopes, his passions.

7

A nd the chance to go to New York comes a few months later. It's the summer of 1914. World War I has just broken out in Europe. Our Introdacquesi have gotten only vague information about it. Pascal has just turned twenty.

Mario Lancia, the squad captain, unexpectedly has to go back to Italy because of serious family problems. The others go through a phase of feeling abandoned. Since they arrived, Mario has been more than a leader; he's been a reference point in their job searches. He's the one who's been taking them from one place to another in these first four years. He's the one who taught them how to send some of their earnings to the family members back in Abruzzo.

Lancia's departure signals the first, gradual breaking up of the group, which decides to move to New York. One of them would have preferred to stay in Tuckahoe, the last place they have found work. This little town, recently a village of just some dozens of inhabitants, in 1914 was in its infancy. Officially it was incorporated in 1911.

Tuckahoe is a tidy, anonymous town in Westchester County, close to Bronxville, and about an hour from Manhattan. This whole area, a peaceful residential zone surrounded by green, is today the home of many people of Italian origin, scattered among the nearby cities of Yonkers, White Plains, Mount Vernon, New Rochelle, and Scarsdale, in addition to Bronxville and Tuckahoe. The Bronx River can be found just a few minutes from these last two towns.

Pascal in the meantime has become a kind of advance agent for the entire gang, and frequently it's he who goes out looking for new job prospects, and he's the one among all of them who's learned the most English. One weekend, finding himself with some free time, he goes to spend a couple of days with some fellows from his area back home who live in Shady Side, New Jersey, on the west bank of the Hudson River.

Once this region was mostly desolate and impassable. Some shantytowns sprang up, spreading over a strip of hilly land thick with scrub and dangerous cliffs that extends for some miles along the banks of the river. Seeing them from the northern part of the island of Manhattan, just up from the massive George Washington Bridge, even now it looks like a kind of wall, prickly with wild vegetation, amid which now and then, and more and more frequently, skyscrapers, futuristic buildings, and other complexes were built, with every modern convenience. These new developments swept away all the squalor of a hundred years ago, when the only things standing there were crumbling shacks that seemed to be holding each other up on top of the cliffs.

This is where the name comes from: the Palisades, which is to say an impressive series of crags and steep precipices that resemble a real fence made of rocks on the point of sinking into the river.

Pascal is staying with a family there, including one Saverio, a genuine Neapolitan a few years older than him, well versed in New York living, who generously offers to be our young man's guide. Together with his inseparable work buddy Federico, who already likes Pascal very much, they decide to leave the shanty town of Shady Side and head toward George Road and from there to go on foot to the dock at Edgewater to take the ferry to Manhattan.

It's Saturday afternoon. The three are pretty excited about the excursion and get ready to go. After a bit, as spruced up as they can be given their financial circumstances, they're all set to leave. Saverio, with his hair all pomaded, casts a glance at his houseguest and motions to him to follow him. Pascal doesn't understand, but his buddy goes into the bathroom, smiling, and grabs a can, opens it, and hands it, still smiling, to his friend. Pascal says,

"What's this stuff?"

"Brilliantine," Saverio replies, squinting at him. "Stick some in your hair!"

Pascal does so and, taking a comb from his pocket, gives his thick mane a finishing touch.

So, the three bold lads, a bit cocky, head out to the street. They pass several rooming houses, piled up here and there along the lane that leads to George Road. These shanties, looking like beehives, resound with many voices. Someone shouts from one house to the next, someone else is plucking away at a guitar, someone eating and smoking, another fighting over nothing.

Along the street men and women bump into one another, mostly Italians but also Hungarians, Poles, and other ethnicities harder to determine, all of them bit by bit returning to their hovels after having left their workplaces.

Shady Side was, a hundred years ago, a giant industrial district, just this side of an important railway junction, ending in the nearby flourishing city of Fort Lee. In the whole area, which is almost rolled up in itself, streets, intersections, and viaducts are knitted, almost tangled, together, around great masses of factories, big and small and of every kind, metallurgy offices of iron and steel, giant warehouses in which materials for railway construction were housed (for the enormous Erie line that many decades later would link New York City to that famous lake), huge reservoirs of gasoline, establishments for producing aluminum, smokestacks, carpenters' shops, and even naval construction sites, given that not far from Shady Side even today, though much changed, is the dock of Edgewater. Here is where the ferryboat operates that joins New Jersey to New York.

Right in the middle of this, the cabins, warehouses, workshops, and storage facilities, are the numerous shacks, stinking and crowded, where the workers live. An ants' nest that seems trapped in itself; a hive of bee-people busy with nonstop buzzing.

If you compare this with a dignified form of human existence, the lives of these people can only be considered as mere survival.

Today there's nothing left of this unlikely swarm of hovels and warehouses. It's all gone; dumps, cabins, dive bars, storerooms, and every industrial building. Every one of them, active right up until the 1960s, closed its shutters as a result of industrial globalization. Even the topography has changed radically because of the tugboats and tractor-trailers that crisscross the lanes of Edgewater. One after another, all the shanties disappeared, and the various buildings were torn down or repurposed as luxury apartment buildings, whose windows now have spectacular Hudson River views.

Right at the intersection of George Road and River Road, when the first runs into the second, the three lads encounter an old Italian man. Dressed shabbily in rags, but wearing two golden earrings and holding a knobby cane, he herds a goat up the slope ahead of him, emitting hoarse shouts at the animal; with him is a mutt who runs after and barks at the goat's heels.

At the crest of this hill are some buildings constructed in a semi-circle, one next to the other, as though leaning on one another. Outside, on a small and mangy clearing studded with pebbles, trash, and other refuse, a group of kids is running around. For a moment, only an instant, Pascal is reminded of his town of Cauze, which he used to leave every day to graze his small herd of sheep.

River Road is also home to a number of slightly less shabby houses running along the banks of the Hudson and going directly to the Edgewater jetty.

Evening is falling, and the first lights are being lit in the houses. Someone calls from one of the homes to Saverio. It's his work pal Giuseppe, another Neapolitan and a close friend. The two of them hope to start their own business as mechanics.

"Hey, Save'! Where you goin'? Come on, have some wine with us!"

The voice is coming from the window of one of the shacks, out of which a reddish lamp-light glares. Someone is strumming on a mandolin. Someone else is engaged in a loud discussion on some topic.

The three stop by the window. Saverio thanks his friend but excuses himself; he explains that he can't stay because he's taking his guest to the city and the ferry's about to leave.

The three continue on and soon run across a pair of drunks stumbling around who come up to and almost bump right into them, but instead they go into a bar. It would seem that almost all the houses on River Road have a bar or some kind of joint on the ground floor where someone can get a drink and do a little merrymaking on Saturday night and make some new friends.

On the final stretch of the road the buzzing noise is even more intense; cars, carriages, and simple carts come and go; people are swarming in the direction of the pier, kids are running and tumbling over each other, a prostitute in front of a bar gives passersby the eye, and there are those who accept her offer of company.

Finally the buildings thin out and give way to the barracks of the factories and warehouses constructed close to the pier. Just to one side is the Trolley Terminal. If you go nowadays to see this area, you can still spy, here and there on the ground, although much more mangled than they used to be, the tram rails built for a single coach to carry passengers back and forth.

To the right of the terminal a fairly large construction served as a waiting room. Here would arrive numerous wagons and carriages from the hinterlands of New York and New Jersey to carry merchandise of all kinds, particularly foodstuffs such as fruit and vegetables; a crowded coming and going amid the unceasing traffic of people of many varied occupations.

Pascal is beside himself with emotion. Before him is the ferryboat that is about to carry him to Manhattan. In his heart he's already experiencing the American metropolis with all his senses. The glittering city lights can be seen clearly in the distance, an enchanting sparkle, irresistible. Both he and Federico stand transfixed, looking at them, while Saverio affects a certain nonchalance.

Built between 1904 and 1905, the Edgewater Ferry Terminal offered ferry service up and down the Hudson from Edgewater to Manhattan. There were two stops in the city: one uptown at 125th St., and the other downtown at Barclay Street, in the southernmost part of New York City.

8

What's Pascal thinking of at this precise moment, as the ferry moves farther from Edgewater and crosses the Hudson headed to New York City? How far away his mountain of Maiella seems now, and his sheep, the witch, the attic in Cauze and the onions under the embers, his entire village life.

His eyes, his mind, his entire being are completely concentrated on the dreamy twinkling of the Manhattan lights, which he can see through the window of the boat, a bit shrouded from steam and spotted from the drops of vapor. His gaze, totally unconscious, is like that of someone who projects himself toward something he wants to conquer that he has already conquered in his heart; something in which he recognizes himself. It's a future/present that to this twenty-year-old already belongs to him, and it makes no difference if he has to go through suffering, sacrifices, deprivations, surrenders.

He has a wad of dollars in his pocket, fruits of his labors: money he was able to save after everyday expenses.

From the windows of the ferry, which run along the entire side of the boat, he continues to gaze fixedly at the island of Manhattan, which hypnotizes and attracts him like a long-desired lover. Saverio, much better versed and expert in New York life, jabs him with his elbow.

"Hey, Pascal. What you thinking about? You look like an idiot." His big face smiles as he says it; he's blowing out mouthfuls of smoke while himself glancing, though feigning casualness, at the American metropolis.

Pascal doesn't respond and continues to look at the scene before him. By this time, as the boat approaches the first stop, Manhattan is a total blaze of lights, and the youth can already clearly see the intense comings and goings of cars and pedestrians on Riverside Drive.

The ferryboat arrives at 125th Street, tooting its long, sad, repetitive horn. Time to unload some people and load again, and then it heads directly downtown. This is where the friends are headed, to the lower part of the city.

They get off at this second stop, Barclay Street, and they blend right in with the feverish Saturday evening crowd, amid the glittering lamps and the crowded lower Manhattan streets. It's Pascal's first time seeing rows of lit-up storefronts and so many elegant people who look with disdain or even disgust at the three roughly dressed men.

A large jewelry shop gets their attention. Federico and Pascal stop, fascinated, to look at the window display, as two exaggeratedly overdressed gentlemen, upon approaching, see them and quickly re-coil contemptuously and then retreat. Behind the two youths, Saverio, cold and unmoved, makes sarcastic comments about the asking price for some little chains on view in the display. Federico remembers an episode in which, just a year earlier, he gave a gold bracelet to a woman he'd taken a fancy to. A bracelet that she gave back to him just two weeks later, angry and disgusted because it had turned black and left a purple circle around her wrist. The two boys now laugh a bit harshly about it. Saverio, behind them, makes some sarcastic comments about the incident, adding a risqué joke in Neapolitan dialect.

Just then all three turn to look at a woman who has momentarily stopped to look in the window herself. She is decked out heavily, and her face is like a terrible mask, yet her vulgar appearance doesn't seem to affect passersby, who don't notice her or give her a wide berth. Our friends are temporarily overcome by her nauseating perfume, which threatens to suffocate them.

Happy and carefree, they resume their walk. They get to Lafayette Street, which immediately entrances Pascal, filled as it is with the roll-ing hum of sound that people make going to and fro. "Where are all these mute people going?" To the silence of people's voices he com-pares the deafening sound of the cars they're riding in. Inside them, they sit like statues, unmoving and looking straight ahead of them, microcosms arrested in time in the center of the extreme mobility of the street.

"Hey, over there. I gotta get something to eat and drink … over there's a very good joint … and there's girls there too."

The proposal comes from Saverio, direct and to the point, his whole personality. There are just a few years between his age and theirs, but his having gotten started on his American experience five years before they did makes all the difference.

The three continue down Lafayette Street for a bit. Pascal gets distracted by another shop window, this time with different kinds of shoes. Then they turn left onto Houston Street. Just on the corner there is a big plant and flower store, but no one has stopped to look in that window, making Pascal wonder if there is something childish or undignified, according to Americans, about stopping to look in a shop window at such pretty flowers. Just then he is reminded of the little bunches of basil, worn behind the left ear, that the men of Introdacqua used to have in the summer feasts in their old country.

Houston Street is a bit less crowded, and it also has a certain ambiguous, enigmatic quality that Saverio doesn't notice. Pascal is distracted again, this time by a couple standing in the shadows and cooing at each other.

They go into a smoky bar. Outside the electric sign, rough and falling apart, says "Blue Moon"; one of the bulbs seems as if it's just about to burn out, and its tremulous bluish light of the first letter blinks on and off every so often.

Inside, which is kind of cramped, there are noisy people of various ethnicities at all the tables. Saverio, who seems somewhat familiar with the place, proposes to his friends that they sit right at the bar, where you can drink and also get something to eat. The place, more a tavern than a pub, appears to be a haven for petty thieves, prostitutes, and pimps. The three friends enjoy themselves, toasting to nothing and everything in their young lives. And they're doing it with enormous tankards of beer, a drink that our Pascal was introduced to in America and that he drinks sometimes on Saturdays with Filippo.

At a certain point Saverio starts eyeing a little blonde woman at the other end of the horseshoe-shaped bar. This woman, sitting not far from him on his right, is flirting in an exaggerated manner with two large men who are gulping down beer after beer. At the same time, though, she is giving Saverio mischievous glances. One of her two companions, a fat man who's moving his hands around constantly, suddenly begins pawing the woman, who bursts into smirks and giggles while also alternating between submitting and theatrically refusing. The scene is not lost on Pascal, who manages to get the woman's name (Susan) and the fat man's too (Tom); from this last Pascal hears a few clumsy verbal advances as well. The other man, meanwhile, is just sitting there peaceably, glancing furtively at the skirmish between the two, drinking beers, and smoking silently.

Saverio is following the little drama and even adds a humorous comment occasionally. Suddenly, the woman takes offense at some patently vulgar thing Tom does. She answers it with a slap. The situation deteriorates because she not only slaps him but takes her drink and hurls it in his face. At this point Tom's friend and the barman intervene; the barkeep is a kind of King Kong type, six feet tall. There's a brief altercation, then the two men leave, throwing their glasses on the table. One of the glasses shatters, but none of the other customers even looks up.

The woman sits down again and starts applying a bit of lipstick, as though nothing had happened, and looking again at Saverio. Some minutes go by. The three friends order another beer. Federico offers Pascal a cigarette, which he refuses.

"Hang on a sec," Saverio murmurs, already set to flirt with the woman. He goes over to sit next to her, and the two of them begin a close whispered discussion, some of which sounds like coaxing.

After a bit, he says goodbye to the woman, who leaves while he returns to his friends.

"Guys," he says, turning to Pascal in particular, "Us three'll go in a bit." And he explains, turning first to Pascal and then to Federico, that Susan will be back soon with a pair of friends they can happily spend the rest of the evening with.

That will be the first real erotic adventure for Pascal in New York, a city toward which he'll always feel both love and disgust.

9

Pascal comes back from Tuckahoe without having obtained any work for his group. By this point he has just one overwhelming desire, to establish himself in New York. He communicates this desire to his friends.

Andrea Lenta, the colossus of the group and the best educated, who also has gone in search of work, returns empty-handed. It's exceedingly difficult, not to say impossible, to find work of any kind for the entire group of men. Still, no one wants to separate from the others, or is ready to do so, after having lived together four years.

Our Abruzzesi pass the entire autumn of 1914 in this way, moving around along little towns in Connecticut and Massachusetts, but only for short-term jobs. Alarming news from Europe reaches them during this time. The war has been going on already for some months.

With the arrival of spring, and no available work, the group decides finally to move to New York City. Here they hope to find some kind of work. They stay on Franklin Street in the neighborhood now called Tribeca, a fairly disreputable area that at that time is occupied by several kinds of immigrants, poor families, outcasts, and vagabonds. The street isn't far from Lafayette Street, which had so entranced our Pascal just months before, but it is so different! The landlady is an old Abruzzese lady with the Homeric name of Euriclea, but everyone in the building calls her Clè.

Clè rents the Abruzzi men a room for fifteen cents a night. In it there are some dirty cots and an old dresser. On one side of the room there is a little alcove; in one part of it there's a wreck of a little kitchenette, and in the other part, marked off by a grimy curtain that flaps around, a toilet with a tiny shower.

One evening, Matteo Rossi, the mellow Ace of Hearts and the most resourceful member of the group, while making his usual rounds about the neighborhood looking for work or at least some free food, runs into Giuseppe Gagliardi, called Pino, who is also looking for a job. Pino, a decent-looking young fellow, tells him he's from Lucania and has just arrived from Italy. He makes a good impression on Matteo, who, generous soul that he is, strikes up a friendship with him and decides to help him as best he can. They toast their new alliance with a couple of beers in a bar on Broadway.

The two of them hang around together for a while in Little Italy, by Mott Street and Mulberry, coming up with possibilities for work, about which Pino seems fairly optimistic.

Now it's evening. It's looking as though it might rain, or snow, or something else, so Matteo heads home, inviting Pino to come along. Once they get to Franklin Street, the Ace of Hearts introduces the young near-paesan to his friends and tells him he can sleep there as many nights as he'd like.

The new arrival, hearty and good-looking, is accepted warmly; he prepays the incredulous landlady for an entire week, astonishing everyone, since the men are used to paying day to day. Euriclea shows him the cot he can use, the one right next to Matteo's. Happy and satisfied, Pino invites everyone for a drink. He has a way with words that's quite charming; he's almost as good as Giorgio, who is the most verbal of the group.

The next day, a cold December morning, the new arrival is up at dawn. Outside it's still dark. He quickly gets dressed and goes out. His companions stay in their warm beds.

When evening comes around, the group reassembles, having spent the whole day looking in vain for work.

Scowling to themselves, they begin to realize that they are facing a long period of forced inactivity; all the while, snow is starting to cover the streets of Manhattan. A few hours later Pino returns empty-handed as well, looking broken and discouraged.

The next morning he gets up again at the crack of dawn. No one, not even the singer of famous Italian songs, Antonio Lancia, hears him rise. Antonio serves also as their watchman, as he seldom is able to sleep past dawn. Before leaving, Pino tells him about a possibility he's looking into with a guy he's on his way out to see at dawn on Canal Street.

A couple of hours go by. The day, rainy and gray, doesn't look auspicious of anything new or good. Bit by bit the men get up, slowly and reluctantly, given the unpromising look of the weather outside.

Matteo is snoring blissfully in his cot. The others are still deciding whether it's worth it to go out for the umpteenth time to look for something to do. The only one who's gone out, apart from Pino, who vanished with the dawn, is Filippo, who now comes back all out of breath, his clothes soaked in rain and sleet. He's back to ask his Uncle Matteo for a nickel. Outside there's a man with a cart selling bananas at a reduced price: a penny for three whole bananas. Pascal, his bosom friend, notwithstanding the odd dust-up, gives him the five cents.

Finally, grumbling and stumbling, the Ace of Hearts gets up and begins his morning routine. He goes to the tiny bathroom for a shower, a habit he's picked up from his earliest days in America. He dresses, has a quick breakfast consisting of a cup of coffee, and announces he's going for a walk, undaunted by the frigid temperature and the mixture of rain and snow that's beating down on the Manhattan streets. He lights his pipe, which fills the room instantly with smoke, and puts on his jacket.

As he's heading out, he instinctively puts his hand in his breast pocket for his wallet.

"Hey," he says, almost to himself. "Where's my wallet gone?" he exclaims, annoyed but still calm. He looks around as if retracing his own movements; then he feels around all his clothes and rummages in all the pockets of his few garments and gropes around the floor by his bed.

"Where'd the wallet go?!" he repeats now in his own dialect. Then, turning to his companions, dumfounded, he says, "They took my wallet. I can't believe it. I had $60, all the money I'd saved!" At the same time, his eyes widen, and he realizes at last who must have robbed him; it could only have been his protégé, Pino Gagliardi.

"I know where I found that son of a bitch, and I'll find him there again!" Matteo shouts in his firm and steady voice, shaking a fist toward the doorway, but without upsetting himself unduly, as he is always a master of his emotions. This is really Matteo's strength, to be able to maintain his composure even in the most difficult moments. Each of his countrymen comes up to him, promising their complete support. They feel the theft as if it had happened to each of them personally.

Sixty dollars a hundred years ago, it goes without saying, was a considerable amount of money, around $900 in today's money.

Matteo goes out, determined to find his "friend." One after the other, the men all leave, each one wishing the others luck catching the thief whom they had offered friendship, kindness, and comfortable shelter.

All day Matteo searches through the Italian quarter: Mulberry Street, Mott Street, Hester Street, and all over the Bowery. Then he goes back to Broome Street until he arrives at Mulberry again and from there up and down the length of Canal Street. No sign of Pino, that polite, affable young man, not even his shadow.

Evening comes. Our friends, especially Matteo, are still hoping that Pino might come back to the house. Filippo keeps saying maybe it's a joke, but time passes and no one knocks on their door.

The next morning when they get up they see that Matteo's bed is empty; he didn't sleep all night and is up at first light, determined to his very core that he will find the thief.

Pascal knows how tenacious Matteo Rossi can be and how fixed of purpose. He is a tireless worker, far and away the strongest of them all, except for Andrea Lenta. He decides to devote body and soul to helping his friend.

The two explore all of Little Italy, inch by inch. And it is on Bayard Street, one block over from Mulberry, that they find him.

"There he is, the bastard," Matteo says under his breath, pointing his paesano out to Pascal. Pino is sitting comfortably in a high seat, getting his shoes shined.

He's calmly smoking a cigarette when suddenly his eyes meet Matteo's. Just then, like a spring, the youth jumps down off the bench to flee but Matteo nimbly grabs him by the arm. Immediately three of Pino's friends come to his aid. One of them comes up from behind Pascal and nabs him, and the two of them roll onto the ground, close to a manhole where water and sewage can be heard running. The other two attack Matteo, while a small crowd gathers and agitatedly watches the scuffle. At a certain point, Matteo punches the more active of his two opponents hard; the other one, witnessing the powerful blow, backs off. Then Ace of Hearts grabs Pino, almost lifting him up off the ground, and recommences hitting and punching him.

A couple more guys arrive on the scene to help the thief, but just then from Mott Street appears Andrea, the colossus of the Introdacquesi group, who immediately fires a punch into the stomach of the first of these guys he sees, causing him to roll on the sidewalk. Pino, meanwhile, held by the collar by Matteo, screams out, "Police! Police!"

The people around him begin to give menacing looks to the three Abruzzesi, ready to intervene, but most of them, seeing Andrea's size, are vacillating. Matteo finally, flanked by Pascal and Andrea, drags Pino toward the police station on Elizabeth Street, not far from Bayard.

Once they get there, he tries with his abbreviated English to relate the story. Pino, on the other hand, settling himself a bit, exclaims in perfect English: "Arrest this man! He hit me without cause. I don't know him!"

Matteo tries in vain to protest. But just then Andrea, the educated giant, with his placid imperturbability, says, turning directly to the police chief: "This man is a liar and a thief."

Encouraged by the calm and steady words of Andrea, both Pascal and Matteo retell the story of the theft, while Pino continues to declare his innocence. The voices overlap until the police chief imperiously orders them to be quiet. After that he proceeds to question them closely, one by one. The thief continues to deny everything, demanding that the three be arrested on the charge of assault. He is searched. Out comes the wallet, which is immediately claimed by Matteo. Instead of the original amount, the wallet contains now only $40.

"How do you know this wallet is yours?" the police chief asks severely.

Matteo, without losing an ounce of aplomb, explains that in an interior fold of the wallet he has inscribed his name. It's the proof that nails the thief.

At the trial of the ungrateful youth, our Introdacquesi friends will learn that he wasn't one of their paesani at all, but a Calabrese.

The episode of which Matteo Rossi was a victim is just one example among many of the scheming that so many Italian (and non-Italian) immigrants fell victim to so often. It's precisely because they were so cut off, herded together to sleep like animals in a single room or in a basement in some New York slum, that they were particularly vulnerable to robberies and violent acts of every kind.

10

The successful outcome of Matteo Rossi's situation does nothing to solve the group's basic problem; finding some kind of work that will allow them to live or survive with some dignity in a cruel and competitive city like New York.

These are sad, dark days, these last days of 1914. It begins to seem clear to them that it's better to separate, so that they might find work in different places. Their savings are starting to dwindle, and some of them, like the jolly bachelor Giovanni Ferraro, have spent everything and are living on credit.

One evening, however, Giorgio, the most optimistic of them and the best speaker, announces to his friends that he's found work for all of them. Someone, knowing how Giorgio likes a good joke, thinks he's kidding. Matteo goes up to him and looks him in the eyes.

"Are you being serious or pulling our leg?"

"Of course I'm being serious," Giorgio replies and places a hand on his heart. Then he adds, "Don't ask me any more details. Tomorrow we'll all go over together to Mulberry Street, and I'll introduce you to the guy who'll hire us. Tonight, all I can tell you is that it's in the South."

"In the South?" Andrea interrupts, "where the oranges grow!" Just then, as if to heighten the contrast, the whipping sound of wind gusts outside makes the idea of a warm and sunny location that much more appealing.

"How much will the trip cost?" Pascal's dad, Angelo, asks. This is what preoccupies the group most: their finances, which have been severely reduced by this point, including what they are able to send back home to their families. But at this moment no one wants to bring up unpleasant matters to take the shine off of Giorgio's good news.

It's barely six in the morning on a freezing day in January. The men are getting ready to go out early, even though, according to Giorgio, their appointment with the job foreman, isn't until nine.

They all gather at Vincenzo Liberatore's place. Vincenzo came to America from Pratola Peligna, so he's practically a neighbor, and he has a little restaurant on Mulberry Street. He's been extending credit to his friends for some weeks now and he's doubly happy at the news of upcoming work, both because they won't have to use credit anymore and also, presumably, because he will at last receive the payment of the debt he's left to the good consciences of his countrymen.

The group celebrates the future job with a big breakfast of eggs and ham. Finally, after one last coffee and some doughnuts, the men say goodbye to Vincenzo and head over toward the "work source," which is on the same street, some 328 feet away.

They get to the front office. The door is still shut. The day's cold and gray; to stay warm, our heroes march up and down, almost in single file, the Ace of Hearts in the lead.

After a bit the door opens. A man comes outside and puts out two placards announcing in block letters the need for manual workers. Inside the office another man, fat and ruddy-looking and seated behind a counter, is straightening up some papers and occasionally writing something in a large notebook.

Giorgio whispers to Matteo, standing next to him, "This is our man, the one with the jobs." The big man signals to the Abruzzesi to come closer, as the room fills up with other job-seekers. Soon the entire place is packed with smoke and people talking.

Giorgio begins asking the recruiter about when they can start work and how much the pay will be. The man sizes up the whole bunch of them and then, in a strong Neapolitan accent, says, "If you want, you can start tomorrow. The job's in West Virginia. Do you know where that is? I'll write you a letter of recommendation, and you need five bucks apiece for the train. It's five if you all buy together on a single ticket, but eight apiece otherwise."

"Five for all of us or five each?" Andrea poses the question with a gentle sarcasm. At six-plus feet tall, he can do it.

The paunchy man, not the least bit intimidated by Andrea's height, silences him with a mocking glance and goes back immediately to his notebook.

The group does a quick mental calculation: The cost of the trip is almost more than they can manage. It's the usual problem they confront when they need to move, at their own cost, from one work-place to the next, always with the risk that, once they get there the living and working conditions will be horrific but they'll be forced to take the job on because of having spent all they had just to get there.

The fat man adds, "The place is in Williamsport, in the Cumberland Valley. The train leaves at three o'clock." Then he looks at the group again. "How many of you are there?"

Suddenly all the men are worried there are too many of them to request that they work together. There's a risk someone will get rejected.

Giorgio interrupts at this point: "Right now there are eight of us …" and quickly adds a little lightheartedness to ease the tension, "but if that's not enough we can easily find some more guys for you. No problem."

"Great! That's great," says the tubby recruiter. "On this list, there are eleven men, so I still need three. Hey! But I want only strong guys, healthy and willing to work."

The men leave the office, where the air has become unbreathable, and get right to work looking for another three guys who are "healthy and willing to work" so as to save the three dollars a head for the group ticket.

They go down Mulberry Street and then turn toward Mott Street. At a certain point they bump into two other Italians, right on the corner. These guys are fairly robust-looking, and they present them with the proposal.

One of the two, making the typical gesture of denial—lifting his chin up—responds, "I'm not going to West Virginia. I don't wanna go to that house of the devil, not even if they paid me five bucks a day."

The other one seems a bit interested. He'll be willing to go if he can afford the trip.

This tentative first go doesn't discourage our Abruzzesi boys, who keep moving and head to Franklin Street, Bayard, Elizabeth, and other streets bordering the neighborhood. Every once in a while they find someone who wouldn't mind joining them but either they can't pay for the ticket or else they're waiting for some other recruiter to contact them about something else, or else they just don't want to leave New York. Mostly, though, it's the cost of the ticket that stops them. If you think about the fact that a hundred years ago a day's work might pay an average of $1.50, $5 or $8 is a considerable amount of money.

The group decides to split up to cover more ground. The search goes on all morning, in vain.

Finally, it's Matteo, the generous Ace of Hearts, who manages to find three men, in a Mott Street dive bar, who are eager to come to West Virginia to work.

A bit tired, but emboldened nonetheless, the magnificent eight, who now have become eleven, head back to the agency, hand over the money to the pudgy Neapolitan, and get the train ticket and the recommendation letter, addressed to a certain Mike Glennon, the commissary man they will need to report to in Williamsport.

All eleven of them go back to Franklin Street. Time is getting short—only three hours until they leave.

On the way back to their house, the Abruzzesi become acquainted with the new men, who have been living on Church Street, parallel to Franklin. One is named Teofilo, from Molise, who is a handyman and who has massive strong arms. Another, Armando, is from Caserta, and he has a bike that he never leaves; it's the only thing he owns and he's determined to take it with him even to Williamsport, convinced that the milder weather will allow him to make some nice excursions on it. The third, Nicolò, also from Molise, is tall and slender, and he has a slight tic in his right eye. Our Introdacquesi are a bit skeptical of his ability to do hard physical labor.

At Franklin Street the men pack their stuff up quickly and get it all into a single case. Everything else of theirs consists of just a few humble items: a pair of worn-out pants out of which one of them made patches for mending their clothes, scraps of an old shirt, various buttons that came off sweaters, and underwear that has fallen to tatters.

To this they add stuff for cooking, some saucepans, some metal plates, silverware, and other modest objects: all of them herded together in various bundles and tied up with string. Andrea Lenta is charged with taking care of the case. He will carry it on his own shoulders.

There are just a few beers left in the kitchen which they open in order to toast their imminent work. The three new guys join them in the toast.

At last they go to say farewell to the ever-busy Euriclea; she's a bit disappointed to see them leave her house. Everyone speaks loudly and happily. Matteo is the only one who kisses Clé goodbye.

And here they are, heading up Broadway, the only street that runs the entirety of Manhattan. Andrea is in the lead, and the group has a certain effect on passersby. More than a few back away almost in fear as they go along or else show signs of disgust at the noisy mass of men dressed in such ragged clothes.

At a certain point in their journey along Broadway, to get to Seventh Avenue, where Penn Station is, Teofilo gets hit by a car. Matteo and Antonio rush to help him. A small crowd gathers, but the car vanishes. Teofilo gets up, miraculously unharmed, and Andrea, putting down the case, momentarily makes as if to chase down the driver. The big guy is always the first to defend others.

They all gather their stuff up again and head directly for the entrance to Penn Station. Giovanni, the carefree bachelor, jokingly pokes fun at Teofilo, who tells them that everyone named Teofilo has seven lives; he himself has already used two—one before meeting our fellows, and the second just then with the car. Smiling, he adds, "I might need the other five where we're headed!"

11

Our workers are in the same mental state on their train ride to Williamsport. The only difference is that this trip is much longer: The train crosses New York and Pennsylvania and then alongside and finally across a piece of Maryland, finally arriving at West Virginia. More than eight hours on the train and some four hundred miles.

When the group gets to Williamsport it's the dead of night. Outside all one can see is a gloomy, desolate, and frozen landscape.

"And where's the warmth we were promised? And the oranges?" blurts out Giovanni, as Andrea's face becomes sad.

Having gotten off the train, the eleven men head toward the little train station, which is dimly lit. An arctic wind whips their faces, and on the ground lies a thick layer of frosty snow.

The station master, to whom Matteo shows their tags for their case, bags, and other bundles, shakes his head: There is no baggage to collect. There's nothing he can do. There's been an error about the baggage service from New York, and all their things have been sent instead to Williamsport, Pennsylvania. The station master adds that maybe they'll show up the next day.

In those bundles and boxes is practically everything our guys need, especially the blankets and some wrappings that, once stuffed with straw or leaves, work as mattresses.

Anger, frustration, dismay invade the hearts of all the men, but there's nothing to do but to walk in the midst of the ice and snow toward the work camp, some four miles away. To make their bad luck complete it's begun to rain: a frozen rain, intense, accompanied by terrible gusts of wind.

Our workers plod forward in single file into the dark and the cold on the reinforced road, which is barely visible, their feet sinking into the snow. In silence, never speaking a word, they trudge onward with their heads down to avoid the wind and rain that pound down on them more and more heavily. It's so cold that the water freezes before it even hits the earth, such that every once in a while one of the men tumbles to the ground.

The road eventually runs into a long bridge that spans the southern branch of the Potomac. A sudden gust of wind, wilder than the others, whisks Pascal's hat off his head and down into the river below. The youth, unlike the rest of the group, is living this situation in a kind of a dream.

At this point they hear the piercing whistle of a train, its dazzling lights full on them. With a leap the men get off the tracks and grab onto the steel and iron fittings that hold the sides of the bridge just as the train passes them with a ferocious metallic boom. After it passes, a violent rush of wind envelops the men. Teofilo's shoulder bag, containing his few personal possessions, takes flight and plunges into the river.

After the river crossing, the countryside becomes a naked and squalid sight, a barren landscape, rugged, completely empty, and desolate, as though abandoned by everyone and everything.

The men continue marching for a long time until in the distance they see the light from a solitary shack. Matteo, followed by all his companions, approaches the hut and knocks on the door. He hopes that they've finally reached their destination.

A Black man of a certain age, tall and with a white beard, comes to the door and, with a kindness that indicates his compassion for the band of down-and-out men, says that they need to go another mile at least to get to the work camp. While he gives a few directions to Matteo, he looks over the group of ragamuffins, trembling and drenched, who, in the heart of the night, are headed toward a place where they will encounter pretty rough work, a place he's heard some talk about.

He wishes good luck to Matteo and his friends and then, just as he's about to close the door, he takes a bottle of Jack Daniels from a cupboard and hands it to Matteo. He gives a hint of a surly smile and, in a low but friendly voice, says again, "Good luck!"

The group sets off again. The bottle of whisky passed from hand to hand does give some brief comfort.

At last they reach a kind of clearing in which five enormous buildings appear in the pitch black, almost like giant barns, made out of tree trunks, their walls all crusted over with ice. A few yards away there's a little shack, badly lit, that also serves as a store for the entire company of workers employed in the camp.

They knock on the door of the first building, and a man emerges. Matteo asks after Mike Glennon, the camp's commissary man. The man grabs a coat and walks over with our men to the next-to-last building in the camp.

Here they find Mike, who just then is opening a beer bottle. With him are another three men, all of whom are playing cards, using a barrel as a table. The man who brought them over goes up to Mike and whispers in his ear.

Matteo introduces himself, hands him the recommendation letter, and lets him know right away that they have no blankets or anything else because their stuff went to Pennsylvania by mistake. The man heaves his entire bulk out of his chair, glances at the letter, and looks a bit suspiciously at Matteo and the others, soaked in water and snow. Then he shrugs and with a grunt says concisely: "Too bad I can't help you. You can sleep in the next shanty where there's room for you." Having said which, he swallows a giant gulp of beer and, burping, goes back to sit with his buddies.

All our men can do is to follow their guide to their shed. Here they find another four men already asleep in their cots. Some rough tables made from pinewood stick out from the walls. These are their beds. Outside, meanwhile, sudden flurries of wind, of an amazing violence, make the entire building shake, constructed as it is merely of wooden boards plastered on the outside with tarpaper.

Frozen with the cold and still in soaking wet clothes, our men look around, dismayed and uncertain what to do. They peer in the darkness to see if there is a stove and they discover one in a corner. But there's no coal or anything else to burn. One of the four sleepers, turns over noisily in his bed, irritated, and mumbles something that Andrea manages to hear: In a shed out back, next to the front door, there's some lignite. Andrea and Giovanni go out and gather some of it. It lights, finally, and there is at least a bit of warmth in the room, in addition to the terrible smell of gas.

Our men try to dry their clothes, at least partly. In the end, overcome with sleepiness and exhaustion, they fall on their pallets, which are covered by a bit of filthy straw.

12

Who is the so-called commissary man? What exactly are his responsibilities? The literal translation in Italian would be just the word *commissary*, an ambiguous word that lends itself to numerous meanings.

In the period when Pascal and his friends are working, the commissary man in the United States is someone who runs the commissary and at the same time a manager of work sites.

The Italian immigrants, most of them manual laborers and unskilled workers, would call this figure simply "the boss," whether he was the one who recruited workers or who ran the work camps. The commissary man is therefore an intermediary between worker and businessman. He's the man who hires the right men for the job. In order to do this, he needs the help of a series of agents spread out across the most important cities (New York, Chicago, Boston, Philadelphia, Baltimore, etc.); in Pascal's case it's the Neapolitan on Mulberry Street. The commissary man is also in charge of the store at the work camp: It's a true monopoly, the profits of which, after subtracting the amount he's entitled to, go directly to the owner. And if that weren't bad enough, the commissary man has carte blanche over the workers. He can hire and fire at will. His power is such that it's easy for him to command the affection of the eager-to-please workers under him; he's the one who pays the weekly wages, the one who writes down in his notebook what the workers take from the store. It doesn't matter if a worker keeps track himself of what he's bought; the only reckoning that matters is the commissary man's. And this leads inevitably to arrogance and thievery. And not only that. Anyone who, in trying to save money, and takes just the minimum from the store, finds himself penalized, incurring totally unforeseen expenses that the commissary man unhesitatingly informs him of. And it's useless to complain unless you want to fall out of his good graces, if not get fired on the spot.

So on Saturday, which is payday, the poor worker who's tried to keep his spending to the absolute minimum is surprised to find a laundry list of stuff to pay for, as though he'd been spending freely during the whole week.

In other work camps it's become the "democratic" rule that whoever doesn't spend enough gets swiftly fired after receiving a couple of warnings about it.

A manual worker, a hired hand, a stonecutter, a simple pick and shovel man like our Pascal is effectively forced to buy things at the company store that in any city in America would cost half as much. Any con-man in New York or Philadelphia or Boston would kill to be in on this kind of racket.

What's left of the workman's weekly pay after the commissary man takes his cut is a miserable sum. And if you remember that almost every one of these men is trying to send something back to his loved ones in Italy, you understand what the living conditions were like for those first immigrants to America.

The commissary man in every camp avails himself of the help of a foreman, in other words a squad leader who, compared to him, doesn't have a lot of power. At the start of the story of our Abruzzesi, the foreman was Mario Lancia, but once he went back home the group was adrift, faced with all the challenges, the movements from one place to the next, the language difficulties, and the hardships in finding work.

Mike Glennon, whom our eleven find in Williamsport, West Virginia, while rough and irascible, isn't any worse than others whom so many Italian immigrants, poor and ignorant—with exceptions like Matteo Rossi, Andrea Lenta, Giorgio Vanno, and our dreamy but hard-working Pascal—unfortunately encounter along the way. It could happen that Mike, when drunk, might threaten a worker with a gun; other times he will jump in and slap the face of some unenthusiastic laborer. Having gone through relocations, being subjected to harsh leaders and suffocating labors, Pascal can only reflect on the cruel system he encounters across the United States, a system that at its most organized and developed is designed to trap pick and shovel men in a type of forced labor. Usually the lure consists of good pay and a chance to travel for free to some remote workplace. Pascal recalls, from his adolescence in Introdacqua, hearing about what happened to his Uncle Giuseppe. Attracted by a chance of working in Florida, he had to give up eight months of salary in order to be able to flee that hell, a place with inhumane working conditions, inedible food, violence, and oppressions of every kind.

The workmen, generally white men, were looked down upon by armed and angry Black men, who with the least provocation would not hesitate to shoot at the white workers, who, at the conclusion of that horrendous work experience, wound up in debt to the company who had hired them!

13

It's January 6, 1915, the somber first day for the eleven paesani in Williamsport. This morning, the Befana has brought them the gift of stabbing pains all over their bodies after a miserable night on wooden tables with no blanket and soaking wet clothes that over the icy night have numbed them and become stiff.

Trying to loosen their achy muscles a bit, the men walk up and down inside their room, feeling their clothes like tiny needles poking their flesh all over. They move a bit clumsily around the bunkhouse, and odd noises escape from their trousers as if hundreds of pins were spilling off their clothes.

But there's no time to refresh themselves properly because Mike Glennon arrives suddenly, telling them to hurry and get some breakfast before time runs out. He looks at each of them to make sure no one is ill. Then he turns to the stove, mumbling something no one catches.

Time to drink some of the black liquid that passes for coffee, and then the work captain arrives. He introduces himself brusquely, saying he's Morten. He is huge and blond, of Scandinavian ancestry. While our men listen to him, pieces of straw that attached to them during the night randomly fall from their clothes to the floor.

Pascal, as usual, is distracted and, halfway hidden behind Matteo and Andrea, looks around closely at the camp, details of which he couldn't make out the night before. All at once the space makes him think of a pigpen like the ones in his home town, only on a much grander scale, and instead of pigs inside it, him and his companions.

Silently and with downcast gazes, the Abruzzesi follow Morten, whom they immediately rename the Dane. He takes them a short way out of the camp. The mirages of warmth and the good life that they have cherished in their minds since leaving New York are well and truly gone now. Then there's also their luggage. Who knows where it is at this point?

They get to a large open area of immense proportions, where other men are already working. The entire clearing is traversed by little trains, nicknamed "donkeys" by the workers, that go up and down, spewing nonstop clouds of steam.

Right in the center of the area there are railroad tracks under construction. Not far away a throng of men are working in a coal mine. Every so often, dark with soot, workers come and go to change the shifts.

Everywhere there's the deafening sound of drills and augers, many of which are busy breaking up the rocky banks of stone along the side of the roadway. A mechanical shovel collects the broken pieces, grabbing them between enormous jaws, looking like a gigantic feeding mouth.

On the sidelines of this huge area two cranes move frighteningly big boulders from one place to another as though they were pebbles. Every once in a while a supply train from the Cumberland Valley line comes by, carrying coal and various other materials.

The whole place, if you could see if from a certain distance, looks like a crazy ants' nest of machines and men resembling nothing so much as self-propelled dolls. All Pascal can do is stare, as though hypnotized, at this unceasing beehive that to his eyes has something cosmic about it, something magnificent and hellish at the same time. It's the first time he's seen a worksite of this scale since he arrived in this country.

And it is in the midst of this tangle of equipment, pneumatic hammers, drills, and railroad cars that he and his companions have to work. Morten, in the meantime, is screaming out the last of the work assignments as they are all crossing the worksite. Suddenly a man rushes toward our group of guys yelling something and waving a red flag. Workers quickly try to take shelter on the sides of the embankment, crouching on the ground. Our men stand stock still, frozen with terror. Morten, imperturbable, says nothing. Then one hears a horrific roar, and a couple dozen yards away a rocky fountain of topsoil explodes in the air with a shower of broken fragments.

The Abruzzesi and Morten are covered in a cloud of dust that darkens the air and brings with it a hail of sandy soil. The cloud slowly settles, and Morten, as though nothing had happened, brings the workers, filthy now with soot and dust, to the area where they'll be working.

While they walk, astonished and shaken, the men silently question themselves. This reality they have fallen into is far more sinister than any of them had foreseen.

The first month in this cursed Cumberland Valley passes quickly. In the souls of our men discontent and physical and psychological discomfort are growing. They've never experienced anything like this before. There aren't any amusements here in the valley, no distractions or city centers in which to spend some happy time. The pay is low (a dollar and fifty cents a day) and the workday horrendous, twelve hours, from seven in the morning until seven at night, with one short interruption for lunch, consisting usually of soup and a sandwich.

Each group keeps to itself, with only the occasional man exchanging words with someone from another crew. The most complete and totally depressing dehumanization reigns over the entire camp.

Our men are hopeful that with the coming of spring something will change, even just that the weather will bring with it some warmth and maybe—the word circulates constantly among the men—there will be some better job postings where they, reduced to beasts of burden, might hope for some more acceptable and more dignified working conditions. But spring is still far away. In this hellish valley the sun never makes an appearance. Each day is like all the others, under an inexorably dark, dreary, and oppressive sky.

One morning two teams are working on an embankment. Above them swings a pulley, used to raise boulders that get carted away by the "donkeys."

Suddenly a violent rip is heard, a dry crack, followed by a workman's terrible screams. One of the cables on the winch has broken and the massive iron structure has fallen down. Workers hasten to the site of the accident. An entire section of the camp mobilizes, and there's a jumble of voices and incomprehensible shouts.

Pascal and Giorgio run to the spot, together with Giovanni by their side. Before their stunned eyes, in the midst of a dense haze of dust, is a hideous scene of blood and destruction. Two men, Teofilo and the giant Andrea Lenta, have been crushed by the enormous pulley.

Teofilo, his eyes staring upward, is already dead. Andrea still shows some signs of life, his face contorting in agony. Matteo is the first to shout for the friends to come. Pascal, Filippo, Giorgio, and Giovanni draw near; they try to pull the mangled body from under the winch, almost succeeding at moving it, but the heavy equipment slips from their hands and again falls on Andrea. All one can hear is the sound of ripping flesh, and the last glimmer of life leaves the giant Andrea Lenta forever.

The accident leaves an immense void in the group, who are now reduced to nine men. The following days go by in silence. None of them dares speak about the terrible incident. One evening, after a long discussion, Matteo and Angelo, announce their decision to return to Italy. The Ace of Hearts concludes the announcement with these decisive words: "It's five years we've been here in America, and nothing's changed for us. Better to end it."

Angelo stays quiet beside him, limiting himself to a nod. A little later, he takes his son aside and asks him to come with them. Pascal doesn't answer. When his father urges him again, he says that he needs to think about it, that he can't answer right away. Angelo, pensive and hurt, doesn't insist. They all go to sleep on their table cots in silence, thinking about Matteo's words.

During the night, a thousand thoughts go through Pascal's mind. It's not possible, he thinks, for my American adventure to end like this. It's not possible that what I've seen and lived up to now is all that America has to offer me ... I'm only twenty-one, I can't go home and take up life again there as if nothing had happened over these five years.

Pascal sees himself again with the beggar Melengo, maybe the only one in the whole village with a a bit of wisdom, but he's filthy, old, in bad shape; who knows if he's even still alive, thinks Pascal. Alberto the shepherd also comes to mind, with his face creased by the sun and his hairy chest, with whom he climbed the Maiella more than once. Alberto, a shepherd like him, with his thoughtful, docile manner that allows him to accept every bad thing that happens to him with the conviction that ills and sickness are inevitable facts of life, that all one can do is accept them and go forward because those evils are designs as incomprehensible as they are unavoidable. No, Pascal says, this is unacceptable. I can't see Alberto or Melengo again, maybe I won't even see Antonio. Pascal thinks back to the ambushes on the witch that he planned with his old friend, boyish things now long ago and far away, and again he sees clearly the witch's frightening face when he gave her a piece of bread on the mountain, her disoriented expression cemented in his mind forever.

I can't go back to Introdacqua—Pascal thinks—with my father, who's fifty-six; sure, he has the right to go back home and embrace his wife—and here there is a flash of emotion in his heart—but me, I'm only twenty-one, I can't go back to my little village with things I haven't done yet, things that haven't happened to me yet. Yes, I have suffered a lot and maybe there's more suffering ahead for me, but it's impossible, Pascal thinks more and more firmly, that this America has only this to offer me. How can I leave this country without knowing everything it has for me? How can I leave without really getting to know it? There has to be something, some path, some glimmer of a chance for me in this enormous land. A path where a little light shines that I will reach after going down this long tunnel so far. I feel as if something in this country has attached itself to me, even with all the hard things I've gone through, something's planted roots in my soul, something that has latched on to my insides, even with all the pitfalls and hardships.

14

The following morning, while they are drinking the usual coffee-like liquid, Angelo, looking heartbroken, approaches his son and asks him if he will return with him to Italy. Pascal, with all the affection he feels for his father, with whom he's shared five years in this foreign country, explains his decision. Angelo, though his heart is in pieces, both understands and respects his son. Old Abruzzese that he is, strong and proud, he remains silent, making no further pleas.

It will be the last time he asks. Between them things have always been direct and clear, ever since Pascal used to help him in the fields.

Two weeks later, the group returns to New York, lately reduced in number because after the departure of Matteo and Angelo—and at the last minute also the "singer" Antonio Lancia and the happy bachelor Giovanni Ferraro—Niccolo' from Molise (the one with the tic in his right eye) and Armando from Caserta (with the bike) are leaving for Utica. Up there in that wooded city in the middle of nowhere out in the farthest northern region of New York State close to Canada, a remote relative of Niccolò has found them some work in a mill.

Our group now consists of just a handful. Besides Pascal, there's Giorgio Vanno, Giacomo Gallina (who used to be crotchety but who has calmed down since the horrible incidents in the Cumberland Valley), and Filippo Rossi, Matteo's nephew and Pascal's buddy.

Unfortunately, work is scarce in Manhattan and the four find temporary and irregular jobs first in Albany, then in Utica. Pascal notes there are quite a number of Italians in Utica, many of whom, instead of working in terrible conditions of the kind he's experienced in factories and on road crews, have started their own businesses. There are barbers, cobblers, bricklayers, a carpenter, a tailor. Someone's even opened a small pizzeria. Of course, with the war on, the times are not prosperous. People are afraid to spend, and everyone tries to keep expenses to the minimum.

One Sunday evening Pascal meets Gaetano, a man from his area in Italy who ended up in Utica while visiting a family member. Gaetano talks to him about some possible work in the freight yard in Shady Side, on the Erie railroad line, about two miles south of the wharf at Fort Lee. The pay is low: a dollar and fifteen cents a day (just a year earlier it had been a dollar fifty, in some cases even a dollar eighty), but the work seems stable and the place isn't far from New York City, where Pascal sees himself settling one day.

The next day the Introdacquesi quartet, at the insistence of Pascal that Utica makes him feel too isolated and far from New York, decides to head to Fort Lee. The long Erie line is under full construction there.

The four friends find themselves a place to stay in a train car that sits on the service track close to the freight yard in Shady Side. In the same car are another five workers: three Poles, one Russian, and a Hungarian. It's really like an elongated room, a hallway.

Inside it are rickety cots, close to one another, not much more than a surface to lie on and a little area for each one of the workmen. No furniture, no bathroom, no electricity. This is basically just a dump. Cold and smelly, filled with holes, it can barely shelter the men who live there. Some mornings (by this time it's the end of February 1916) Pascal finds his cot papered over with a thin layer of frost. The blanket—the one his mother had given him when he left for America and that he has carried with him for six years now—is just shreds.

There are no regular workday hours. What the men need to do is to always be ready, alert for any incident, some kind of an accident, some unforeseen situation that necessitates removal or replacement of material of various kinds, such as freeing a piece of track from some kind of obstacle so as to get it back in working order, taking action in the event of some unexpected mishap or an injury either slight or serious.

It can happen that Pascal has to go to work in the middle of the night, no matter whether it's snowing or raining or if there is a blizzard. Mostly the work consists of lifting the railroad ties that are soaked and rotten and carrying them on your shoulders, while you trip over uneven ground, while the heavy wooden pieces dribble dirty water all over you. Then you need to set the new ones in place with massive bolts. All this material needs to be picked up from a barn that serves as a warehouse, and after your work is done you need to put your tools back there where they belong.

Sometimes a worker, an older guy maybe, isn't so good at moving the ties and slips on the ice. The shouts of anger and rage can be heard all over the infernal place. Everywhere confusion, hissing, whistling, shouts and brusque orders over a loudspeaker, sirens, excruciating sounds and noises in the midst of a general turmoil. Train after train piled all together, heavy equipment that needs to be moved somewhere else, cars in movement that you need to make sure don't run you over.

One moonlit night Pascal happens to see two workmen flattened by a freight car, literally buried under heaps of coal, a horrific scene that the young man will carry with him his entire life.

15

The Erie railway line extends for almost 3,100 miles and links New York to Lake Erie. Its construction began in 1832 and ended in 1960, more than one hundred and twenty years in which almost 2,000 immigrant workers from all parts of Europe died in accidents of various kinds.

The headquarters of this pharaonic enterprise was established first in New York City, from 1832 to 1932, and then from 1932 to 1960 in Cleveland, Ohio. This is the longest railway in all of America, second in the world only to the Transsiberian.

Today, if you go to the great station at Fort Lee and observe the dense railroad network that it characterizes and that from there spreads with extraordinary efficiency and amazing functionality, it's almost impossible to imagine the suffering, the oppression, the hell that Pascal and his friends had to endure the winter of 1916, when this railroad, and the entire latticework of rails that would spread out from it, was at the height of its growth and there was no life insurance and no medical or union assistance.

It is curious and bitterly significant that Pascal in his succinct autobiography makes no mention of the American unions of this era, though they were functioning. His countryman Arturo Giovannitti, the Italian writer (he moved to the United States just a handful of years before Pascal) and fiery anarco-syndicalist orator, was very conscious of their workings. Giovannitti, who is too little known today in America (and even less so in Italy), had a high level role in the union movement during the years between 1910 and 1930.

One occasion will be noted here, the historic strike of 1912 in Lawrence, Massachusetts, named the Bread and Roses Strike, in the course of which an Italian American striker named Anna Lo Pizzo, a fabric worker with strong ties to the socialist movement, was killed. It was a strike in which thousands and thousands participated, workers from many different nations who were fighting against a salary cut imposed by the business owners. Arturo Giovannitti, Joseph J. Ettor, and Joseph Caruso, the three leaders of the union movement, were unjustly accused of Anna Lo Pizzo's murder and thrown in jail.

Giovannitti wrote a famous poem from prison that became known around the world, titled "The Walker," and succeeded in defending himself. During the trial, he refused an assigned attorney and displayed his exceptional eloquence. His self-defense, which alarmed and enchanted the judge and jury, allowed him to avoid a certain death sentence. A very different outcome would transpire for Nicola Sacco and Bartolomeo Vanzetti fifteen years later; they were executed by electric chair, having been falsely accused of murdering an accountant and a guard at the Slater & Morril shoe factory. Fifty years after they were killed (August 23, 1977) Michael Dukakis, governor of Massachusetts, would recognize the errors committed in the trial, clearing the names of Nicola and Bartolomeo.

Our young dreamer Pascal D'Angelo, during the frigid winter of 1916, seems totally ignorant of these workers' struggles, and his English is still fairly uncertain. In the train car in which he lives with his Italian and Polish companions that winter, all they talk about day after day is how to clean the mud off themselves.

16

After some months the four Introdacquesi men leave the railcar in Shady Side and move a bit further north in New Jersey, not far from Saddle River. There's been a call for workers here, mostly stone-cutters, drill workers, diggers, and cement workers, all for the job of building the new American freeways.

Pascal finds a job as a cement worker. The highways go as far as the eye can see. It's necessary not only to flatten the land but, in the case of underground streams, to channel them into manholes made especially for the site. There are no concrete mixers available. The concrete gets mixed by shovels and spades. A miserable task, especially when done during a broiling summer, as that of 1916 was. This is an endless job apart from the briefest pause at midday, thirty minutes to eat a hero sandwich and swallow a few liters of water. A continuous motion, with the workers coming and going under the sun carrying on their shoulders dusty bags filled with cement, while another group continues mixing the concrete. The faces of these workers, reduced to simple robots, look like so many colanders, and the dust gets plastered on their entire bodies, causing an unbearable burning.

Pascal is trying to mop off his face and throat with a handkerchief that quickly becomes a soggy rag. Every once in a while when he's soaking with sweat, he lies down on the grass to dry off, while under the burning rays of the sun the sacks of cement keep moving. Once dried off, Pascal realizes his handkerchief is stiff as a board.

But woe to anyone if the foreman catches sight of you. He's a bulldog who won't stand even for a worker taking the time to dry off.

A guy named Domenick has been assigned as group captain of Pascal's squad. He's of Italian origin and has absolutely no compassion for the workers, even less if they also are Italian. He yells clipped orders at them in Calabrese dialect mixed with some kind of American slang, constantly swearing. This bulldog is a massive man with outsized shoulders, abnormal features, and bloodshot eyes. The workers know him well, and no one dares to hope for an act of clemency from him.

They all just obey him with their heads down, because they're afraid of getting fired, which would mean the nightmare of endless wandering around searching for more work, weeks or months of forced idleness and begging here and there for some job or other.

One morning, during a particularly cruel heat wave, they need to build some foundations for a manhole in a hurry. Domenick is yelling and threatening to get rid of anyone who dares to stop, even just to mop the sweat off his brow.

In the process of digging, the workmen come across veins of subterranean water. At a certain point, the Bulldog orders some of the men, Pascal among them, to go down into the hole and dig. Down in there there are occasional pools of murky water. Almost all the other workers aside from Pascal have rubber boots on. The youth has a moment of hesitation. Domenick pounces on him, yelling, "If you want your ten hours put down in the time book you better go down and dig, and hurry up about it!"

All Pascal can do is go down in the hole and dig, dig, dig, muddying himself up to the calves under the sneering smirk of Domenick.

The culmination of this everyday brutalizing comes a few days later. In order to get up on top of the foundations, the group of workers assigned to the manholes needs to climb onto boards that are set more vertical than horizontal. Suddenly a summer storm comes up, a real tempest. To go up and down pushing the handcarts filled with cement becomes a titanic task, because the rain makes everything more difficult. The wheels barely turn, stuck in the massive amounts of sludge.

Pascal's job is to push the carts, full of cement, up to the top of the bulkhead and then pour the mixture down inside. It's a harsh and unceasing job. You barely have time to turn around with the cart before there's another one, overflowing, that you have to deal with. Really a job that tests human limitations, given the state of the boards and the vertical bulkheads that it's necessary to cross while pushing these carts filled with cement.

Domenick realizes all of a sudden that one of the loads is a bit lighter so as to be easier to manage. He starts raving, shouting down into the hole, and walks up and down screaming like an animal at the men below.

When he comes back next time, Pascal finds the cart so full that it's overflowing. He hesitates a fraction of a second and glances at the foreman, who continues screaming down into the hole to Pascal to keep working. Pascal tells him that the cart is overfilled and too heavy to move on the wobbly boards. There's a chance the carts will tip over. By way of answering, the hot-tempered Domenick jumps on him, grabs the cart, and pulls it up by the handles, yelling in a voice filled with scorn, "Heavy, right?"

Pascal dares to retort, "Well, yeah, that's easy, the hard part is getting it where it needs to go...."

"I'll show you," Domenick curses. He gives Pascal a hard shove and grabs the handle of the cart and pushes it across the wooden boards. But here the man swerves a couple of times and he almost slips to the ground. Suddenly he stops and, almost as though to himself, he shouts, "But why should I be the one doing this? What do I have you here for? I'm the foreman."

In the meantime, another worker, a bit more daring than Pascal, a friend of his, hurries to take some of the cement off the cart. But Domenick catches him. Cursing like someone possessed, he threatens to fire the entire group and forces him to replace the cement he took off. Then, turning back to Pascal, he orders him to push the cart. All the youth can do is obey.

This obvious abuse will remain forever stuck in his mind. What can he do? For a moment the young man considers throwing the whole thing over and leaving. The rain keeps pouring down. Pascal doesn't even look at Domenick, who is observing him, trembling, and he grabs the cart and pushes it up. But just then, just at he reaches the top, it slips and loses balance. The cart falls into the hole. Pascal barely has time to let go and grab desperately onto the wooden structure to keep from collapsing. A nail goes through his right hand, mixed with mud, rain, and sweat, and the blood spurts out wildly, coloring the whole hand and forearm red.

Domenick rushes over. "Get out of here, you idiot! You don't work here anymore!" he screams like a madman.

Soaked, in pain, totally spent, Pascal goes back to the deserted sleeping quarters. His hand, which has begun to swell, hurts him dreadfully. In the neighboring village there's no pharmacy, but there is a general store. From there he gets a bottle of hydrogen peroxide.

He goes back to his cabin. He disinfects the wound as best he can. Inside the building there is a stove, but it's unlit. No way to dry his clothes, which are dripping all over the place. The youth disrobes and wrings his clothes out as best he can. There isn't even a place to hang them up for the night. Finished, he stretches out on the cot, which is made of two planks nailed together.

In this way he passes a couple of hours in total silence like a dog curled up in a corner licking his wounds. Every so often the muffled sounds of voices reach him. Outside, the rain continues to fall mercilessly. The pain in his hand is piercing at times and Pascal even forgets his hunger. Anyway, if he wanted to eat something, in the barracks there's only a piece of stale bread and a morsel of half-moldy Italian salami.

He curls up on the cot and alternates dozing and feeling acute pain in his hand. His thoughts wander in a kind of dark and infinite space.

Finally, bit by bit, the first friends of his from the squad return, sopping wet from the rain but happy to be inside. The place quickly fills with their racket, with the smells and the steam of worn out bodies after a long day's work. Someone lights the fire, someone else shouts, and someone goes to get food from the store. Fat sizzles in a giant frying pan.

Giorgio comes over to Pascal's bed, asking how his hand is doing. Then he brings him a sandwich and a piece of omelet. He says something encouraging to him, but he too is exhausted from the day. Slowly, slowly, the sounds quiet down and everyone goes to his own cot.

Midnight has just passed. Pascal can't manage to close his eyes, but the pain in his hand is less intense. Finally he feels sleep coming on. The silence is broken only by the continual sound of the rain tapping on the roof and by the trickling of water in some corner of the barracks.

17

It's five in the morning, and one of the men in the hut begins to get up in the midst of the general noise of his companions. Another man, a bit later, begins to make his own breakfast and a sandwich to take with him for the lunch break. There's also someone humming to himself as he boils some eggs in a pan. Eggs are the best bargain that these men can avail themselves of, aside from soft sticky white bread, an occasional piece of cheddar cheese or a salami sold "Italian style," or some bologna.

Outside, the rain has stopped and the weather seems vaguely promising. The dripping inside the barrack has completely stopped.

It's not even six yet, and some of the men have already gone out to work: ten long hours of manual labor. Dawn is arriving. The sky is gray, covered with clouds and fog. Little by little the barrack empties.

Pascal remains on his own. Eventually he decides to get up, despite his wounded hand. He dresses quickly in the still damp rags he wore the day before. The next shift starts at seven. The youth hopes that the squad leader will have cooled off and can give him a task suited to his condition.

He hurries over, running toward the work site, and gets there at 7:01. Dominick yells down at him: "You're late. You can come back at noon."

Pascal calmly replies: "Why dock me the whole five hours? If I'm really too late for the 7 shift, can't I start at eight? It's only seven...."

"I said noon," Domenick curtly interrupts. Then he turns his back without so much as another glance and walks away.

Pascal, who is mild by nature, would like to respond, even physically, to this pointless and obvious mistreatment, but his innate calm prevails, and so he returns to the sleeping quarters.

At five minutes to noon, he presents himself again at the work site. He's wrapped a rag soaked in hydrogen peroxide around his swollen and purply hand. The sky looks bleached, a merciless sun beating down on the sweaty faces of the men in Pascal's group.

The scene from earlier in the morning repeats itself. The fore-man, with no hint of compassion and without even looking Pascal in the face, orders him to pick up a shovel and get to work with the rest of the group mixing the cement.

"Actually," Pascal ventures to reply, "couldn't you assign me some other task?" He raises his arm to show his bloated and band-aged hand. "Maybe, just for today, I could carry water to the men … or something else, as long as it isn't shoveling or pushing the cart."

"No!" Domenick replies drily. "If you can't use a spade, then go home and heal your hand." Having said as much, he leaves Pascal and heads over to his lookout post over the men.

For a moment, Pascal loses his grip on reason and feels like jumping the foreman … who is armed, like all the foremen. But it's only for a second. He stands looking at Domenick walking away. "Go home." How can he call that heap of a sleeping quarters "home"? It turns into a sieve every time it rains. Work is in short supply, Pascal reflects. If he fires me I'll have to start from the damned beginning all over again looking for a job. And he remem-bers the long, extenuated days of that frustration.

Finally evening comes and with it the workmen, exhausted and swaying on their feet like so many wild beasts going back into their barn. Pascal watches them come in in groups: There's the Poles, the rowdy and show-offy Irish, here the Abruzzo team … the weather is mild. Since the afternoon, the day has regained its summer splendor. When the weather's like this, the men prefer to be outside. They light fires and bunch together according to ethnicity; someone's curled up on a rock, writing a letter.

Pascal keeps to himself, seated on a stone, his bad hand hanging over his knee. He hears the crackle of the fire and for a moment is transported back to his village, when they would light the bonfires for Saint Anthony in January. In the half light he sees the outlines of his companions, someone getting more wood, someone fetching water, someone else cooking his simple supper. But it will be a while before supper's ready. The wait is so long sometimes that, weary from effort, some fall asleep while the pot continues puffing and snorting on the two red-hot stones. Sometimes it even catches fire and the smoke wakes the sleeper with a start, his supper irrevocably lost in the depths of the ruined saucepan.

This evening, with Pascal seated on his rock observing it all, is enchanting, the sky lit up with stars and the jolly noise of the men. But theirs is a strange gladness, mixed with a deep dejection that flies around in the space outside the sleeping quarters. Despite the sweet mildness of the hour, many of the men are in a bad mood. Even the night before, when the rain soaked their clothes on their backs, they seemed happier. Now some are sitting in silence, closed off, as though this magic night had awakened in them the old dream of a more secure place, a place with no foremen, where no one ever felt alone and everyone helped one another.

One man, older than Pascal, comes closer to him, asking about his hand: It's Giorgio Vanno. He tries to encourage him as best he can; not for the first time he offers to go with him to talk to some other foreman. No two areas at the site are the same. Each has its own special part of the job to do.

The foremen don't live in barracks like the ones these men are herded into like animals. They live in little farmhouses, close to the store, three or four to a house. Their salaries are nothing like as low as the workers'. Besides, each one gets a bonus for supervising the men assigned to him.

Some of these foremen, the more cynical and conniving among them, including Domenick, falsify the number of hours they put down in their logbooks. As Pascal learned in Cumberland, it makes no difference at all what a workman writes down in his records for the hours he worked. Only the logbook of the foreman counts, and you'd better not dare question it or you'll get fired instantly.

Once the workday is over, the foremen go back to their lodgings, where they find dinner ready and a clean bed to sleep in, not the grimy cots made of boards, heaped together one next to the other, where the pick and shovel men take their rest.

18

Pascal thinks about everything Giorgio said to him. In the end, he decides to follow his advice. He gets up off the rock and proceeds to the foremen's housing. He walks down a lane that's cooled by a refreshing summer breeze. The full moon has just appeared, and it shines on every ravine on this rocky and winding road, with embankments that look like heaps of silvery topsoil. All around the wide lane, thin sparse trees stand and long stretches of fields extend as far as the eye can see.

Suddenly the youth sees the stumbling silhouette of Domenick, the source of all his anger, his problems, of all his humiliation. The Bulldog is walking in front of him, staggering and plastered drunk. On the worksite word's going around that he has something going on with a woman in the village.

Pascal, observing the man's sloppy bulk, feels his anger rise again and, like a reflex, he experiences a stabbing pain in his hand. He quickens his pace to catch up with the big beast. In his head there are various impulses warring confusedly, among them the idea of attacking Domenick now, breaking his face, and making him pay for all his suffering.

But just then he feels a hand on his shoulder. The young man, lost in concentration, starts, turns, and sees the big smiling face of Giorgio Vanno, who has followed him quietly, without Pascal realizing it. Giorgio looks at him fondly. Guessing his state of mind, he invites him to sit down with him on a couple of big rocks by the side of the lane. His benevolent and reassuring manner makes all of Pascal's anger disappear.

"What do you want to do, son?" he asks, looking him in the eyes and keeping his hand on his shoulder.

Pascal is silent. He doesn't know how to answer this calm question. He picks up a twig and starts doodling in the dirt in front of him. Giorgio consoles him with words that Pascal will remember for the rest of his life.

"I understand, believe me, that you're thinking about some stupid act that will make you lose your job and not only that, you might never be able to get another job. You might even get deported or thrown in jail."

He stops. Then, as though pursuing a line of thought, he adds, "Yes, it would end very badly indeed, my dear Pascal. Don't be depressed. The god of New York is testing you."

The young man now unloads everything, telling him not only about all his rage, his frustration, but also about the abysmal pain of his hand. Giorgio looks at him a long time and then, as though absorbed in his own thoughts, he continues, "A senseless world, many centuries ago, drove nails into the wrong hands ... the wrong hands."

Pascal is only twenty-one. He doesn't completely understand the significance of these words, but he does feel love in them and above all hope for a better future. He understands that they come from a man who could be an older brother to him, particularly now that his father has returned to Italy.

Then Giorgio, to break the tension a bit, makes a joke about the bulldog Domenick, a sarcastic comment about his relations with the woman in the village and his rough and unlikely capabilities as a lover. The two of them burst into a gale of laughter that refreshes Pascal. After which Giorgio bids him goodnight, returning to the barrack, adding once more the exhortation to go talk to a different foreman; they aren't all of them the same.

Meanwhile, Domenick has disappeared around the corner, beyond which can be seen the vague light from one of the houses.

Pascal feels the night close in around him, little by little, as though it had arms, like his mother's when, in his childhood, she would hug him to comfort him. In that moment Pascal feels himself overcome by a terrible, compelling homesickness. He turns his gaze to the moon, still in the sky, and in her sees again the moon that would mysteriously illuminate the Maiella, among other peaks in his home region. And he sees himself, sitting again on the steps of his house, and he is astonished to see the shack itself, and he doesn't know why this image should mesmerize him so.

Finally he gives himself a shake. I'm not here to gaze at the sky, he says, coming back to himself. He puts out of his mind every useless fantasy he had had and heads over to the farmhouses. He speaks to the first foreman. No can do, he says. They already have a water-carrier in his group. The second one he talks to lies and tells him his group is too small to need a water-carrier. The third one won't even talk to him and shuts the door in his face.

Discouraged, Pascal quits and goes back to the barrack. He barely has put his foot inside the door when Salvatore, one of the workers, a Neapolitan man who's recently taken a liking to Pascal, says to him, "Hey, Pasca'. Didn't find anything?"

Pascal just shakes his head no. Next to Salvatore there's an older man, a foreman named Anthony, Neapolitan also, a man Pascal's seen only once before. "What's this guy lookin' for?" he asks Salvatore.

Salvatore, who seems to know him well, tells him in a rising voice and in a colorful mixture of Neapolitan and American slang, "I'll tell ya what he's lookin' for. First of all, you foremen are like the bosses here, you're like kings or emperors. Now, listen to me. This boy here yesterday hurt his hand, see it? It's all swelled like a balloon. He's lookin' for work that's better for that, but nobody'll listen to him. That bastard Domenick told him he's gotta keep mixing cement with the spade but he's gotta heal his hand first. Now, if he's come here with no money, what the hell's he supposed to eat in the meantime? Antonio, you get it. What the fuck's this poor shmuck's gonna do?"

The speech has the desired effect. Pascal realizes he's in front of a foreman who's different from the rest of them. And, in fact, Anthony looks kindly at him and says, "OK, kid. Tomorrow come work for me, in my team. There's a lot to do at our worksite. We need workers."

Pascal begins the morning in a new way, with a small amount of enthusiasm and optimism. He changes the handkerchief he's wrapped around his hand for one that's a bit cleaner after rinsing it out in hydrogen peroxide. In an old pan, with some oil still left in it, he cooks two eggs for a kind of omelet, slimy and a bit smelly, which he puts between two pieces of stale bread. He looks around for a piece of paper to wrap it all in, but he can't find any. He spends a couple of precious minutes looking. His fellows are already heading out to the worksite. Pascal tries to hurry. He knows he has to go farther away to reach his new site. He absolutely does not want to show up late. Finally, exasperated, he pulls the old kerchief spotted with blood out of his pocket and wraps his lunch in it as best he can.

Anthony gives him a spot with the diggers. It's a tough job, but easier than mixing cement or pushing overloaded carts, also because from time to time you get a brief break.

The new foreman quickly develops a liking for him and treats him, apart from a few rebukes, more or less kindly, and in the course of a couple of days Pascal manages to get his Introdacquesi buddies transferred to this group too, also to do digging work.

And so two weeks go by. The hand wound starts to heal over. The whole squad is waiting impatiently for payday. Among them there's the happy prospect of being able to buy something good from the wagon that comes by every week selling meat, fish, vegetables, and fruits, among other things.

But on the evening of the last day of the second week of work, the foreman, looking nervous, tells them that the contractor has sent a telegram saying that it was impossible to come that day but that he'd be there for sure the following day. The men accept this pretty well. After all, it's only a matter of waiting one more day.

The next day, immediately after the end of the work shift, a man arrives out of breath at the sleeping quarters saying there's been another telegram. All the workers, with the foreman in the lead, go outside. At the end of the path there's a little crowd of people. Here they find the superintendent, looking pale, reading a telegram out loud.

Everyone is quiet, concentrating hard to hear the message. The superintendent, a good little fellow in jacket and tie, with a placid and firm manner, announces that unfortunately the entire project has gone bankrupt, all the work is stopped, in fact today is the last day, and there is no pay forthcoming.

Anthony, cursing out loud, throws himself on the guy, asking for a more detailed explanation. It's not just his workers who aren't getting paid, he isn't either. The argument between them quickly becomes heated and comes to blows. The men have to separate the two combatants.

In grim silence, like a pack of beaten dogs, the workers return to their quarters, heads filled with questions, downcast and unsure of what to do.

19

We can easily imagine, after all the first rage has been burned off, the state of confusion, even of shock, that reigns in the barrack.

It's the middle of the night. Almost no one can sleep. Pascal too is wide awake, but unlike the others, he feels no desperation. Where can this type of interior serenity come from, this almost Olympian detachment in the face of unforeseen dramatic events that could change one's life like out of the clear blue sky finding oneself penniless and out of a job?

Moments ago, while the others were inside in groups discussing what to do and still others were gathering their things together, ready to leave the next day, he went out into the open to get some fresh air.

It's a beautiful summer night. The sky, in the absence of lights from the building, seems even more resplendent, all quilted with stars and a sickle of waning moon to conjure up an infinity of dreams.

Never before this late summer night has the young Pascal felt such an intense connection to this land. He pictures the ways in which this night is like a beautiful but haughty and indifferent woman. She's turned away, wearing a bright-colored dress of light transparent silk, and he can admire her but he doesn't dare approach her. He would like to love this creature, to sit next to her on the grass in this immense field, to embrace her tenderly, to weave a wordless dialogue with her, created just from the smallest gestures, the lightest ceaseless caresses.

But at some point he also feels the desire to shout, to yell at this world that is forgetful of or ignorant of every shortness of breath, every effort, and the smallest of miseries. And maybe also to laugh, laugh, laugh till his sides split, at these misfortunes, which suddenly seem so insignificant, so paltry and fleeting compared to the boundless beauty of the sky above him. What to do? Where to go now? Pascal knows all he really needs now are food and work. And all at once he begins to think about going back to Fort Lee. In the end, he thinks, better to be back there with work (even though low-paying) and living in that miserable boxcar in Shady Side than to stay here, worn out and never even paid.

The next morning, having gathered up their things, the four Introdacquesi head for New York. The road to Shady Side is twenty miles, on foot and, as fate would have it, in the heat of the summer. They are all hoping that somewhere along the way they'll run into some other job prospect, temporary work in the fields, maybe, or on some farm. They set off in good spirits and even manage to exchange a joke or two.

It seems like an interminable march, with frequent stretches to be crossed in the blistering heat of the sun. The partly paved road goes through immense tracts of land, some of them cultivated and others left as though abandoned.

In the afternoon they reach a clearing with a little farm on it. There's a drinking trough where one can slake his thirst. Next to the front door sits a tranquil-looking farmer, a young man. They ask him, fruitlessly, if he has work. It's the third person they've asked already today. He has nothing to offer them, but he asks them, in a friendly way, where they're going and what their plans are.

"We will just keep going … on foot. We don't have a choice," Giorgio replies simply.

The farmer goes inside and emerges again with a kind of old handkerchief filled with plums and apricots. Smiling, he hands it to Giorgio, who thanks him on behalf of the group and asks him about the best way to reach Shady Side.

It's five in the afternoon and our travelers set out again. They keep going until twilight. They throw themselves down in the middle of a charming meadow and, after having finished all the fruit, they fall asleep in the open air. None of them has the strength or desire to say anything on that endlessly long day.

The next morning they wake to the chirping of the birds flying around in the branches of a tree they've slept by. They're all ravenously hungry, and they seek to allay it with long drinks from their water canteens. They try to figure out the next move to make. Giorgio would have them go directly to New York City, but in the summer the city is an oven and it's hard to find a job. They need to calculate how much money they have. Everyone empties his pockets of his few remaining pennies. Barely eighty cents: not much, but it might be enough for a couple of sandwiches to split among them.

So, they set off again, heading toward a little town that the farmer from the night before told them should be about four or five miles away. It's called Dumont, but as the hours go by it seems like more and more of a mirage, another four or five miles!

Like Shady Side, Dumont is a little town tucked into the greenery that is part of Bergen County. At the time our heroes reach it, after those four or five hours, it boasts about two thousand inhabitants.

They get there finally, spent, stumbling, and ravenously hungry. It's a muggy day in August. They immediately set about trying to find the general store so they can get something to put in their stomachs.

After some verbal back and forth, after asking a passerby for directions to the store and having him mistake them for rough vagabonds, they find the store and go inside. To their surprise they discover that the owner is from their area in Italy. They hurriedly tell him the terrible situation they find themselves in, all their misadventures and misfortunes, culminating in the final, totally unexpected one of not being paid.

Nicola, an Abruzzese from Aquila, not only gives them abundant refreshment, he also offers them hospitality for the night, letting them sleep in real beds, fairly comfortable ones, an experience none of the men has had for a long time. The next morning he even gives each one of them enough money to catch the bus to the train depot at Shady Side. And it's there that they have decided to stay for now. The boxcar that we know so well awaits them.

The routine at the freight yard in Shady Side is exactly as Pascal left it a month earlier, except this time he is experiencing and living it differently. After all the injustice and suffering he went through in Saddle River, now he knows how to laugh at it. If a foreman raises his voice here, Pascal doesn't worry about it. If he needs to carry some heavy railroad tie from one place to another, he does it without thinking too much about it. In detaching himself from these things, he has learned to take refuge as in a bubble where he can pursue his fantasies without thinking about the hard work that is keeping him there. Also, he's discovered a kind of hangout in Hudson Heights, which he can reach in less than half an hour by the Edgewater ferry, a place managed by a woman from his region named Gina, a happy and good-natured person. Pascal comes here every Saturday evening to spend some carefree time having fun and joking around with his friends. It's actually because of one such joke that his life begins to take an unexpected course.

A group of Mexicans arrives at the freight yard, recruited directly from the south and put up in sleeping quarters close to the boxcar. He soon strikes up a friendship with a fellow his age named Fernando, who fought alongside Pancho Villa and was taken prisoner by the Americans.

A few weeks later Fernando and an older friend of his named Tomás are transferred to board in the already crowded boxcar with Pascal. The two are high-spirited guys, and they like to sing and play guitar after dinner. Tomás likes to tell stories about his life and experiences, and Pascal listens to them with great interest, sometimes even falling asleep to their rambling—also because of the mixture of Spanish and English that Tomás uses. Our youthful friend thus begins learning a bit of this new language.

Every week Fernando receives a Spanish-language newspaper from Texas. Pascal really enjoys listening to his friend read the paper out loud. Over time he begins to get used to this language and starts comparing Spanish words to their Italian counterparts. Up until recently newspapers had been for him just a means of lighting a fire, but now they are a source of real joy and learning. He finds, moreover, that English is even more pleasing and attractive to him than Spanish, and he decides to get an English-language paper every week. It's not easy reading, and often many words evade his comprehension so he acquires a second-hand dictionary. Reading this little dictionary, which also has in it the basics of English grammar and a list of irregular verbs, slowly becomes a regular exercise. Pascal learns page after page by heart.

With the help of the dictionary, reading the paper becomes much easier. He takes to writing, in big letters on the crumbling walls of the boxcar, words he's just learned the meaning of. These are words that he reads and rereads continually, having them always before him when he's in the car.

One day a friend of his who works as a bartender in many of the bars on River Road takes him to a variety show in Italian. In addition to the main show, there's a short comedy sketch and the recitation of some poems.

It's the first time Pascal has ever set foot in a theater, even though it's a run-down Bowery theater. During the performances, he begins to intuit an entirely different world of expression, one in which he feels completely at ease. He has a flash of insight. Hearing some intermission recitations, he becomes convinced he could do better.

In the next weeks, working doggedly every Sunday, he writes, in very approximate English, something like a cross between a burlesque and a comedy sketch, and when it's finished he reads it aloud to his friends in the boxcar, to their immense enjoyment.

In the area around the worksite, people begin to talk about Pascal as someone who can write a good joke or funny stories. Every so often one of the youngest workers brings him reams of paper on which to write his stories. Every day now Pascal is getting more and more confortable in English. He continually writes down new words, wherever he happens to be: on the inside and outside walls of the boxcar, on the railroad ties, in the margins of the newspapers he reads, and on page after page of notebooks. He's like an obsessed man, feverish with the desire to gain better and better knowledge of English until he has mastered it all. He frequently lobs unusual words at his friends, the more obscure the better, then patiently explains the meaning of each one, enunciating them letter by letter.

Over the short span of a few months Pascal becomes the "teacher" of all the laborers in the freight yard at Shady Side: an unusual teacher, funny and quirky, who never tires of posing questions of every kind and writing odd compositions, caprices, preposterous pieces, occasional verses.

One evening—it's gotten to be autumn by now—he comes home with the three musketeers Giorgio, Giacomo, and Filippo, after having visited Gina, and he chats a bit with a couple of brakemen who are getting ready to go on the night shift. They're Americans, from Vermont, big guys who appreciate Pascal's creative side. At a certain point, Pascal turns his face to the sky and exclaims, "The stars are marching over the deep night. With whom are they going to war?" The young men are perplexed and, half joking half serious, they ask Pascal who indeed the stars are going to war with. And he responds ecstatically, "With the Emperor of Eternity! Death!"

The two, along with Filippo and Giacomo, burst out laughing, but then one of the two suddenly stops and, speaking a bit tentatively, says to Pascal, "You're really a crazy man."

Now we are in December of 1916, and Pascal is more than ever set on immersing himself in writing this language in which he continues to make enormous progress. However, work in this same period is nonstop. Some days it becomes unbearable, partly because of the severe cold. There are accidents on the rails every day. Pascal suffers tremendously from not being able to devote all his time to his creativity. No sooner has he settled down to some concentrated time in the boxcar than he hears a throat-rending shout about this or that accident, most of them in tunnels or further down the tracks. In these cases one has to move immediately, and Pascal has to put aside his dreaming. By this point he has set down, in a notebook he bought at the small stationer's on George Road (the same place where he got the second-hand dictionary), a collection of short humorous stories, little scenes of various types set out in joking fashion, song lyrics, notes, and extravagant long poems. The experience of the theater has also instilled in him the desire to compose an ambitious tragic play.

Also on George Road there is a tavern run by a huge Hungarian man of few words and his wife, Mascia, who is submissive but also attentive and who works at the cash register. They have a daughter, Margit, who helps them out. After his inseparable friends Giorgio and Giacomo have said goodnight, Pascal spends some time with her, along with Filippo, chatting. Margit is around twenty years old and has beautiful dreamy blue eyes, and she is secretly in love with Pascal. She feels an enormous tenderness for this slightly bizarre young man, as he is prone to fantasy and, above all, totally different from everyone else who comes to the tavern.

The place has a back room where, Pascal dreams, one could put on a theatrical show. He mentions it to Margit and right away she enthusiastically agrees; besides, if people paid to see it, her parents would make a bit of money. And who knows, Pascal wonders, if that might make the giant dad a bit more inclined to like me. Naturally, he would be the author and director of this passionate tragedy, our grassroots author, Pascal D'Angelo (he would later write his surname in publicity sheets without the apostrophe). Obviously Margit would play the female lead, with her parents' permission. And just as obviously, the other actors would be his friends Giorgio, Giacomo, and Filippo.

Over the following days he works feverishly on the play, which he decides should take place in New York City. He quickly writes the scenes of the first act, in which a homeless man, owing to the vicissitudes of life, is constrained to sleep in the subway, and his sleep and dreams, presented at the beginning via monologues, are continually disturbed by the noises of the wheels.

One Saturday evening when he finds himself free from work, Pascal decides that he should spend a night in the subway himself so as to get some inspiration and words that he can use in the monologues. As a companion in this wild idea, he enlists Giorgio, who has long since become a kind of big brother to him and who fears that Pascal will run into some unpleasant situation while doing this.

Sadly, this project runs aground almost immediately, despite the fervid support of his friends, on account of a terrific wintertime intensification at the railyard and the parallel increase in construction on the Erie railroad. All around in the air, in the middle of the deafening sounds of drills and augurs, there is the uninterrupted traffic of trains, single carriages, small locomotives, cranes, pulleys, and donkeys, a cacophony of industry that frequently robs Pascal of even Sundays or the few hours of daily rest when he comes home, exhausted, to the train car after twelve hours of work.

The culmination of this endless fervor comes a few days before Christmas 1916, with the arrival in the yard of a team of inspectors who have come to confer with the various foremen.

And yet, even in the midst of this infinite raucous beehive, Pascal continues to enrich his English, utilizing what little pieces of time he gets. His Webster's is in tatters by this time, though he never stops patching it. Some evenings, even when he is dead tired, he tries writing his first poems, which he stealthily gives to Margit. He feels the purest love for her, mixed with the pain of knowing that nothing can come of their relationship. What can he promise the girl, he, a manual laborer, a stonecutter, a pick and shovel man?

One Saturday night their story ends brutally. While they are hidden in a dark corner outside the tavern, cooing to each other, Margit's father appears. In his unhinged way, in a language of mixed Hungarian and American slang, he shouts something at the girl and begins hitting her. Pascal tries to intervene, and her father literally picks him up and begins slamming him violently against a stone fence. Pascal feels a cutting pain in his shoulder, and at the same time he glimpses in the darkness the index finger of the Hungarian's warty hand pointing at him as he says with animal-like fury, "Get out of here! I don't want to see your face ever again, you dago bastard!"

Pascal never sees Margit again. In vain he looks for sign of her when he goes past the front of the Hungarian tavern in the following days. There's no trace of the girl. It's as if she has evaporated into nothing. And no one can give him any news of her.

The boxcar also disappears a few days later. One morning the foreman arrives and brusquely says that there are new work assignments. Everyone who's been living in that hole has to leave. They need to get their stuff and be ready by six the next morning. They will all be transferred to a new site, further north on the railroad line, where they will work as manual laborers.

To the pain of having lost his girl now is added the nightmare of forced transfer to a place in Pennsylvania—as he is told later on—called Carbondale, a place he's never heard of and the sound of which he doesn't like. The name makes him think of coal. And the whole hellish experience in the Cumberland Valley comes back to him, and he imagines himself as a miserable laborer all filthy in black and covered in soot.

Our Introdacquesi consult with one another. While Giacomo might be disposed to try this new venture in Carbondale, Filippo and Pascal are totally against it. Giorgio is uncertain what to do. At forty years old, he has become a de facto guide of the group. He wants to reflect calmly on the new situation. "The night will bring good counsel," he says at last to his companions. "Tomorrow we will decide what to do. In the meantime we have a lot to do to get our bags ready."

While gathering his things together, Pascal thinks a million thoughts. Finally, perhaps because of the frustration of his recent separation from Margit, he shouts, with his voice broken with emotion, "I'm not going to Carbondale. You guys do what you want, but I've made my mind up."

It's the first time that the youth, of a mild and obliging disposition, has had such a peremptory reaction to anything. His companions come over to him, realizing he's having some kind of nervous crisis. They all consult with one another. Finally Giorgio speaks up, putting his hand on Pascal's shoulder: "OK, that's fine. Forget Carbondale. Let's finish getting ready and then we'll go talk to the foreman, get the pay we're owed, and we can get going today."

It's noon. Our quartet has found a bit of serenity and they are even feeling optimistic. They've gotten their pay and are now sitting in a restaurant on George Road eating spaghetti and meatballs. They're talking over the future that awaits them in Utica, for this is where they've decided to go. Giorgio says that in that city, which is in the full throes of industrial development, there must be good prospects for work. A guy he knows, someone from home, might be able to find them something in a factory or at least get them some kind of work, even if it's temporary.

21

The four men stay in Utica only a short time. From there they go to Troy; finally, after having roamed between Pennsylvania and Massachusetts, they wind up a bit more permanently in New Haven, Connecticut.

Pascal, however, isn't satisfied; he's very conscious of the precarious nature of these jobs. Besides which, the call of New York City is too strong. In his heart of hearts, he wants to go back as soon as possible, once he's saved a bit of money. The idea of becoming a writer is growing inside him, even though he still isn't sure how to undertake the profession. His notebooks are filling up with incredible lists of English words he's memorized, as well as with a dense mass of notes, jottings, stories, and poems.

They spend some weeks in relative peace in New Haven, a nice city all in all, where they run into enough immigrants that they feel fairly at home.

One day, Giacomo confesses to his friends that he's fallen in love with Ruth, a resourceful brunette he met in Troy and whom he's stayed in touch with. Ruth, a hairdresser in a very nice shop downtown, has managed to find him a good job working in a steelmill. It was love at first sight for both of them, and even after just a few days of seeing each other they began planning a future together. Giacomo also really likes Troy, a pleasant city with a magnificent view of the Hudson. One day, when walking by its city hall, he was struck by an inscription on the building's façade that reads "Ilium fuit, Troja est: Ilium was, Troy is." For someone who studied a bit of Latin in grammar school and who has loved the *Iliad* since boyhood, this looks like a sign from destiny.

In the first days of March 1917, he bids farewell to Pascal, Giorgio, and Filippo and leaves for Troy. He friends will never see him again.

Giorgio, however, wants to stay in Connecticut. New Haven is a pleasant city and he's quickly gotten used to it. He's made friends with two Italians, Gennaro and Amalia, who own a little trattoria on Grove Street where he often goes to drink a glass of something and chat with Gennaro. And then he also runs into an old friend of his from Sulmona who emigrated here just a few years before he did.

One evening, the last day of March, comes the stroke of luck of his whole life. Gennaro introduces him to his brother Franco, called Frank, who has a plumbing business that's gotten off to a great start. Frank likes him immediately and hires him, teaching him the tools of the plumbing trade, which Giorgio picks up readily. It's the turning point of his life. In a few months he's one of the most sought-after plumbers in New Haven. During the summer of 1917, after having acquired a lovely house on Church Street, with a view of the sea (to be precise, Long Island Sound), he will be able to fulfill the dream he has cherished all the years he's been in the States, of sending for his wife Giulia in Introdacqua. He goes to get her himself and bring her to America in the summer of 1917.

At just over forty, Giorgio will begin a new life, and Giulia will give him two sons. The first will be named Gennaro in honor of the friend who did so much to shape the course of his life.

Unlike Giorgio, who is so happily situated in New Haven, Pascal is thinking more and more about going back to New York. He has made enormous improvements in his English. He's got a new Webster's and some more secondhand books, including a history and anthology of English literature, which he reads and makes notes in every Sunday. He's working now in a small machinist plant and manages to save some money. But he hasn't managed to make any close friends in this place, just some fleeting acquaintances. He has an instinctive reticence that makes him avoid Italian Americans, among others, whereas his pal Filippo feels totally at home in such groups.

One evening the two go out with a couple of young women, one of whom has been flirting with Filippo for a while now. Thinking he's doing something nice for Pascal, with whom he's been sharing a tiny apartment in Chapel Street, Filippo asks his girlfriend to bring a friend of hers to join them on their usual Sunday date. But the meeting produces no effect. Pascal still cherishes the memory of the sweet-faced Margit and finds the bland and vulgar conversation of this woman Giovanna Amanda distasteful and the fact that she'd rather be addressed as Giamandy utterly absurd.

One morning, after a night when his decision to leave New Haven comes to a head, he announces the fact to Filippo, knowing already that Filippo won't be going with him.

The day he leaves, Giorgio drives him to New York in his first new American car, a brand new Chevrolet, a little less than two hours from New Haven.

Their farewell is quick and emotional. In a confused but also determined manner, Pascal tells him he's sad to be leaving him but at the same time very happy to be going to settle permanently in the great American city.

"And what are you gonna do on your own?" Giorgio asks him, smiling, but also with some concern.

"I don't know yet," Pascal answers. "I want to do something that gives me satisfaction, something creative ... but first and foremost I have to learn the language of this land better. I want to give my life more meaning. Right now it feels incomplete."

"Remember that if you change your mind, I'm always here. No matter what you need. OK?"

"Thank you very much," Pascal replies, hugging his friend, a man who practically is a father to him.

"No problem," Giorgio says, mixing some English into his Italian. Then he adds, "I'll come to visit you. Don't forget to let me know your new address in New York."

PART THREE

New York City and Brooklyn 1917–1922

1

Pascal is now truly alone in New York. He walks down Broadway
feeling a sense of intoxication mixed with a strange nervous excitement. A thousand thoughts fly through his head as he wends his
way, carrying his suitcase, through traffic. It seems like an eternity
since he left the city. In actuality it is only a matter of months. Now
he knows, whatever he decides to do, he has to face it alone, without
consulting anyone else. There won't be any Ace of Hearts to guide
him, nor Giorgio, or the powerful and educated Andrea Lento to
protect him—or to teach him anything new. Thinking of Andrea
suddenly pains him; he remembers the horrific cry of agony as he was
crushed beneath that damned winch in Cumberland.

Nor will he have his father, who's back in Introdacqua now,
probably still cursing his American experience, but also enjoying being with his wife and his other son, Felicino, who's grown to be a
hearty lad of nineteen and can be counted on to help his family out.
Pascal thinks for a moment about Felicino; it seems impossible that
his little brother, who was just a child when he left, is already nineteen. But Pascal's fondest thoughts are still for Giorgio, to whom he's
only just said goodbye, the only one of the entire group who's really
had good luck.

In Pascal's suitcase, aside from some thrown-together garments,
are his beloved Webster's, some other books, including the one of
English literature, and two newly minted notebooks, one red and one
blue, that he bought in New Haven, on College Street, close to Yale
University. He fell in love with the notebooks the minute he saw
them in the window. He fantasizes about writing in them, who knows
what? In the center of each cover there's a plate on which is printed
COMPOSITIONS. Underneath are three lines reading, "Name,"
"School," and "Grade." Pascal doesn't go to Yale, nor will he write
any papers in these books or receive any grades from professors. He
bought them simply because he liked them. He's never seen any

notebooks that looked like these, but something spurred him to get them. Something still vague but somehow urgent told him to do it.

Pascal continues to walk happily through the streets of New York until his steps carry him mechanically to Little Italy, the neighborhood in New York he knows better than any other. He rents—by the day—a room on Bayard Street, and he spends his first New York days wandering around the streets of midtown and downtown.

One morning, September 10, 1917, Pascal is walking along Fifth Ave at 42nd Street. At a certain point he suddenly finds himself facing the majestic New York Public Library. He stops in front of the building. He stares, fascinated, at its architectural features, particularly the imposing columns of the entrance. He walks up a couple of the stairs and regards the two great lions, one on either side. In his entire life he has not seen anything remotely like it. Along the top of the façade, just above the columns supporting it, he sees six statues and wonders what they represent. It will be some time later that he'll discover that the ones he admires most—the sculpture is by Paul Wyland Bartlett—represent Poetry (to the left) and Tragedy (on the right). These are the two forms of art that resonate most with him and the ones he will aspire to learn to write.

The youth feels a bit dizzy and hesitates to go any further up the staircase leading to the entrance. Inside he feels something has stopped him, possibly even prevented him, from reaching the doors.

2

Officially established in 1895, the New York Public Library is, after Washington, D.C.'s Library of Congress, the largest library in the world. At the time when our Pascal saw it for the first time about a hundred years ago, the building housed ten million books, in addition to magazines, newspapers, and other publications of various types. Today it has close to sixty million, and there are eighty-seven branches all over the city of New York.

In order to realize this pharaonic construction, the best architects of the age were invited to compete, among them Henry Bacon, who some years later would conceive the Doric-temple-shaped monument in Washington dedicated to Abraham Lincoln; George B. Post, the architect of the New York Stock Exchange on Wall Street; and the firm of McKim, Meade & White, who had already designed the famous Boston Public Library. Actual construction, on designs from John Merven Carrere and Thomas Hastings, winners of the competition, began in the spring of 1899 and lasted twelve years, during which tons and tons of marble were transported from Vermont to New York.

This majestic building was formally inaugurated on May 23, 1911, in the presence of US President William Howard Taft and New York City Mayor William Jay Gaynor. Gaynor is famous for having declared, "Who can pass by this building for the first time without stopping? I almost said kneeling down, but we don't kneel down as easily as that in New York."

During the last decades of the nineteenth century and the first of the twentieth, New York City was (and continues to be) a nonstop construction site: Among the most spectacular of the urban projects to be built in this period, aside from the NYPL, were the glorious Brooklyn Bridge; the monumental Grand Central train station on 42nd Street, with its magnificent façade designed by Whitney Warren and Charles Wetmore (whose firm was responsible for some of the most impressive buildings not only in New York but in a number of other important American cities); and Penn Station on 7th Avenue, the other significant railroad terminal in the city; all this without mentioning some of the wonderful skyscrapers, among them the Chanin Building, the Empire State Building, and the Chrysler—this last still considered the most elegant skyscraper in the country.

When Pascal first set foot in the New York Public Library, it had been just seven years since its opening.

3

Pascal moves through the vestibule of the library in a daze. He takes in the grandiosity of the architecture, with its neoclassical flavor and sober geometry. He continues to admire the elaborately decorated ceiling, the stuccoes, the various sculptures, the enormous lamps, the windows, and the variety of elegant furnishings.

He turns to the imposing staircases, symmetrically placed on the two sides of the room. They are very similar to the stairway designed by Jean-Louis-Charles Garnier for the Paris Opera (Garnier is responsible for many European buildings, among them the spectacular façade of the Casino of Monte Carlo). Finally, across from the various reading chambers, he reaches the great reading room.

The first thing Pascal notices is the silence in all these spacious rooms. A spacelike, profound silence, accentuated only by the light rustling sounds—the muffled steps of visitors, some delicate buzzing here and there, the barely perceptible riffling of book pages. It seems like a miracle to him to see the coming and going of so many volumes all at once. He is struck by the absorbed concentration of the readers at the long tables, consulting or taking notes or simply reflecting on the books and notebooks in front of them.

In the large antechamber of the reading rooms, an entire wall is made up of numerous shelves containing books for ready consultation. Above them is a plaque reading: REFERENCE BOOKS. They are mostly encyclopedias, manuals, guides, dictionaries, almanacs, and resources of that variety. Pascal is amazed that all these massive publications are immediately available to all. They can be picked up without asking permission of anyone, taken to a reading room, and examined by anyone who wishes to.

To the right of this giant scaffolding are lined up, one next to the other, additional pieces of wooden furniture, all identical, and with a myriad of drawers, each marked with a letter of the alphabet. These are the catalogues of the books housed here, each one of which is assigned a card containing the bibliographical specifics and its location. On top of the catalogue cabinets sit two boxes, one of little sheets of paper and the other with tiny pencils in it.

Pascal watches as the visitors look through the drawers, holding a pencil in one hand and the sheet of paper in the other, and making a notation. After which they go to the counter of the reception desk, leave the sheet with an employee, and then sit down to wait on one of the benches in front of the desk for an employee to retrieve the requested book.

This entire process unfolds before his eyes like something magical, wrapped in a kind of cocoon, in which he feels himself to be more and more enfolded. The sensation of being enveloped is so strong that he feels he can't escape it, and he has no desire to.

Almost unconsciously, he slowly approaches the catalogues. He looks at them as if in a dream, and yet he senses everything around him. He runs a finger along the surface of the drawers, the soft, highly polished wood that has something about it that feels familiar, and yet distant too. He seems to recognize the heavy warmth of the wood of the drawers, their age, their tangibility, as when he was a boy and he would caress his mother's face.

At last he shakes off his dreaminess and walks over to the reading room, feeling a certain lightness. It's an ambience in which he feels peaceful and perfectly at ease.

This first dazzling impact of a book, an object that is visually multiplied by infinity in the library, is what electrifies Pascal's attention. This is the first, most real, complete, irrevocable encounter of Pascal with the world of books. The young man, on that 10th of September, 1917, will happily spend the entire day in this immense library. He will spend hour after hour exploring the depths of an enormous volume on the art and poetry of the European Romantic period that he found among the reference books. He is captivated by some of its illustrations, particularly works by Caspar David Friedrich, Gustave Courbet, and above all Theodore Géricault, whose *Raft of the Medusa* he finds profoundly moving. Among the poetry, he is drawn most to that of Keats, Byron, and Shelley, whose work he has encountered in the second-hand anthology he picked up in New Haven. Throughout the day's reading he has wandered around among the halls and smaller reading rooms and decided his favorite is

the immense consultation room in which, carefully laid out and ordered, one can find so many newspapers and magazines. He admires
the paintings and prints on the walls of the long and airy hallways
leading to the bathrooms. The perfect cleanliness of the space, the
fact that he can avail himself of it whenever he wants to—he is re-
joicing in a sense of comfort he has never experienced in his entire
life.

4

Having encountered and become acutely aware of the New York Public Library, Pascal experiences a drastic change in the course of his life. Not that he suddenly decides to change his profession and find one different from his own of laborer and stonecutter, the only one he knows and that earns him some money, but rather that discovering the library as a magical and attractive place where he can find all the books and newspapers and magazines he wants (and that interest him) brings about in him the birth of a powerful and imperative motivation, a new and decisive meaning to his life. With all his physical and emotional strength Pascal is choosing a road of no return, a road that gives his existence a decisive direction.

The young man spends weeks this way, all day and every day, inside the library. Sitting at one of the long tables, he takes page after page of notes: thoughts, verses, bits of dialogue, short stories, or just English vocabulary words, words whose numbers grow and grow each day and that he quickly memorizes. In the library Pascal has truly found the ideal interior habitat that can satisfy his omnivorous appetite for reading, writing, and learning.

Some mornings his new life seems like a dream. How far away seem the events of the Cumberland Valley or of Saddle River, New Jersey! It's as though a spell made everything disappear: the superhuman efforts involved in the nonstop picking and shoveling, the deafening noises of the drills, the winches, the pushcarts and augers, the endless humiliations and difficulties provoked by foremen, or rabid dogs like Domenick.

Pascal knows very well that this new experience of being a reader and writer can't change his pick-and-shovel existence, at least not right away, but these weeks of tenacious study are changing his attitude toward his life; they are giving him his deepest reason for existing. And this reason is concentrated in the increasingly compelling desire to write, write, write, every day. He thinks of nothing else. And this is the state of mind in which he spends the final months of 1917, a turbulent and historically memorable year for the United States as it takes part in World War I.

Pascal's attitude about the war, which he reads about every day in a variety of publications, has always been fairly detached and disinterested. In the spring of that year, when President Woodrow Wilson officially declared war against Germany, he was in New Haven with Giorgio and Filippo. Giacomo had just left for Troy to join his girlfriend.

The entry of America into the war took our Abruzzesi by surprise. Pascal was very aware of the growing state of confusion and agitation in the streets of New Haven, especially those close to Yale. In that area he had seen more than one group of students yelling and protesting against Germany. It could happen that even on a seemingly calm day, some unexpected act of violence might erupt, as he had seen occur one tranquil April afternoon. It's a Saturday. Pascal is walking down Sachem Street. Just a bit earlier he had gone with Filippo to a pharmacy, but he left him there so he could walk around a bit on his own. Once he gets to the intersection of Prospect Street, he runs into a group of students shouting anti-Germany slogans and also inveighing, so at least it seems to him, against certain professors at the university. A lot of what they are yelling he can't understand; some of the students are threateningly waving American flags. In front of a store, a man of a certain age shows some disapproval of the group's behavior. Suddenly one of them, a stocky young fellow, goes up to the man and punches him in the face. The man falls to the ground, his mouth bloodied.

There are days in which, for the first time, Pascal argues about the war with Giorgio and Filippo. In the local papers he's read about heavy enlistment numbers, even of men his own age. Most of them are Yale students. In his confused and essentially peaceful mind, he struggles to understand what exactly is happening and in what way it might interfere with his life. But he does it in a detached and reserved, almost an indifferent way. He can't understand the patriotism of those shouting students nor can he feel, unlike Filippo, an Italo-American hatred for Germany. For him Germany is just a geographical place, one where, Pascal remembers well, some of his countrymen went in search of work.

One night when they are having dinner at Gennaro's house, a violent argument breaks out between him and Filippo: Their attitudes about the war are completely opposed. Giorgio tries in vain to make peace between the two of them. Pascal sits in perplexed silence. Filippo jumps suddenly up from the table and announces that he's going the next day to the police station to find out how to enlist. Giorgio, trying to calm him down, says jokingly, "Hey, kid; did you come to America to work or to fight a war?" Filippo, completely serious, glares at him. It's the first time he has gone against Giorgio.

Two weeks later, Filippo will say goodbye to his friends and to his crying girlfriend. He'll leave for Washington, D.C., together with other young men from New Haven who have signed enlistment papers, ready to join the American troops sailing to Europe.

5

Day after day, Pascal sees his savings diminish alarmingly. Even though he's saved every way he possibly could, the stash he had set apart is now reduced to just a handful of dollars. Nevertheless, he isn't about to give up his new way of living, which in addition to just feeling right, is also the only path to realizing his dreams. At the same time, he knows he can't spend every day in the library. This knowledge pains him, as he has really discovered the true joy of time spent there.

Lately he's been staying for long hours in the periodicals room. He assiduously reads the newspapers and journals, keeping abreast of what's happening across the world. In a separate little notebook, he begins noting the addresses of publishing houses that issue works of fiction as well as poems and short stories. In his fevered mind he imagines sending them some of his own compositions. He has also discovered that at the library there's a room full of typewriters available for anyone's use. All you have to do is bring some paper with you. This is an extraordinary discovery, and not a day passes that doesn't find him there practicing on the machines, which to him seem like fantastic inventions.

One day, with his savings reduced to just some pocket change, he inquires about work from a neighbor of his on Bayard Street, a man from Lucania named Pietro but called Peter here. Thanks to him, he finds some work on a construction site in Brooklyn where they are building footbridges over the water near the South Brooklyn Marine Terminal. The pay is low, but it's not very strenuous work, and it leaves him free Saturday and Sunday, which are the days he takes the train over to hunker down in the library.

Living in Brooklyn is much cheaper than living in Manhattan; so Pascal decides to leave his place in Bayard Street and move to Prospect Avenue into a tiny two-story house. The landlord is a Greek American named Demetrius Zodiatis, who lives on the top floor, and on the ground floor, where the kitchen and servants' quarters are, and next to a backyard, he's carved out a little room that Pascal rents from him. He shares the kitchen with Zodiatis. The only inconvenience is the bathroom, a narrow and smelly little cube built in a corner of the backyard. In it is a Turkish toilet and a small sink with a tube you can hook up to the faucet if you want to take a shower. Apart from this nuisance, it's cheaper than the last place, and Demetrius is an easygoing guy whom Pascal gets along with right away.

Some months go by, during which Pascal's English improves even further. He puts most of his efforts into composing his first poems, which eventually he reads out loud to Demetrius. Demetrius is his first reader, and he listens carefully while he chain-smokes cigarettes. He's a cultured person, he speaks excellent English, and he frequently has some good feedback for Pascal. Not only that, but in his living room there is a little library he lets Pascal use. His passion is classical music. Sometimes on Sundays he gets out his old and bulky Victor V gramophone, which still works perfectly well, and listens with Pascal to various symphonies and lyric operas. Demetrius, although a bit deaf, likes Schubert best of all, while Pascal immediately falls in love with the operas of Puccini and Verdi. Zodiatis is in his mid-seventies and a widower. His wife Eufrosine died three years earlier. He has a son living in Philadelphia. Reading, smoking, and listening to classical music are his only joys in life, apart from good food.

The two men often pass the time sitting on the room's only two couches, discussing poetry and music, although Pascal is constrained, on account of Zodiatis's deafness, to repeat himself sometimes. Zodiatis, smoking stubbornly, sometimes gets up to go to the kitchen, lighting matches directly on the wall. The marks of these countless strikes appear like so many scratches on the wall to the right of the stove's burner.

The second person Pascal reads his poems to is Lynn, a nice girl who works in a bistro close to the Marine Terminal. Idealizing her, Pascal dedicates some of his poetry to her and flirts cautiously. She isn't pretty and she has none of the dreamy charms of Margit, but in exchange for his kindnesses to her, she gives him extra-stuffed sandwiches and the fullest glasses of beer.

In the evenings after a long day's work Pascal prefers to stay at home in his room. If it's nice out, he'll sit and write in his little backyard. He takes the only chair he has in his room and sets it up out there so he can write in his notebook.

By this time it's the fall of 1918. The sun is staying out long enough that the youth will be dreaming and writing until nightfall. Far from the continual noise of his coworkers on the site, and far from the street noise from his road, which skirts the bay and which will in years to come become the Gowanus Expressway, Pascal closes his book and looks up at the sky. Ever since boyhood he's loved the stars. He recalls enjoying staring up at the luminous sky, rendered more magnificent by the fact that Cauze had no electric lights to interfere with the starry splendor. Who knows, he thinks now, how many worlds there might be up there? How many stars and planets, with how many eyes looking up in my direction contemplating the same moment? Maybe somewhere in space our gazes are meeting and we'll never know. But suddenly a dog begins barking, disturbing these fantasies.

6

One day, a Saturday evening in January 1919, upon coming home from work, Pascal learns from Demetrius that in a theater close to Sheepshead Bay they are performing *Aida*. He himself doesn't feel like going, but he encourages Pascal to. All at once Pascal feels himself overwhelmed by a wave of joy mixed with excitement. He's never been to the theater in his life and, with the encouragement of Zodiatis, he decides to give himself this experience. Aside from anything else, the next day he is entirely free. He has heard Verdi's opera, from listening to it with his landlord on the gramophone, and knows the story of Aida and Radames well. He's also read the libretto, which Zodiatis has in his library.

So, the next evening, after having dressed up as much as possible, and following his landlord's directions, he heads out to the theater. He gets a bit lost in the labyrinth that is South Brooklyn, but he asks help from a shopkeeper who steers him in the right direction, and he gets there just in time, finding a seat close to the orchestra.

That night will give Pascal his first taste of true artistic beauty, something beyond the insignificant stories and poems he's been showing to Lynn or reading to his work buddies. Pascal perceives, albeit still in a slightly nebulous way, how this beauty should and can be, what the nature of its power is, the great creative spirit and the discipline that go with it. It's something that up to this point he's associated only with Percy Bysshe Shelley.

That unforgettable experience will spur him to buckle down even further in his study of poetry and the writing of it. He buys more books and a new Webster's, much bigger and more satisfying than the tattered previous one, and his thoughts fly frequently to those gorgeous arias he heard at the theater and that he continues to savor with old Zodiatis. By this time Zodiatis has developed a real paternal affection for the boy. One evening he gives him an old but very elegant pipe, used just once by him before he returned quickly to his favorite Lucky Strikes.

On certain days when work is especially arduous and the deafening noise becomes unbearable, Pascal contrasts it in his mind with the divine melodies of Verdi and Puccini. His pages of notes and writings grow more every day. Sometimes in the evenings, when he feels the powerful desire to try to write an opera himself along the lines of *Traviata*, *Aida*, or *La Bohème*, in order to release the tension he goes out wandering the streets of Brooklyn, prey to a thousand questions, dreams, illusions, projects. His love of music and poetry reaches an impossible peak with the passing of time. He burns to write a great opera and would love to fashion a libretto, but for his utter lack of musical knowledge.

One Sunday afternoon in April of 1919 he sees a sign go up in the window of a building advertising a private music institute. In it they will teach harmony and counterpoint. He knocks at the door, without result. He asks someone passing by if he knows anything about the school. The person tells him the school's closed on Sundays. Pascal showers the man with questions he can't answer (How long does it take to learn music? How much do lessons cost? Does he know *Aida*? etc.)

A little further on, he discovers another such sign, this time on a private house. He rings the doorbell. An elderly woman opens the door and looks in horror at Pascal. Only in this moment does he realize what a shabby picture he presents: a sweaty shirt with no collar, pants covered in patches, ratty shoes, an unkempt beard, and tousled hair. But he doesn't lose heart. With great politeness he addresses her:

"Good evening, Madam. Pardon me for disturbing you. Do you teach music?"

"No," the woman replies, looking at him with a kind of disgust.

"But," Pascal insists, "on the sign it says lessons in harmony are given here."

"Maybe," she says shortly. And then she adds, "What music do you know?"

"Truthfully … none," he replies, dejected.

"My dear young man, it would be better if you learned a bit about music before dedicating yourself to harmony."

"How? What must I do?" Pascal asks earnestly and desperately.

"Learn an instrument, what I do I know? A piano, the trumpet, the violin …"

The woman abruptly ends the conversation by shutting the door in his face.

This episode tamps down the enthusiasm and desires of our aspiring composer for some days. The following week he sees in the window of a thrift store a second- or third-hand violin. After some bargaining, he manages to buy it for five dollars. For some additional charge, he also gets a small book of beginners' music lessons. Triumphant, he goes home to show his trophies to Demetrius. Zodiatis turns the violin around in his hands, tests the strings, holding the instrument up to his ear, and finally good-naturedly congratulates Pascal. Pascal retires to his room and immediately sets about familiarizing himself with the instrument.

From that day onward Pascal dedicates himself exclusively, in his free time, to that violin. He practices certain harmonies over and over and then starts stealing some of his nighttime sleeping hours studying the manual and trying, sometimes until he becomes exasperated, phrases and passages of music. Zodiatis leaves him to it, lover of music as he is himself. He tolerates all the dissonant notes, which are quite muffled by the time they reach him anyway, because of his deafness.

Once, however, in the middle of the night, there comes a furious knocking on Pascal's door. It's Patrick O'Malley, an Irish beanpole of a man who lives next door to Zodiatis. The man, tall and strong, faces Pascal, who's a bit shocked, and threatens him, wagging his finger in front of his face, shouting at the top of his voice that he has to get up at five every morning to get to his factory job in Long Island City.

Pascal stops practicing at night but still works at it during the days, especially on the weekends, when he tries to get in as much practice as he can.

One Sunday afternoon, Patrick presents himself again, this time knocking quietly on Pascal's back door. Pascal, not leaving the chair in which he's been plunking away, calls out, "What do you want?"

"I want to talk to you a second."

This time Pascal isn't intimidated at all and goes to open the door, ready to fight.

The Irishman greets him liltingly and even goes so far as to offer a vague compliment, indicating the violin. Then he says, "It's really nice, your violin. I'd love to own it. Say … would you sell it to me? How much do you want?"

Pascal retreats a couple steps, seems to caress the violin slightly, and then, almost speaking to himself, murmurs, "It's a good violin. It's worth almost $10."

"Well, that's an exaggeration; what about $6?"

Pascal hesitates, and then O'Malley says brusquely, "All right; $7 and we won't discuss it anymore."

He takes out his wallet and removes seven one-dollar bills. Radiant with happiness, Pascal puts aside his hesitation and attachment to the instrument that has been tormenting him for a month or more. He takes the money and hands the violin over. O'Malley looks at it, thumbing the strings for a moment. Then suddenly, as though having a seizure, he raises it and breaks it against a rock in Pascal's backyard. Pascal is slack-jawed. Then, walking back toward his house, O'Malley shouts, "At least I'll get some blessed peace this Sunday!"

The next day Pascal returns to the used-instruments store. He goes in and walks around listlessly. At last he notices an old guitar. He considers buying it, but a little voice inside him dissuades him. He feels he's gone through his music mania. It's a field that's beyond his capacity. He decides instead to redouble his efforts at writing literature and recommences his visits to the New York Public Library.

7

Pascal decides that, of the English Romantic writers, whom he has been studying systematically, it's Keats and Shelley he feels most passionate about. He's already discovered Shelley's lyric verse drama *Prometheus Unbound*, a work that profoundly fascinates him.

It so happens that one Saturday afternoon, August 4, 1919, he unearths on a table of used books in Bryant Park—the great open space behind the library—a pocket edition of Shelley's drama. Filled with joy, he buys it for mere pennies. He considers this circumstance irrevocable proof of his destiny, and he immediately links the date, August 4, to the same date of the poet's own birth.

That night, in the silence of his room, he reads with renewed attention the life of Prometheus as related by Shelley. To him it seems a very complex work, written in a nineteenth-century English he finds hard to understand, but with constant reference to his Webster's he manages to grasp it. He feels a great power in the work, a cosmic spirit capable of elevating itself above the world's human miseries. Obscurely, but also more and more clearly, Pascal associates the titanic spirit of this mythological figure and his superhuman ability to undergo any torment with his own fate. He too, like Prometheus, must resist and go against every force of adversity in a life that wants to destroy his ideals. As far as he is concerned, these ideals of becoming a real writer, a great poet who, freed from every bond, from every vexation, oppression, persecution, will succeed in allowing Good to overcome Evil and to establish Love overall.

In the continual rereading of this work of Shelley, Pascal finds analogies even with *Aida*, in particular the protagonists' heroic and sentimental impulses. He deeply feels the values animating them as they are gradually frustrated by obstacles that our young friend associates with those in his own life. The harder they are to overcome, the greater will be the spirit of resistance to confront and vanquish them.

So, every time he visits the library—by now he is going every Saturday—he immerses himself in reading about Greek mythology, a subject he is wholly ignorant of but that he feels resounds within his own soul and his powerful desire for consciousness, and that, apart from everything else, is a fertile source of inspiration for his poetic imagination.

One day on returning home from work he finds a letter from Giorgio under the door to his room. In it he learns about Giorgio's life and of the birth of his first son, named Gennaro, who by this time is two. Giorgio chides him over how seldom Pascal writes with his own news. Pascal spends so much of his free time wrapped up in his reading that he has little time for writing letters to his old work buddy. Giorgio writes about his own plumbing business, which is doing wonderfully. The war's been over for some time now and, at least in New Haven, it seems there's been a certain economic upturn. He tells Pascal that he plans to spend the Labor Day weekend on Long Island. In Bridgeport, about a half hour from New Haven, there's a ferry that links Bridgeport to Port Jefferson. His friend Frank—now also his business partner—the one who got him into the plumbing business and from whom he's learned all the tricks of the trade, recently bought a house in Cedar Beach, Long Island, and he's invited Giorgio and his family to spend the holiday weekend. In Cedar Beach, close to Port Jefferson, there's a beautiful stretch of sand. Giorgio warmly encourages him to take the train from Brooklyn down to Huntington or to Port Jefferson. He can pick Pascal up in the car and take him to Cedar Beach in no time. Frank wants to have a nice homecoming celebration, including a big barbecue. Together they will celebrate the holiday.

The letter concludes with a P.S., which Pascal reads more than once.

My dear Pascal, unfortunately I have some bad news. Some months ago I learned that last year our Filippo died in France, in the battle of Belleau Wood ... I am sorry to have to give you this news. Gennaro was right (remember that night he and Filippo fought?) when he said war is a bastard. May his soul rest in peace.

8

Pascal spends several days going over Filippo's death in his mind. Some nights he tosses and turns in bed, while memories of things he and his now dead friend went through together run through his thoughts. Of all his Abruzzesi group who came to America, Filippo was the one he spent most of his time with.

He recalls little things, even the tiniest details tied to their shared experience: the arguments, among them the memorable fistfights in Hillsdale, New Jersey; the fun times drinking together; some dustups when they both went after the same girl; jokes played on Giacomo, before he went to Troy; the hellish work in Cumberland Valley; and at last the heated discussion about the war and their radically diverging opinions on it.

For days and days Pascal will think again about his friend, wondering about the exact circumstances of the battle in which he died. One morning in the library, he spends more than an hour poring over a map of France in a huge atlas. And in the end, having found the Belleau forest, just a few kilometers from Chateau-Thierry, where his friend died, he fantasizes, in front of the open atlas on the reading-room table, how that dramatic event came about, its dynamics, its tragic end ...

Sometimes, in dreams, the shining, agile figure of his friend appears. He sees his cocky smile, sometimes a bit ironic, sometimes more scornful. Other times, while falling asleep, he tries to imagine Filippo's dead body, asking himself painfully where—or even if—it might be buried. And what if it is still there, abandoned on the battlefield, out there in the open exposed to all the elements?

More than once, after being suddenly awakened with a start during the night, he can't go back to sleep. So he turns on the small bedside lamp and immerses himself in Shelley or in his beloved Webster's or an English grammar book he recently bought. But the words seem to swim in front of his eyes. Then he tries to write something; or another time he tries reading over and polishing some poems he's written. Suddenly the verses seem so meaningless, and then, unexpectedly, his mind goes back to some moment with Filippo—even some banal situations that Pascal thought were buried in his memory.

And in the end his thoughts almost always go back to that drastic and swift decision of Filippo's to enlist in the US Army. Pascal wonders now if he made a mistake in not accepting Filippo's heartfelt plea to join him. Who knows? Maybe Filippo would still be alive today, or maybe both of them would be dead for a cause that would have ennobled their lives and given some dignity to their miserable immigrant existence, some respect and recognition much greater than any they had ever obtained in America.

And yet Pascal, even in that hovel that he shared with Filippo in New Haven, had found moments of sweet tranquility, of human togetherness and domestic well-being, a type of security and warmth that he could trace back to the little house he lived in as a child in Cauze, a security he isn't sure he will ever find again.

These dreamlike memories and imaginings, so vivid, tied to Filippo weave themselves oddly on occasion with thoughts of Prometheus's eviscerated body, the way the poet Shelley had portrayed it: Prometheus, condemned to be chained forever to a rock with an eagle feeding on his liver. But he heroically endured his torments in the hope that they would end once Jove, symbol of Evil, was dethroned in favor of the forces of Goodness, as foretold in a prophecy ... Verses Pascal has reread so many times that he has memorized them roll through his mind:

> Whilst me, who am thy foe, eyeless in hate.
> Hast thou made reign and triumph to thy scorn,
> O'er mine own misery and thy vain revenge.
> Three thousand years of sleep-unsheltered hours,
> And moments aye divided by keen pangs
> Till they seemed years, torture and solitude,
> Scorn and despair—these are mine empire.
> More glorious far than that which thou surveyest
> From thine unenvied throne, O Mighty God!
> Almighty, had I deigned to share the shame
> Of thine ill tyranny, and hung not here
> Nailed to this wall of eagle-baffling mountain,
> Black, wintry, dead, unmeasured; without herb,

Insect, or beast, or shape or sound of life.
Ah me! Alas, pain, pain ever, for ever!
No change, no pause, no hope! Yet I endure.

The autumn months pass by quickly. Pascal decides not to go to Cedar Beach with Giorgio on Labor Day morning, even though Giorgio has written to him several times about it and gotten no reply. Instead he spends the holiday wandering around the streets of Brooklyn. In addition, the evening before, old Zodiatis, although not feeling well, left by train to visit his son Michalis in Philadelphia. Michalis and his wife, Zyranna, a sweetly spoken woman, have a nine-year-old daughter, Arianna, whom Zodiatis is devoted to and likes to go on long walks with.

Demetrius will spend a whole week in Philadelphia, partly because he also needs some medical tests that will be done at the nearby Hahnemann Hospital. When he comes back to Brooklyn, Pascal notices he seems thinner and has an unusually grave look on his face.

9

During the second-to-last week of November 1919, the foreman calls together the workmen under him and tells them that, as of December 20, there very probably won't be any more work for them. The job site has to shut down work related to bridge construction, and that work won't recommence until the following spring.

It's bad news for Pascal. He's used to this type of work of low pay but with weekends totally free for him to do as he likes. Also, he's recently struck up a friendship with a man named Felice, who everyone calls Felix, a strong, outgoing type to start with whom work has reduced to a husk of a man, although he's retained his dignity and shows occasional flashes of uncommon intelligence. He's the only one of the workers Pascal has told of his ambitions to be a writer. And it's he, Felice, who is responsible for generating some respect among the workers for Pascal's talent. The youth becomes an object of discussion for them. Some of the men encourage him to look for a better type of work, given how well he speaks and writes in English. Others believe that if you're born poor you're destined to stay that way. The more optimistic ones think Pascal is wasted on this job and should try to become a foreman. But Pascal in his heart knows he has no ambition in the sphere of construction, and no desire to take on some office job.

One evening, having finished work, Pascal and Felice stop at a bar close to the work site to talk and have some beers. Pascal tells him once again about his dreams, his passion for literature, for theater, and in particular for poetry. Then he takes some sheets out of his pocket, the latest things he's written. At a certain point Felice interrupts him good-naturedly and says to him, "Your poems are nice, Pascal, but it's hard, it's very hard. Look reality in the face. What kind of hopes can guys like us have? We who are and who've always been stonecutters, manual laborers? Look at me. Apart from being semiliterate, look at what I've become. I walk like a duck now, I've got a hunchback, just last month I almost got smashed by a carriage. The other night the watchman mistook me for some young thug with who knows what kind of stolen goods slung over my shoulders. My hands are so numb I couldn't even write the letter 'O' using the rim of this glass. Sure, you can write and speak English, but what are you going to do if you keep rotting here? You gotta go, Pascal. Go far away from here, but do it now. Don't wait till you've gotten like me. Look what I've become, look closely, Pascal. You're looking in the mirror at your future self. Get away from here. Find yourself some kind of work in an office where you can improve your English. Think about it, my boy. Think now!"

Felice's words leave Pascal shaken, and in the coming days his resolve grows to become a writer at all costs. The desire to write, write, write occupies his mind all the time. He thinks of nothing else. But at the same time he realizes he needs to learn English better, to master the grammar and syntax, to be able to put in order the mess of feelings and thoughts that stir his mind and thus to give them a coherent expression that is also original, to know how to formulate his world in a personal way and the best way to express it.

One particularly cold evening, beaten by a face-searing wind, Pascal heads home after a hard day at work, which he has spent entirely outside. All the footbridge building takes place outside. At lunchtime with the usual hero sandwich the workers gather together and light fires in large bins. Around these, one next to the other, they rub their hands and seek to warm themselves a bit before going back to work. The day before there's been an intense snowfall, but the workers don't get a day off. They have to work as usual on the footbridges under the shouts of the foreman amid the cursed snowflakes.

Frigid with the cold, Pascal walks along the way from the job site to his house, lost in his own thoughts. The streets are deserted, and the silence is broken only by the crunch of ice under his feet.

He finally reaches Zodiatis's house. When he's about to go into his room via the backyard, the blast of heat from inside the house almost pushes him backward. The heat and some faint noises from another part of the house practically blister his ears before the rest of his body adjusts to the temperature.

From his room adjoining the kitchen and the servants' quarters, he can hear some strange sound, like a continual rasping noise, coming from the kitchen. He opens the door and calls to old Demetrius to ask if he wants some hot tea. But his voice sticks in his throat before he can even pronounce Demetrius's name. Zodiatis is lying on the ground scratching nervously with the fingers of one hand on the floor as though he wants to get someone's attention or is desperately trying to get up.

10

The next morning Pascal decides not to go in to work, taking an unpaid day of "vacation." The events of the previous evening turn over and over in his head. Everything happened in a quick and abstract sequence, something unreal that he seemed not to be a part of. And yet it was he, Pascal, who rushed to sound the alarm, calling Michalis, who got there not long after the ambulance that carried Zodiatis away.

Demetrius is now in Brockdale Hospital Medical Center. Pascal can still see the entire scene to which he, as though in a trance, was witness. The attendants who went to the old man lying on the ground, the quick examination from the doctor who arrived with them, the old man carried out on a stretcher, the rapid arrangement within the ambulance. Pascal barely had time to take Demetrius's hand. The old man looked at him with a confused expression and a weak smile. A funny kind of look, almost sweet, was on his face, and his gaze moved, lost, off into nothingness.

Three days after the episode, Michalis comes to see Pascal. He briefly describes his father's condition and says that he'll be transferred right away to the rehabilitation center at Hahnemann Hospital in Philadelphia, which is the best possible place for him to recover and which is also very close to Michalis's home. Zodiatis has had a stroke, and the entire right side of his body is paralyzed. He can't speak, and it will take a long period of rehabilitation before he can regain use of his words and his ability to move. Pascal listens silently to what Michalis says while looking at the kitchen floor, on which there remain signs of Zodiatis's scratching. Instinctively his eyes move up to the wall on which one can still see the many marks of the matches Demetrius lit there. For a second Pascal's mind wanders and he doesn't hear Michalis's last words, informing him politely, but firmly, that he has to leave his room by the end of the year. The house has already been put up for sale. Zodiatis isn't coming back to live there, and Pascal won't see him again.

These are sad, cold days for Pascal, who can't even chat with his friend Felice. For some reason, he doesn't know why, Felice hasn't been at the work site. Like Pascal, he also didn't show up to work the day after the incident with Zodiatis. But whereas Pascal came back to work, Felice hasn't been seen again at the South Brooklyn Marine Terminal. No one can explain his absence or tell Pascal where he went, or give even the slightest information about him. It's as if he's disappeared. All Pascal knows is he lives near Bensonhurst, a grim slum in the eastern part of Brooklyn.

Bensonhurst is a rundown quarter where in the first years of the twentieth century mostly Italians and Jews began to settle, families of the lowest extraction looking for a cheaper place to live. Families that after decades would multiply and remain there for generations, seeking to improve their quality of life and little by little improving also the whole area, although it can still look like a jumble to today's visitors.

One morning Pascal talks briefly with his foreman. Maybe, he thinks, he can tell me something. But instead he cuts him off brusquely. "What do I know? It's not my business. To me, Felice is just a worker; I don't know anything about him! Get to work, Pascal."

11

It's a frigid Saturday, December 20, 1919. Pascal has been out of work for some days in advance of the shutting down of the construction site, which is happening this very morning. He still has heard nothing about his friend Felice. Old Zodiatis is at the rehabilitation center at Hahnemann Hospital in Philadelphia.

Pascal is in his room, intent on organizing all his things in preparation for yet another involuntary move. Yesterday a truck arrived and three movers got out and quickly emptied the entire house, including his room, in which just a bed and chair remain. Pascal's stuff is stacked up in bits here and there.

After being laid off, Pascal spends the next few mornings in the New York Public Library, intensifying his readings and study of English. He's also typed up his best poems. In the afternoons, he's walked around Lower Manhattan and Brooklyn looking for a new place to stay. One time he finds himself having walked all the way to Bensonhurst in a vain search for Felice. No one there could help him. He comes back to his room after three hours of walking, feeling grim.

Now he's sitting on the edge of the bed contemplating his situation. For a moment he thinks about going back to New Haven. He knows he can depend on Giorgio to help him find some kind of work and maybe even to give him a place to stay just until he gets on his feet. But he gives up on the idea. He doesn't want to go back there. He doesn't want to leave New York. He likes Brooklyn, even though he no longer has Zodiatis or Felice to talk to. Even more, he can't bear the thought of leaving the library. It's the only place he feels like himself, where he feels nourished and his imagination stirred. He knows its rooms intimately by now and feels entirely at ease there. It's there that he's discovered the writers he loves so well, and he feels he owes everything he's learned to the library. To stop going there would be like abandoning himself.

Finally he gets up and gathers his books, his notebooks, and his few clothes together and puts them in his raggedy suitcase. Then he dedicates himself to his papers. He's been accumulating notes and writings of various types since he's been back in New York. First he sets aside the typewritten pages that contain his best poems. He rereads them carefully and then puts them in a folder. Then he examines a bunch of other sheets with fragments of verse, reflections, notes, and so on that need correcting or amplifying, including a series of dialogues he has in mind for use in a future opera. These are all the things he's collected for the past two years and has not gotten to yet. Suddenly many of them seem insignificant to him, naïve and filled with errors, even grammatical ones, and they no longer speak to his state of mind.

He begins, therefore, after having carefully looked them over, to discard them a few at a time, tossing them in a corner of the room. In another folder he puts together some pages that he thinks have a decent potential. He rereads "Midday," a poem of his that he likes very much:

> The road is like a little child running ahead
> Of me and then hiding behind a curve—
> Perhaps to surprise me when I reach there.
> The sun has built a nest of light under the eaves of noon;
> A lark drops down from the cloudless sky
> Like a singing arrow, wet with blue, sped from the bow of space.
> But my eyes pierce the soft azure, far, far beyond,
> To where roam eternal lovers
> Along the broad blue ways
> Of silence.

Pascal spends several hours of the day doing this meticulous work without realizing it, until the first pangs of hunger hit him. There's nothing left in the house. He goes over to the little store nearby, buys a sandwich, takes it back and eats it in silence. Then he returns to looking over his papers and getting rid of a bunch more of them.

Now in a corner of the room there's a messy mound of papers. Pascal looks at them a long time: This mound seems to him like a symbol of his past, at least his recent past, the last two years of dreaming and writing in the library or in his room. Evening is falling. Pascal carries the mound bit by bit out to the backyard and then lights a fire. The blaze, once released, reminds him of a kind of purification ritual, the general cleansing of all the filth, all the physical and ethical ills he's had to endure up until that moment.

From the mass of papers, reduced now to ash, a thin column of smoke arises. Pascal stands looking at it mutely. Then comes a powerful voice from behind him. It's Patrick O'Malley, his Irish neighbor, returning from work. He's smelled the fire in the next-door yard and come over to check on what's happening.

"What the hell are you doing?" he says, looking, perplexed, from Pascal to the remains of the fire.

"Nothing ... just burning up my life," responds Pascal distractedly. Then, seeing Patrick's confused face, he tells him briefly about the recent events: Zodiatis's illness, the fact that he needs to find a new place to stay and also a new job.

Patrick shakes his head slowly and strokes his reddish beard, saying, "Well, if you want, I can rent you my basement for whatever you were paying Zodiatis; my basement is bigger. Want to have a look at it?"

The Irishman's unexpected offer is as sudden as it is welcome. Pascal will save not only the trouble of moving but he'll also be able to stay in the neighborhood he's been living in for more than a year.

After a moment of hesitation, Pascal accepts the offer to look at the basement.

"Okay," Patrick says. "Come with me."

So they begin to walk over to his house, when suddenly, after just a couple of steps, the Irishman stops and looks sideways at Pascal and then in a stern but also somewhat joking tone says, "Hey, youngster, let's be clear. No violin in my house. Okay?"

And as if to reinforce the admonition or the threat, he waves his hand in the air as though to give Pascal a thwack. Then he bursts into a great guffaw.

12

Pascal's new lodgings are quite a bit bigger than his previous ones. It's a basement, clean and dry, with a bathroom and shower, a small kitchenette in the corner, and a separate entrance. Pascal will enter by going downstairs in the back of the house which lead to the door. The only disadvantage is the poor light in the room. It gets light only from two rectangular windows set high up on one wall. An interior staircase connects the basement to O'Malley's residence upstairs.

Pascal likes the place and quickly brings his things over. Before leaving Zodiatis's house he wants to make a quick visit to the living room there. The room, never big to begin with, is now empty, but as in a mental movie, Pascal can once more see Sunday afternoons spent there with the old man, especially the ones when they discussed the poetry of Shelley.

Patrick presents his wife, Edna, a jovial and affable woman of about thirty-nine. Pascal is amazed at the woman's thick bundle of red hair, her full lips, and her long red fingernails. Edna and Patrick invite him to stay for dinner to seal the new arrangement they've just made.

At the table, in between courses (Edna has made a wonderful Irish stew), Pascal learns a bit more about his new landlords. Patrick is a rough and ungainly man, but overall not a bad guy, apart from when, according to Edna, he drinks and can easily become a handful. This tends to happen on Saturdays—like today—when her husband can drink a few more beers, not having to get up in the morning for work.

O'Malley came to New York when he was just a boy. His parents, like Edna's, live on Jackson Avenue in Queens, where there has been, and still to some degree is, a dense concentration of Irish. It's here that Patrick and Edna met, at the famous Trinity Grace Church, and there that they were married.

During the conversation, Patrick is drinking beer after beer, and frequently breaks into loud laughter, with very little provocation. His laughter resounds like thunder in the kitchen, which is also the dining room. Very proud of his Irish heritage, O'Malley tells Pascal the story of St. Brendan, the Navigator, while Edna observes their guest with great curiosity. Every so often she asks him a question, sometimes fairly personal or else peculiar, such as whether he can sing any Italian songs. At that singular request, O'Malley gets up abruptly from the table and asks Pascal if he knows Al Jolson's music. Pascal's heard the name from some articles in a newspaper and rotogravure.

While Patrick begins messing about with an old gramophone, Edna brings two magnificent desserts to the table, an Irish coffee cake and an apple amber cake, which she cuts in generous pieces to serve to Pascal while she asks him archly if he has a girlfriend and if he ever takes her to nightclubs in Brooklyn or Manhattan. She talks about jazz and musicals, two forms of entertainment about which Pascal knows little or nothing. She tells him enthusiastically and somewhat vainly about the musical comedy *A Night Out*, featuring the music of Cole Porter, whom she is mad about.

In the meantime Patrick has got the beat-up gramophone working, and soon the warm and smoky voice of Al Jolson can be heard, occasionally broken by some scraping of the needle on the disc. Patrick even begins to dance a bit, and Edna asks Pascal if he knows how to dance, meanwhile giving him a come-hither look. Very different from Beethoven! Very different too from *Traviata* or *Aida*, listened in religious silence with old Zodiatis. A new world opens before the increasingly confused Pascal, a more electrifying world, a new way of enjoying life. All in all, it's been a long time since he's spent such an evening of good humor and the most complete relaxation.

The dinner concludes with the gramophone still squawking and Patrick bringing out of a cabinet a bottle of moonshine, the typical Irish drink, more properly called poteen, a drink of great alcoholic strength imported to the United States with the first Irish immigrants. It's called moonshine because you make the illegal liquor by the light of the full moon! Confused, amazed, almost incapable of reacting, but also in a way intrigued, Pascal takes in this domestic scene while

Edna keeps giving him sly looks and O'Malley continues to refill his glass with moonshine.

It's an evening that the youth will long remember and that finally ends with more exhortations on Edna's part to sing and the rough encouragement of O'Malley, who at a certain point tries himself to sing "O' Sole Mio," explaining between burps that he and Edna had had the good fortune three years ago of seeing and hearing Enrico Caruso, on the memorable occasion of an exhibition of the great tenor with the Victor Orchestra, directed by Walter B. Rogers.

At long last, weaving about a bit, Pascal bids goodnight to the couple, not without noticing, a moment before going downstairs, an obscene smirk that the tousled Edna gives him.

13

It's been only a few weeks since Pascal moved over to the O'Malleys'. He's spent several entire days in the basement, reworking his poems.

One morning in early January of 1920 Edna comes downstairs to the basement. Something is not working with the heater. She's freezing and she suspects it has something to do with the central heating of the house, located in a corner of the basement. Pascal watches as she fusses uselessly around with the knobs on the enormous metal burner. He gets up from his desk to give her a hand, even though he knows nothing of heaters. Edna, in the meantime, gives his back a little rub. Pascal doesn't know if she does it casually or on account of the cold, or for some other reason....

"But aren't you cold?" she asks, looking coyly at him.

"No, I am okay here...." Pascal responds. In the basement it's fairly warm. A strange silence hovers calmly over the whole space. One hears only the occasional gust of wind from outside.

"Ah, right. You Italians have hot blood...." Edna says, almost as though she were talking to herself, and at the same time gives him a look full of meaning.

"Feel how cold my hands are!" Edna puts one of her hands on Pascal's neck, and suddenly the shiver of the cold mixes with a different kind of shiver along his body. And before he even knows what's happening, he feels Edna's full lips on his and hears her murmur, "Oh, why don't you give me a bit of your warmth?"

Pascal tries clumsily to shield himself. He is totally unprepared for this situation. But Edna seems possessed. She begins licking and biting his chin and then moves to his earlobe. Pascal feels her breath on his neck while her hands frantically rummage over the lower parts of his body. The youth pulls back slightly, stumbles, tips over a shelf, and falls on the couch while Edna collapses on top of him.

Edna comes back in the following days. Pascal endures these sudden intrusions with growing annoyance and guilt. For him at twenty-six, this almost forty-year-old woman has quickly become a source of discomfort. Aside from everything else, he sees his savings growing dangerously thin, by now he's down to pennies, but before he goes looking for more work, he wants to finish revising his writings. He's decided to select from among them pieces to send out to newspapers and journals both great and small. At the library he's copied out the relevant addresses. Having paid close attention to what gets published in them, he's convinced his are as good as some that are regularly printed even in the ones that are supposed to be the best periodicals. He is also developing little by little a very personal critical sensibility at the same time that his English is reaching more dignified expressive forms.

Sometimes on the weekends Patrick will come down to the basement to fetch some tool for the house. These are short encounters during which the Irishman exchanges fleeting words with Pascal. The youth is extremely embarrassed during these moments. He feels guilty toward a man who has offered him a roof over his head, even though he's paying for it, and unwittingly his wife as well, who is starved for sex. O'Malley doesn't notice his tenant's awkwardness.

One splendid Sunday morning at the end of January, Pascal decides to find another apartment. It's 8:00 a.m. The house is empty. Patrick and Edna have gone to spend the day with some relatives in Flatbush. He puts his things in his beat-up suitcase and tidies the basement a bit. In his heart he hopes to find another place that same day and maybe even also a job. He'll return for the suitcase later. In his pocket he has just the few dollars he owes in weekly rent to O'Malley every Monday.

Determined, he walks down 19th Street. His destination is the South Brooklyn Marine Terminal. At the intersection of 19th and 4th Avenue, he turns left and walks to 35th Street, which goes directly to the port area, which he's very familiar with. Reaching the terminal, he sees the footbridges he worked on in recent months. Since it is a pleasant sunny day, some families are walking about. A young boy insists to his parents that they take one of the footbridges, which are coated with a thin layer of ice. For a second, Pascal is distracted watching them and daydreaming. At twenty-six his own father was already engaged to his mother, Anna Felicia, and they were married a couple of years later. But the daydream lasts only a few moments. Now he has other dreams and ideals whirling about in his mind.

Pascal heads toward the water. A group of starved gulls gathers on the jetty. He stops to watch them, in a kind of spell. The loud, almost alarming sound of their flapping wings impresses him, as does their chasing one another in endless droves.

At last he comes to a building with a little shipyard, totally deserted, nearby. A man, wearing a pair of torn gloves and a woolen cap, is carrying long wooden shelves inside, along with various other things that are scattered here and there near to the door. A little dog tied to a stake keeps him company.

Curious and hopeful, Pascal comes over and exchanges some words with the man. Then, encouraged, he asks politely if there might be some work available.

"What can you do?" the man asks, stopping what he's doing and looking at Pascal somewhat perplexed.

"I've done a bit of everything in a bunch of places ... I have strong arms. Last month I was working at the Marine Terminal, but then the construction site closed. We were building footbridges."

"Okay, give me a hand here and then we can talk," the man cuts him off. He's a stocky guy with a brusque but courteous manner.

Pascal accepts happily and limits himself to silently doing what he's told to do. The two spend some hours moving a variety of things from one place to another and putting discarded materials into a dumpster. Very short breaks. During one of them the man lights a cigarette and motions to Pascal, offering him one, but he refuses politely.

"Good. You're smart not to smoke," the man says. "I started very young. Sometimes I think about quitting, but I can't do it. ... It's a filthy vice. Good for you for not doing it."

"Well," Pascal says, patting the dog, "I don't have that one, but I have other vices. By the way, we haven't met. I'm Pascal."

"You're right. Excuse me. I'm Benjamin, but call me Ben. They all call me that here," and he shakes his hand. "Come on, let's finish up. Then we can go get dinner."

The inside of the building is like a warehouse of a variety of artifacts, mostly having to do with seafaring. Pascal realizes that it's a warehouse for the nearby construction site.

At around 2:00 Ben stops the work and invites Pascal to go with him to a little place on 53rd Street, just a few minutes away. As they walk, the man chats with Pascal and tells him a bit about himself.

Ben's from Abruzzo and came to America in January 1900, when he was just three, exactly ten years before Pascal. He speaks good English (Pascal notices right away), and he's married to the daughter of his father's best friend, a carpenter, who died in a car accident some years ago at just forty-four years of age.

Pascal in turn tells him about his leaving Italy and the hardships he went through with his Introdacquesi group. He's quiet, out of modesty, about the subject of his ambitions (his "vice") of being a poet or a writer. Ben listens to him with interest and seems to take his situation to heart.

Soon they're at Linda's, a run-down place with people of all kinds coming and going. Suddenly the whole area, which had seemed empty, is electrified. Before they go in, Ben asks Pascal to wait outside a moment and, without waiting for him to reply, he heads quickly off to a little house a few yards past the diner. He opens the door and lets the small dog inside. Then he comes back, smiling, to Pascal.

"My wife's with her parents today, along with our son Dante, and it's not good for me to leave the dog alone at home.... Go on in, you're my guest. You'll see it's not a bad little place."

Pascal says affably, "You've given your son a great name."

"Eh, yes and no. It's my father's name; he was named by my grandfather, Stefano, who had a particular love for the *Divine Comedy* ... he knew parts of it by heart!"

No sooner have they gone in than they are enveloped in a swirl of sounds, smoke, smells coming from the kitchen, the clatter of plates and silverware. At one table, four men are playing cards, and every so often one of them complains to his buddy. Behind the counter, where the beers are flowing freely, there's a wall on which paper plates are tacked up, as though they were extravagant round decorations. On each one is written the name of a meal and underneath, its price, and are all incredibly cheap.

"Pick whatever you want," Ben says to him, waving his arm toward the plates on the wall.

By now it's almost four in the afternoon. The place is less crowded. Pascal and Ben are getting along well, after having enjoyed a massive cheeseburger and fries and drunk a few beers.

"Well, now I got to go, Pascal," Ben says finally, putting out his cigarette in the ashtray and picking up his jacket, gloves, and hat. The two head for the door. Before saying goodbye, Ben looks at Pascal in a friendly way and says, "Listen, I'll tell you what. You show up tomorrow at seven. I can't promise you anything. I'm just the janitor there. Sunday mornings I just go clean up. I do a bit of everything, and I know the boss, Jimmy Lo Pianto, well. I've known him for more than ten years ... he was one of my dad's closest friends. Before coming to work at the dockyard he was his right-hand man in a huge warehouse. I do well at the site. Jimmy's a good guy. Tomorrow morning I'll tell him about you and we'll see what happens."

"Thanks, Ben! God bless you!"

"No problem," Ben says with a half smile. Then, shaking his hand, he gives him a five-dollar bill, saying "Thanks for your help today."

14

Pascal heads toward home feeling his spirit refreshed. The prospect, however vague, of a new job gives him hope that he might be able to have a certain independence. He goes up 4th Avenue as high as 20th Street. By this time the sun has set. The sky's become milky, and all around there's a feeling of snow, and in fact soon afterward some sporadic flakes begin to twirl here and there in front of him.

Having gone a short way down 20th Street, he sees not far away a small card attached to a little gate halfway open that he hasn't seen before. Curious, he goes over. The card bears faded writing saying "Rooms for Rent." "Wow!" Pascal thinks, "This is really my lucky day!" He goes down the little path leading to a doorway. To one side of the door there's an arch through which he can see a little courtyard. Pascal rings the bell, and an imposing woman answers, rather old and with her head covered in curlers.

"Good morning, I mean, good afternoon," Pascal says quietly. "Forgive me for bothering you. I saw the sign on the gate and ..."

The woman looks at him, almost with disgust then she turns her head and shouts, "Gordon!" Then without a further word, she disappears inside and leaves him on the porch.

A big solid man appears, wearing an undershirt, despite the cold, and with a big cigar in his mouth.

"Good afternoon," Pascal says again. "I wonder if you have any available rooms ... I saw the sign. My name's Pascal D'Angelo, and I'd be interested," he holds out his hand.

The big man gives his hand a surly shake and replies, chewing his words, "Pleasure. Gordon Parker. There is a room left, but...." The man hesitates a bit. "Okay, I'll let you see it now. Then we can talk. Hang on a minute." He stammers something incomprehensible and then reaches an arm out to a coat rack and grabs a beret, which he puts on his head.

Without putting anything else on, he leaves the house and walks with Pascal. They pass under the archway and emerge in the back courtyard. Here there is a kind of rectangular hut that runs horizontally across almost the whole space. This coop, long and low, has three doors one next to the other.

"We rent three rooms," the man says, still chewing his words. He points to the central entrance, a simple, rough door. "The left and right ones are taken. There's just the middle one."

Gordon pushes the door, which was only half-closed, and Pascal is surprised to see, instead of a room, a bathroom, with a sink, an obliquely hanging mirror, a shelf, and a Turkish-style toilet. In the air, there is an unbearable stench. On the wall across from the entrance there's a door, closed and locked, which Gordon opens, grumbling. "This is the only room still available. To get in you got to go through the toilet, which you have to share with the other lodgers."

"But isn't there another way in?" says Pascal, a bit aghast.

"No," Gordon replies drily. "Unless you want to climb through the window ..." and he gives a hint of a smirk that should be an ironic smile. Then he adds, "Eh, it's not like the toilet's always busy. Like I say, we have just two other tenants, and with you it'd be three, and anyway one of them is away a lot."

Pascal looks at the little room, whose furniture consists of just a cot, a chair, and a cupboard. On the wall a shabby painting hangs by a string. The only window, to the right of the bed, is open and at this moment is letting in gusts of freezing air. Over its panes a thin curtain flutters, little more than a rag. The man hastens to close the window, although with some difficulty. Pascal looks hesitantly at the room, which is a narrow little dump and badly lit. He glances in the cupboard and looks around, uncertain what to do. Suddenly he's startled by the rough and strangled voice of the man who speaks without ever removing the cigar from his mouth.

"Well? What are we gonna do? It's five dollars a week. In advance."

Pascal does a bit of figuring. It's exactly half of what he's paying Patrick O'Malley. That's a good savings, and besides, he thinks, I'd be rid of Edna. Gordon, from the middle of the little room, watches him silently, showing some signs of impatience.

In the end Pascal takes out the five dollars and gives it to Gordon, who gives Pascal the room key, with one piece of advice. "The bathroom doesn't have toilet paper. Or soap, or washcloths, or anything else. Those are things each lodger brings himself when he needs them."

It's six o'clock. Outside it's dark. Pascal has just moved into his new place. After talking to Parker, he goes home, writes a note to Patrick and Edna, leaving it in plain sight on their front door. He's taken his suitcase and come back to 210 20th Street. That's the address of his miserable new dwelling.

15

The following morning Pascal gets up a little before dawn. Crumpled up in his cot, he looks at the window. In his tiny room the cold, which is intense and brutal, has coated the overcoat he uses as a blanket with a freezing dampness. Outside there is an opaque light and an unreal quiet. At last he decides to get up. Pushing aside the raggedy curtain, he looks outside. Along all sides of the foggy window a rim of solid, transparent ice has formed. His breath leaves his mouth in cloudy little puffs, which add to the fog on the glass.

The window faces out on a side street, deserted except for an occasional small shack. On the right is a run-down building, a barred garage with an enormous lock attached to a long bar that spans the wooden door. A few yards from this garage there's a junkyard with a rusty wire gate. Inside this dump a second-hand dealer comes every day, a German man named Heinz, who peddles used goods of every variety, mostly old bikes and some broken-down motorcycles, pieces of construction material, hardware, accessories, tools, and scraps of all kinds. A compact white layer of new snow covers the streets and the entire place is immersed in a livid, almost milky light.

Freezing, Pascal reflects on his new situation. For a moment he mourns the snug basement where he's spent the past weeks. He also feels a slight guilt, owing to having left the O'Malley house almost stealthily, like a fugitive. But at the same time he forces himself to fall in line with the decisions he's made. The most important thing now, he thinks, is to have a job, hopefully not too demanding, and to dedicate himself completely to writing. This is his main objective.

He goes out in plenty of time to get to the work site. Gordon, who is shoveling the snow in front of his own home, sees him crossing the entryway and pretends to be looking somewhere else.

For Pascal these days between the end of January and the beginning of March 1920 are among the coldest and loneliest. Thanks to

Benjamin, he is taken on at the construction site, where he does manual labor Monday through Friday, loading and unloading by means of a pushcart or in certain cases loading on his own shoulders different kinds of materials. It's a long and monotonous kind of work, and his mind is elsewhere. Few breaks, few chances to talk to anyone, including Ben. During a fleeting pause, sitting on a bench inside the warehouse, eating a sandwich in silence, the young man writes down some phrases in a little notepad he has with him: stubs of verses and wandering thoughts, or else he reads his pocket Webster's. In his room he has the much larger one he bought in New Haven. His only joys come from the hours that he spends in the library. He goes there regularly on Saturday and Sunday. Here, apart from all else, he can enjoy the use of a real toilet without having to endure the repellent stink of the latrine by his room, where he hasn't got even a little table to read or write on.

In the evenings he goes back home, bringing some warm soup with him. He sits down to eat on the edge of his bed or else on the single chair. In the cupboard, not having much in the way of clothing to put away, he has arranged his few beloved books, papers, notebooks, and whatever other little miserable possessions he has. In a corner, some old photographs of his family and the pipe Demetrius Zodiatis gave him, although he's never used it.

One Saturday morning Pascal makes a firm decision. It's the first day of a cold spring. He decides it's time to launch his first attack on the editorial fortress of New York, which consists essentially of some journals and newspapers that he's singled out in recent months. He has no doubt in his heart that he will succeed. For some time he's been collecting envelopes and stamps with George Washington's face on them: He considers this strongly symbolic, associating himself with the figure of the victorious warrior leader of America. After much reflection and evaluation, he's chosen two newspapers and two journals to send some of his poetry to. In the preceding weeks he has duly typed up copies of them.

For some days on the way home in the evenings, he has asked Gordon Parker if there is any mail for him. But each time his landlord has answered with a shake of the head.

Pascal is so persistent in asking after mail that after a certain point Gordon begins to suspect something fishy is going on. And in fact, when after two weeks a parcel does arrive for Pascal, Gordon doesn't resist his temptation to open it and snoop around inside. He delivers the envelope one Saturday evening while Pascal is returning from the library. Pascal hurries to his room, and while he turns on the gas lamp with one hand, he tears open the envelope with the other. But what he discovers is his poems and a very courteous message from the editor-in-chief thanking him for his work that he has considered for publication.

Pascal's dejection is strong, but it's accompanied by a renewed fervor. It's the first official response he's received from a renowned publication, and he finds it gratifying to have been thanked and to be treated like a professional writer in his very first literary experience.

Galvanized by this first response, despite the rejection, the next morning Pascal prepares two more envelopes and puts his poetry inside to send to other publications. The list of places he's put together is long, and his war's just begun. The ritual repeats itself over and over. Pretty soon Pascal finds himself with a stack of letters, all very courteous.

Days and then months pass, marked by efforts and moments of bitter delusion. And yet, every time Pascal is on the point of giving up on the idea of a literary career, an irresistible inner voice convinces him to persevere. At the same time he can't help but be aware of the fact that he is one of many, too many, aspiring poets who populate the Big Apple.

One cold Sunday in November 1920 while he's wandering aimlessly around the Village, he stops by a large newsstand. He decides to buy a weekly, one of the most famous and respectable of all. Then he goes to sit on one of the benches in Washington Square. Pascal likes this park and goes there whenever he can. He enjoys walking on and sometimes scattering here and there with his old shoes the different colored leaves heaped on the ground. It's a big leaf party. All together they form a yellow and red quilt, sometimes with vivid gold edges, that adorn every walkway in this great park. It's what in America is called fall foliage, and the young man knows it well, having enjoyed it during his various work postings in Connecticut, southern New York, and Vermont.

Pascal especially likes to sit on a bench on the pathway to the right of the grand arch dedicated to George Washington. From this bench he enjoys observing its powerful marble features. This monument always gives him a feeling of serenity, power, and faith. Not far from the arch stands a statue of Giuseppe Garibaldi, albeit in a kind of clumsy pose, which strengthens these battle-like sentiments in him. If he, he thinks, can be a hero of two worlds, then maybe I too can be a hero. I'll be the poet of two worlds!

But his exultation fades suddenly, when he begins paging through the journal he's just bought, and he reads a poem published on one of its inside pages. He is instantly filled with scorn. How is it possible, he asks himself, trying to analyze the situation calmly, that something like this can get published, while I am struggling in vain? Then he bursts into wild laughter. If this woman, he thinks with sufficient irony, has so bewitched the editors that they in desperation agreed to publish this garbage, well, then I will bewitch them too. I won't release them from the spell until they agree to publish me!

More determined than ever, almost jaunty, he goes back to his hovel and cuts the poem out. He reads it again, shaking his head. Then he attaches it to the door, so as to have it always in front of his eyes as a disgusting example of something he never could and never would write.

The next day, a Monday that seems to announce the coming of the first cold of winter, he quits his job. He explains to Benjamin, once more, what his aspirations are, and his dreams of being a writer. With the passing of the months the two have become good friends, and before they part ways, Benjamin tells him he can have his job back whenever he wants it, if he wants it.

16

More resolved than ever, armed with an iron will that grows stronger with each rejection, Pascal spends the next months with increasing determination to preserve his dream of being published and recognized as a poet. He's set aside his meager savings from the preceding months of work. According to his calculations, by spending as little as possible, he can dedicate himself solely to writing without having to work as a manual laborer for at least the next four to five months.

One morning in February 1921 he decides to show up in person at the offices of an Italian-language newspaper that's been published in New York for several years. He's been reading it in the periodicals room at the library for some time. It also publishes some poems, which Pascal judges to be fairly mediocre. He's convinced that if the paper publishes his work, it will be a step up in quality for them. He's been thinking about this for a while, and if he hasn't done it before now it's because he writes solely in English. He knows his Italian is a bit rusty, and since he's been devoting himself to improving his knowledge of the language of Keats and Shelley it's only gotten worse; really, it's almost disappeared. But in truth he has no interest in becoming an Italian writer. That morning, after having gotten together some pieces written in a passable Italian, he goes to the newspaper's office. The name is displayed in huge brass letters on the plaque at the entrance: *Il Progresso Italo-Americano*. In his heart he's hoping to get some encouragement at least from someone with the same roots as himself.

To the doorman, who eyes him a little suspiciously, he asks to speak personally with the editor, a man named Carlo Barsotti, originally from Lucca, who's made his fortune in America. Pascal has verified that it's thanks to him, via his newspaper, that in recent years powerful campaigns have been launched in the Italian community to erect monuments in various locations across Manhattan dedicated to illustrious Italians, such as those of Giuseppe Verdi (whom Pascal loves) in Verdi Square; Christopher Columbus in the middle of Columbus Circle, beneath which Pascal has frequently stopped during the course of his wanderings around town; Giovanni da Verrazzano (which in the States they insist on spelling with just one "z") at Battery Park; Dante in the park of that name, which however went through some trouble before going up—but Dante was a poet, and poets, as Pascal knows only too well, have difficult lives. And finally the clumsy monument to Garibaldi, which Pascal is familiar with.

Il Progresso Italo-Americano, with its daily circulation of 100,000 copies, is far and away the biggest foreign-language daily in America, and particularly on the East Coast. The editor, Barsotti, in addition to founding the publication, also established the Italian American Bank. All in all, he is one of the most well-regarded people in New York's Italian community. Also, Pascal thinks, since he's so involved with the Dante monument, surely he's a poetry lover!

"Whom would you like to speak with?" the doorman says, giving him a quick look up and down.

"I'd like to speak to the editor ... Cavaliere Carlo Barsotti," Pascal responds somewhat audaciously and, indicating the sheets he's carrying, adds, "I have some of my work to present to him."

"The editor isn't in today. Come back tomorrow," the doorman cuts him short.

"That's fine," Pascal replies promptly. "Please let me speak to the associate editor, Adolfo Rossi." Pascal has memorized both names.

The doorman is mildly surprised that Pascal knows their names. He listlessly rises from his chair and says, "Okay, wait here a moment and I'll see if he can see you," and he disappears behind the guard's booth.

A moment later Pascal finds himself in a soberly decorated waiting room. Behind a desk there's a man with a small, pointy mustache looking at him, puzzled, with a certain curiosity.

"Good morning," Pascal says, holding out his hand. "Are you Adolfo Rossi?"

"No, I'm not Mr. Rossi. He hasn't come in yet. Make yourself comfortable. Pleasure to meet you. I'm Alfonso Buttafuoco," the man says somewhat ceremoniously. "What can I do for you?"

"I've brought some poems to submit to your paper ..." Pascal hands Buttafuoco his folder.

"Poems? Poems written by whom? By you?" he says aloofly, taking them and glancing absently at them. "You must know our paper publishes only works by well-known authors. There's nothing we can do for you."

"Listen," Pascal insists, "there are American publications that pay $5 to $10. I'd be happy with whatever you offered ... whatever you deemed fair ... I also write in English."

Buttafuoco bounces out of his chair. "Ten dollars! Why, not even ten cents," he says suddenly with a brutal arrogance. "I'm sorry. We're not interested. Try some other paper."

17

Some months go by, during which our budding writer visits other publications, always receiving the same treatment. Summer 1921 arrives. Pascal decides to send his submissions to places outside New York, with the result that rejection cards and letters begin coming from all over the country. In more than a few the editors request repayment for the mailing expenses.

Even in the face of all this, Pascal doesn't give in. On the contrary, his heroic purity still tells him that sooner or later fortune will smile on him. In the darkest moments, when he feels most disheartened, he glances over at that poem on the door.

At the beginning of autumn his savings are noticeably low. He begins to think that soon he will have to ask Benjamin for more work. And yet, the more his resources diminish, the more stubborn he becomes. He believes blindly in himself and in what he writes every day. Maybe this is what America has taught him: to have faith in a better future, to fight and confront life without losing courage in the face of hardships. Even if circumstances get worse, the moment will come when things turn around. What's important, he thinks, is not to surrender, never surrender, especially when, coming home from the library to his wretched room, he has to face the horrid smells going through the bathroom—which even passersby sometimes use—in order to get to it. Sometimes the putrid, stinking water overflows and comes in under his door to stagnate in malodorous pools, even under his bed, a place infested with cockroaches and other hard-to-identify insects. There is no way of heating the room, not even a stove, and when it's freezing outside (by now it's mid-December 1921), Pascal wraps himself up in his overcoat, which also serves as his blanket. In the mornings he feels completely numb, covered with sharp folds like blades of ice. The most uncomfortable thing, though also a bit tragicomic, is having to shave while wearing his coat, or else moving clumsily around his little room.

The few friends he has who come to visit him in his hovel, including Benjamin, can't hide their dismay at finding him in this horrific place.

"You have to be out of your mind," Benjamin says to him one evening, "to live in this hole, without even a stove, and with the toilet dumping all this crap on you. You're going to get sick! Why don't you find somewhere else? Dammit! Why don't you ask around if there are other places available? You want me to ask at the job site if someone can rent you something decent?"

Ben has taken his friend's cause to heart. He respects and understands his ideals. Sometimes he brings him a hot meal or some leftovers from home. Before saying goodbye, he asks again: "Now, Pascal, have you decided to find a new place to live? You want me tomorrow to get the guys at work to see if they can get you somewhere better than this hole?"

Pascal always shrugs when he gets these questions/offers. He knows his finances won't permit him a more luxurious place, and anyway it would mean going back to being a pick and shovel man, which he's done for so many years already, and possibly even having to work on the weekends when he likes nothing better than to be at the New York Public Library, his sole refuge, for some peace, warmth, and comfort. In those beautiful reading rooms he can think and read completely at his ease. If his body is forced to submit to the horrid reality of his miserable home, then at least his soul, when not inside those crumbling walls, can rise nobly and imagine other, more sublime worlds.

It's the week before Christmas. New York seems paralyzed by an arctic coldness, but at the same time seized with the mania of frantic acquisitiveness. In the midst of it all, Pascal is heading over to the editorial offices of another important and world-famous publication. After having spoken with the doorman and handed him a folio of his manuscripts, he is sagging, closed inside his thoughts, waiting for someone to come and tell him they've been rejected. At one point a jovial, bold young fellow passes in front of him and, catching sight of him, stops, taken aback by his unhappy demeanor. Pascal rises from the chair and looks at the man's face with a questioning air and, at the same time, a vague hopefulness.

"Can I do anything for you? You don't look well. Maybe you are sick?" the man says to him, hypocritically thoughtful.

"I am okay," Pascal says with a faint smile, "it's my poetry that's sick … and it can't find any recognition."

On hearing the word "poetry" the young man chuckles, his face wrinkling into a sneer while he looks upward, as though following some invisible point. Then, by way of taking leave of Pascal he says, "I believe you've come to the wrong hospital, my friend."

A little while later the man to whom he's given his manuscript reappears in the waiting room and shows Pascal into an interior office. Here he is met by a man with a calm, reassuring air, like a family doctor. He looks at Pascal for quite some time, almost benevolently; then, in a tranquil but firm voice, he tells him, almost as a doctor might talk after having examined a patient, "I am very sorry, sir, but I'm afraid we can't help you. This publication's procedure doesn't allow … what I mean is, it's not our policy to publish pieces written by outside writers. I wish you good luck."

It's a scene Pascal has seen and lived before, with only the slightest variations, in the preceding months. But similar treatment, even repeated several times in different ways, can't discourage him. In his mind he's set aside a fixed thought that spurs him not to give up. Even if ninety-nine offices—he thinks—reject my poetry, there's always the possibility that the hundredth will accept them.

That evening upon entering his frigid room, Pascal has as his only comfort the encouraging knowledge that there are still some editors in New York to be contacted.

18

Pascal decides to reduce his spending as much as possible, so he gets it down to his rent to Gordon Parker, the cost of taking the subway to the library and back, and his daily food. He goes to the library every other day, a decision that pains him, but it does save him the subway fare. Then, unable to reduce the rent, he aims at spending the absolute minimum on food, which is already next to nothing, and so limits himself to a single daily meal.

So he begins roaming around the worst, most rundown neighborhoods in Brooklyn looking for some store that will sell him some food for just a few cents. During one such excursion, he finds a tiny deli on 39th Street, run by an Indian man, where he can buy a meat and vegetable soup, of an uncertain flavor, but capable of filling his stomach. Thirty-ninth Street goes by Green Wood Cemetery and when, with his container of hot soup in his hand, he passes by that gate, beyond which he sees the rows of stones, he can't help but reflect that if his life continues like this it may not be long before he joins the ones buried in that old graveyard.

He tries also to limit the expense of bread, which is his main food. He checks all the bakeries nearby, comparing them and trying to figure out which one is the cheapest. It's a process of minute sifting, causing him to examine the entire area around his house. One day, intuiting his restricted means, a baker tells him he can come and get stale day-old bread at a reduced price or even free. This discovery will certainly make a difference, however small, in his daily expenses.

Those terrible days of December 1921 mark one of the coldest winters in recorded history of America. The days creep along with exasperating slowness, endlessly, in contrast to the mad, furious rush of people in the Manhattan streets preparing for the end-of-year festivities. To Pascal it feels like being inside a dark tunnel with no light visible at the end. He knows he is fighting a fierce battle in the name of an ideal and that his mission is to hold out at all costs, living the most basic life he can. He goes from day to day, eating his semi-warm soup out of paper containers in which he puts little pieces of his day-old bread to soften them up. Once in a while he "splurges" on some expenditure like overripe bananas, which cost almost nothing. The good ones cost a nickel for twenty, but these browned ones that Americans spurn are a delicacy for Pascal, who is fighting for his life. The fruit vendor who sells them to him from his cart asks him one morning, "Who are you giving these to, a dog?" And Pascal shoots back, "No, a wolf!"

Sometimes Pascal's hands, when he's carrying home his soup, begin to tremble, whether from the cold or from the heat coming from the container or from his fear of being stopped by patrolmen and having the container searched and then maybe even getting arrested. The broth in fact does sometimes surpass the fermentation levels permissible by law. When this happened, all Pascal could do was throw it away, having ascertained, at home in his wretched hole and tasting it, the acrid acidity of the slop, filled with picked-over bones, chicken feet, pieces of offal, and other strings and bits of dubious origin. In the face of that disgusting mix, Pascal is forced to resign himself to his lost nickel and go to bed hungry. But it doesn't bother him so much: The more obstacles and hardships this meager existence foists upon him, the longer he stays on his feet, undaunted, believing wholeheartedly in himself.

With the raging of that winter, at the terrible end of December of 1921, his situation becomes desperate. On account of the arctic cold and the brutal, icy humidity, mold is damaging his few books, his papers, his scant belongings, and, together with them, his increasingly weak body. Some nights he can't even bring himself to stay there. He goes out, wrapped up in his overcoat, and walks like a lunatic over to the subway station at Flatbush Ave, over three miles on foot, to find a bit of warmth.

On a particularly frigid day, he might decide not to leave his room at all. To save even more, he goes less and less to his beloved library. In the meantime, the rest of the city is celebrating the feast of Saint Sylvester.

One morning, after getting up, he realizes he can't even wash. The water has frozen in the pipes. This freeze lasts for three days, during which Pascal doesn't go out and eats crusts of bread he's saved and the worst of the ruined bananas. He's reached the depths of desperation, but even now there is still a thread of hope, hope battling all the adversities, a thread of hope that doesn't want to die.

19

The morning of December 23, Pascal is intently reading newspapers and magazines at the New York Public Library. Turning over the pages of *The Nation*, he sees notice of a literary contest sponsored by that publication. A glimmer lights in his heart, a mirage, that pushes him to enter the competition. The best poem will win $100—a sum, he thinks, that would last him several months, and besides, he would get to know the New York literary world.

So, he spends the last week of the year prey to the blackest desperation mixed with an unusual agitation, which drifts at times into a kind of delirium of the imagination. As the days pass, he feverishly and impatiently wonders what will become of the three poems he's mailed to the journal. At the same time he despairs of ever gaining any recognition.

December 31, a gray and anonymous day to close the year, he decides to spend in the library. He hasn't been there since mailing his pieces in to *The Nation* on the 23rd. He's spent the past week in his room, waiting vainly for news of the results.

Before going out, he sticks a piece of bread in his overcoat pocket, leaving another piece under the bed for when he gets back. He counts his remaining money, bringing with him only what he will need to take the train. The rest of it, the few pennies left, he puts in the cupboard. Then he heads out on the long trip to the Flatbush station under a milky white sky that promises nothing good.

Immersed in his thoughts, reading, and writing in his notebook, Pascal spends the whole day at the library until it closes, which on December 31 is 8 p.m.

This is the day Pascal is robbed of the little money he needs to take the train home. Someone takes it out of his coat pocket when he gets up to go to the bathroom. It's the day Pascal has to walk all the way home, in the midst of an apocalyptic storm of snow and ice. The same day that began this story.

Pascal will spend the day and night of the first of January 1922 weakened, without food, crumpled over, as in a trance, on his bed: immobile, his head wrapped up in the moist peel of his overcoat. It's in this state of semi-consciousness that he greets the first glimmers of dawn on January 2.

Feverish and dopey, as though wasted away in his room, Pascal opens his eyes halfway and the first thing he sees is the poem he's attached to the door. That piece of paper has been his despair and his obsession this whole time.

He stays in bed until the time when the mail usually comes. The mailman is punctual, but there's no letter for him, no communication at all, no pre-stamped envelope.

A bit later Pascal leaves the house like an automaton, on his way to the library. At the Flatbush station he drinks a big cup of very hot coffee and gets to the library as though encased in an air bubble or in a sack of dizzy, liquid lethargy. He goes straight to the typewriter room.

20

Brooklyn,N.Y.January 2,1922

113 Prospect Avenue

To the Editor of The Nation,

   Dear Sir:—

      I have submitted three poems "For The Nation's poetry
prize," within the established period as described in the columns
of "The Nation." Not having heard anything from your editorial
office,I would be much obliged if you should inform me on the
matter.

      I hope you will consider them from a view-point that they
have been written by one who is an ignorant pick and shovel man who
has never studied English.If there are not too many mistakes I must
warmly thank those people who have been kind enough to point out the
grammatical errors.I am one who is struggling through the blinding
black flames of ignorance,to bring his message before the public—
before you.You are dedicated to defend the immense cause of the
oppressed.This letter is the cry of a soul stranded on the shores
of darkness looking for light—a light that will point out the path
of recognition.Where I can work and help myself.I am not deserting
the legions of toil to refuge myself in the literary world.No! No!
I only want to explain the wrath of their mistreat.No! I seek no
refuge! I am a worker,a pick and shovel man—what I want is an
outlet to express what I can do beside working. Yes. To express all
the sorrows of those who cower under the yoke of doom.

      I suffer. And there are no words that can fitly represent
my living sufferings.No! no words.Even the picture loses its mute
eloquence before this scene.I suffer:for an ideal,for freedom,for
truth,that is denied by millions,but not by the souls who have the
responsibility of being human.Yesterday,New Year's Day,I only had
5 cents worth of bananas and a loaf of stale bread,for food.And
to-day:a half quarter of milk and a loaf of stale bread.All for the
love of an ideal.Not having sufficient bed clothes for a stoveless
room like mine,I must use my overcoat as a blanket at night and as
a wrinkled coat during the day.The room is damp—and my books are
becoming mouldered.And I too am beginning to feel the effects of it.
But what can I do? Without a pick and shovel job and without a just
recognition! And besides,the landlady has notified me to leave her
room not later than January 10,1922.She may have someone who can pay
a little more than me.So I must go where another room can be found.
Perhaps it will cost more than this.How can I afford it? Without
work and without a recognition that will allow me to work!!!?

      Please consider my condition and the quality of work I
submit.Then say if I can be helped without expense on your part.

You can do.Then do something for me.Even in this horrible condition
I am not asking for a financial help,I am not asking for pity,nor am
I asking for an impossibility.I am only asking for a simple thing_ a thing
which you are giving away free.While you are giving it away free,why
not see where this thing can help the most? I am not coveting the
prize because of the money.No! But because it will give me recognition
a thing that I cannot do without.If it's given to me,in this helpless
state I can go around to all the Editors,and say that I have been
awarded "The Nation's poetry prize." When I say that,they will hear
me—they will consider my works—they will begin to accept them.Then
dominated by an impulse of encouragement I will write:a novel,two,3
who knows how many! But how can I go on now,without an introduction
of this kind? They don't hear me.If ask them to see my manuscript
they say they are busy,or else they let me leave some poems and then
they put them hatching oblivion in an obscure corner of their
editorialocratic drauers.When a certain time they might accidentally
happen to see my poems they glance at the name,and see it's an unknown
one.Then return them without reading them.What do they know what I
have written? Must it continue like this forever? That is why I am
asking this help from you.If it's a help without expenses why not
help me!? Makes no difference to whom is given,it does not the same
help that gives to me!Because there is no writer in this condition,
and can present the same quality of work.Then let this prize break
those horrible barriers before me,and open a new world of hope! Let
this prize,(even if an honorary one) come like a bridge of light
between me and a waiting future.Let me free! Let me free! free like
the the thought of love that haunts millions minds.If it's without
expenses on your side then:give,give me an opportunity.You are the
man of the hour!This the moment when for nothing you can give me all
When for nothing you can put me into a place where I can work hard
to make enough money to have a musical education.For I want to compose
music.And yet I do not know the difference between one note and
another.What bars me from doing so? When I know music then I can
glorify the immense cause of the many.Then I can vilify the horrible
injustice of the vile few! Then give me! give me an opportunity and
see what I can do! Oh! please! hear me I am telling the truth,and
yet who knows it? Only me.And who believes me? Then let mn soul
break out of its chrysalis of ignorance and fly toward the flower
of hope,like a rich butterfly winged with a thousand thoughts.
Remember! what I want is a help without expenses:the honor of the
prize.Please hear me! who can see those weights of duty that crush
down and yet I cannot perform.I am not a spendthrift,$.100 will
last me 4 months.I am not asking for an impossibility.Let me see
what I can do? O! please let the strength of this prize lift me,
and place me on the pulpit of light.Where I too can narrate what
the Nature-made orator has to say in me!

Pascal D'Angelo
210—20th Street,
Brooklyn,N.Y.

P.S. Please after January 2,1922
do not communicate to this address
anymore.New one will soon be given.

21

It's midday. Pascal has just come out of the imposing post office of Grand Central Station just a few blocks from the library. He's just mailed the letter to Carl Van Doren, executive editor of *The Nation*.

It's a cold but clear morning, January 2. He moves through the crowd like a drunk in the grip of a colossal bender. A moment later, suddenly, he notices nearby a man looking at him kindly, shaking his hand, smiling at him. The man helps him up from the icy sidewalk on which he's slipped and fallen.

Pascal spends two days almost in a coma, without once leaving his hole. He's buried in a state of calm despair, without pain and without thought, a void in which he's serenely benumbed, since he has lost all desire for anything. He spends almost the entire time in bed, sleeping or drowsing, while in the morning he is shaken by a continual, brutal knocking on the door, a pounding that becomes more and more furious. Pascal drags himself to the door. Gordon stands outside, looking angrily at him but also looking quizzical. Annoyed, he hands him a letter, special delivery. Pascal, eyes half-closed, sees the letterhead of *The Nation* on the envelope. It's Carl Van Doren, the editor himself, who's written to him. He invites him to come to the office, with date and time specified.

Two hours later, Pascal, emaciated, trembling, skeletal, his head in the clouds, is in Carl Van Doren's office. Despite his deterioration, there's a soft smile on the spectral face of the young man. Van Doren is welcoming him kindly. He immediately orders coffee and donuts, which arrive in a flash. To the young man looking at him, bewildered, he says, "I was touched by your letter ..." At the same time he is shaking his hand and telling him that he, he himself, is the winner of the poetry contest.

Pascal is almost not listening. He looks around him as though in a dream. A beam of sunlight comes diagonally through the large office window and his mind gradually clears. Van Doren is continuing to talk affably, to ask him questions, to encourage him, and to advise him to tell his life story in a book, which he personally will mentor. Pascal thanks him, still somewhat fuzzy-headed. Then a thought comes to mind: I don't have to go knocking on the door of some Great Publication anymore. I never have to eat stale bread again, never have to shovel, dig, tunnel, endure ill treatment ... Yes, I can write, think, as much and however I want to, and about what I want to. It's Van Doren himself, he thinks, who's saying it and repeating it. No more obstacles in my way as a writer.

Pascal knows this very well, because just a few hours later with his beat-up suitcase, in which he's gathered his papers and meager belongings, he's leaving his room. The courage he possessed in the past has returned to him as if by magic, and now he feels ready to live out his life, day by day, as though born into a new existence.

As he passes his landlord standing at the gate and watching him curiously, he speaks in a low voice. "Farewell, Mr. Gordon," he murmurs.

EPILOGUE

It seemed right to me to leave our poet (however unwillingly and maybe even a bit abruptly) at the moment when he parts ways with his landlord.

Thanks to the support and encouragement of Carl Van Doren, Pascal will go to live in a slightly nicer room in Brooklyn, where he will feverishly write, in a few weeks, his autobiography. The book, *Son of Italy*, published by Macmillan, was reviewed in a number of papers. Suddenly the name Pascal D'Angelo began to be heard around, be it cautiously or sometimes with a certain fastidiousness, in U.S. literary circles. His poems appeared, as if by magic, in addition to *The Nation*, in important dailies and American journals—*The Century Magazine*, *The Literary Review*, *The Bookman*, *The Measure*, *Literary Digest*, etc. Pascal included some of these poems in his autobiography. That "God of New York," who seemed indifferent and who ignored him for so many years, turned his face toward the poet now. Pascal gave a memorable reading, presided over by Van Doren, at the Poetry Society of America. To those present he seemed, in a faintly surreal atmosphere, an awkward and emaciated young man, but his voice was altogether different, firm and very sweet, like the rest of his nature, and he began his reading with one of the three poems that won him the prize in *The Nation*:

> In the dark verdure of summer
> The railroad tracks are like the cords of a lyre
> Gleaming across the dreamy valley,
> And the road crosses them like a flash of lightning.
> But the souls of many who speed like music
> On the melodious heart-strings of the valley
> Are dim with storms;
> And the soul of a farm lad who plods, whistling,
> On the lightning road
> Is a bright blue sky.

But over the course of a few years the name Pascal D'Angelo was quickly forgotten. He never married or had children. He never went back to Italy. On the morning of March 17, 1932, having been exhausted by an impoverished lifetime, he was found dead in his little room by his landlord, and only with the help of his few remaining friends was it possible for him to be buried in Green-Wood Cemetery in Brooklyn.

All that's left for me to do is put away the various papers on his life. I wasn't able to trace very many documents relating to his stay in New York, this New York that changes its face so often: stores and houses that I saw just a year ago disappear almost instantly. You can't find them anymore. You instead find an empty space or another building, or a restaurant or a simple diner, maybe a small hotel or a coin-op laundromat. And this *is* the city of New York; these are the most changeable zones: Queens, swarming with people, which used to be the last suburb of the city, today is a natural extension of it; Little Italy, an area where in Pascal's day only Italian regional dialects were spoken, now is swallowed up by Chinatown; Staten Island, which has always encapsulated itself; sensual, fleshy Harlem; the huge, fearsome, and variegated Bronx; teeming Brooklyn, a borough of several million inhabitants, a city within a city and within still another city, like some infinite Russian doll incorporating itself continually.

Left to me are only these papers on Pascal and above all the story of my grandfather Giorgio who was close to him until 1917, when our stonecutter decided to leave Connecticut and move first to Manhattan and then to Brooklyn, having decided to follow his star. He never visited the man who was like a father to him, not even years later when, having fallen in love with Cedar Beach, Long Island, my grandfather bought a house there where he spent the rest of his life. Pascal, invited many times, never visited. Destitute in his miserable little room in Brooklyn, he wouldn't even send my grandfather his address.

I'll put away, then, in a big box, the possibly useless photos of houses, streets, and neighborhoods where Pascal hung out, places that were very different ninety years ago. I put away the notebooks and postcards bought at an old shop in Brooklyn, a thrift store. I'm putting away photocopies of some letters, handwritten by Pascal, that I found in libraries. And I also put away now, dear reader, this story you've just finished reading.

But today there's one more thing I want to and must do before I say goodbye to Pascal. I go to the garage, get my bike, and go down Shore Road. Eventually I make my way to Harbor Beach Road, which runs along the entire length of Cedar Beach. Soon I reach what used to be my grandfather's house, a cottage that, after many owners, belongs now to a shopkeeper from Manhattan.

I leave the bike next to a streetlamp and venture along a path among the dunes on this large and beautiful beach. Along this long varied pathway they've installed benches spaced just a few yards apart and facing the ocean, or actually Long Island Sound. On the back of each one of these benches is a brass plaque with the name of someone to be remembered.

Here's the bench I'm interested in. On the plaque it says *GIOR-GIO VANNO (1875–1965)*, and beneath it *In memoriam*. I sit on the bench, which feels like it's mine in a way; in front of me stretches the vast ocean that joins two continents.

Around me there's only peace and silence, barely interrupted by the constant sound of the low waves and here and there a gull's strident cry. It's a late morning, crystal clear. From this vantage point I can see the coast of Connecticut and even New Haven, where Pascal and my grandfather lived. My *nonno* was probably the only one of the group from Introdacqua in 1910 who really made his fortune in America. I mentally thank him for telling me about Pascal, and I sit there looking peacefully out at the space around me until the air begins to grow dark.

AUTHOR'S NOTE

I wrote this novel inspired in part by the structure of my friend Sebastiano Vassalli's *La notte della cometa* and in part by Pascal D'Angelo's autobiography, *Son of Italy*, which was published in New York in 1924. Born in Introdacqua (L'Aquila) in 1894, Pascal emigrated to the U.S. at sixteen and died in Brooklyn, in desperate poverty, in 1932. The events related in the part of this novel covering his emigration and early life in America are real, as are some of the characters—friends and companions with whom D'Angelo shared his emigrant's tale. Various other episodes described in the novel are invented, based upon research I undertook and on the cultural and historical record of New York in the 1920s.

In Italy, among the few people whose work relates to D'Angelo, I must mention Vassalli, who brought attention to this wretched but also visionary "Italian poet who wanted to be American" (comparing him to Dino Campana), in one of his *Improvvisi* in *Corriere della Sera* (November 21, 2001) on the occasion of the appearance of *Canti di luce*, a slim volume of D'Angelo's poems edited by me and published by the courageous Il Grappolo Press in Salerno, which had just two years earlier produced *Son of Italy* for the first time.

D'Angelo's letter, included in the penultimate chapter, is the original he wrote to Carl Van Doren on January 2, 1922. Van Doren was at that time the editor in chief of *The Nation*, whose archives, at Princeton University, contain the original pages Pascal typed it on. I'm grateful to the Firestone Library of Princeton for giving me permission to consult Van Doren's archives, and also grateful to the New York Public Library, which conserves the microfilms of the major Italian newspapers published in New York in the 1910s and '20s.

My thanks also go to the Pro Loco of Introdacqua for their indispensable help in my research and for giving me the precious volume titled *Introdacqua in History and Tradition*, by Gaetano Susi. Thanks also to the widow of Rino Panza who gave me his book *The World of Pascal D'Angelo*.

Special thanks go to Maurizio Vignola, Salvatore Violante, Charles Franco, Rosanna Liberatore, and Annalisa Macchia for their cooperation. I am also grateful to my friend and colleague Anthony Julian Tamburri, dean of the John D. Calandra Italian American Institute, for having provided me with specific details about the procedures at Ellis Island—particularly at the beginning of the last century—in use when immigrants, be they Italian or otherwise, poured into the United States from the various nations of Europe.

LUIGI FONTANELLA lives in New York and Florence, Italy. A professor of Italian Literature, he has been the chair of the Department of European Languages, Literatures, and Cultures at Stony Brook University. He has published collections of poetry, essays, and stories. Among the most recent titles are *Pasolini rilegge Pasolini* (Archinto, 2005, translated into several languages); *L'angelo della neve. Poesie di viaggio* (Mondadori, Almanacco dello Specchio, 2009); *Bertgang* (Moretti & Vitali 2012, winner of the Premio I Murazzi); *Migrating Words. Italian Writers in the United States* (Bordighera Press, 2012); *Disunita ombra* (Archinto, 2013, winner of the Premio Nazionale Frascati); *L'adolescenza e la notte* (Passigli, 2015, Pref. by Paolo Lagazzi, Pascoli Prize, Viareggio-Giuria, Prize); *La morte rosa* (Stampa, 2015, Pref. by Maurizio Cucchi); *Monte Stella* (Passigli, 2020); *Raccontare la poesia 1970-2020. Saggi, ricordi, testimonianze critiche* (Moretti & Vitali, 2021); *Tre passi nel desiderio. Tre Atti Unici* (Neos, 2021).

He has published the following novels: *Hot Dog* (Bulzoni, 1985, translated into English by Justin Vitiello and published by Soleil in 1998); *Controfigura* (Marsilio, 2009) and *Il dio di New York* (Passigli, 2017). He is the Senior Editor, for Olschki Publisher in Florence, of the international journal of poetry and poetry studies *Gradiva*. Email: luigifontanella02@gmail.com.